THE LAST WAR

THE LAST
WAR

Book One of The Last War

Peter Bostrom

www.authorpeterbostrom.com

Summary: Earth is under attack. 20 years after the American-Chinese war devastated our worlds, we finally have a tense peace. But legendary American Admiral Jack Mattis, on his inspection tour of the first joint American-Chinese space station, finds himself in the middle of the unthinkable: an alien invasion. Their ships are powerful, their weapons overwhelming. And in the confusion, our tentative peace with the Chinese is shaken to the core. Taking command of his old battleship, The Midway, Admiral Mattis races the alien fleet to Earth, desperate to prevent the utter destruction of humanity's home. And in Earth's darkest hour, Mattis must unify and lead old adversaries to the fight against a common enemy, one that doesn't care about flags or borders. An enemy driven by malevolent hate and a thirst for blood. An enemy that cares for one thing only: Earth's destruction.

Text set in Garamond

Cover art by Tom Edwards

http://tomedwardsdesign.com

ISBN-10: 1545124361
ISBN-13: 978-1545124369

Printed in the United States of America

For my three favorite admirals: Kirk, Adama, and Ackbar

Prologue

Operations room
Station 43
Capella System, 42 light years from Earth

"I can't believe you've done this." Petty Officer Third Class Leonard Alexander Jacobs jabbed a finger at the game tile on his duty monitor, as though the computer would change its mind. The tile stayed red. "Admin *is* a word."

"No, it's a contraction," said Petty Officer Third Class Suhina Iyer beside him, her thick Indian accent almost smothering her words, tapping on the key that denied him his precious points. "It's not a word. Doesn't count. Only *administrator* counts and you, my friend, are missing a T."

Every day was like this. Even among distant systems, Capella System was considered the back-end of nowhere. The frontier's frontier, the only human presence a tiny space station orbiting the gas giant Euphrates. A giant coffin where the thirty-odd staff had nothing to do all day but perform the meaningless drudgery that counted as work, play stupid games they were bored of, and consider the chain of bad life decisions that had led to them being posted out this far.

And arguing. Oh boy. Nothing kept the mind occupied like a good argument. All around him, the other station operations crew chatted away, also trying to stave off boredom.

"Admin is a shortening," said Jacobs. "A contraction is like…something else. Like how *do not* becomes *don't*."

"That's the same thing."

"No, it's not," he said patiently. "Admin's like radar. It counts because it's a word in common usage."

"Radar is an acronym," said Iyer. "Totally different."

Oh, this was good. Jacobs readied the next chain in the argument he'd prepared, but then something flashed on the edges of his screen.

The radar program was trying to tell him something, almost as though it had been summoned by the use of its name. He switched between programs, bringing up his actual work.

A faint reflection, out near Euphrates's third moon, right on the horizon of the gas giant. The size of a small ship or large fighter. A gunship?

He almost ignored it, but even this tiny blip was more excitement than he'd had in a long time. "Radar contact," Jacobs called out, trying to sound less bored than he felt. "494,400 kilometers distant, bearing 96.229 mark 11.812. RCS suggests gunship class."

The general hubbub of the operations room ceased. Everyone cast aside whatever tool they had been using to keep themselves from going mad and focused on work.

"Confirm that," said Lieutenant Ellis, stepping up behind him. Ellis was their short, nasty CO with the face only a mother could love, like it had been run over a couple of times with a cheese grater. "Iyer, send another pulse, maximum power."

The radar pulsed again, and this time, nothing came back, even with the higher power. That area of space was empty.

"Again," said Ellis. Another pulse. Another nothing.

Iyer was staring at him. In fact, everyone was. But he was sure the ship had been there.

"No transports or shuttles are due today," Iyer said. "And they wouldn't come that close to the gas giant if they were. Not picking up any distress signals, no transponder codes. Nothing."

"Petty Officer," said Ellis, gently patting the headrest of his seat, "I think you've been out here on the edge too long."

Haven't we all? Maybe his mind was playing tricks on him. Maybe it was the damn rats chewing on the network cables again. Who needed the Chinese when they had rodents sabotaging every system on the station?

"It was faint, ma'am," said Jacobs, banishing the doubts in his mind. He'd definitely seen it. "If it was a recon gunship, we might have been seeing a refraction through the gas planet's atmosphere. There could be something behind the horizon, observing our radar pulses without reflecting them. The Chinese used to do the same thing, back in the day."

"This isn't back in the day, Petty Officer, and the Chinese are our friends now." The tiniest hint of sarcasm slipped through Ellis's carefully chosen words. "Stand down. It's probably just a bounce from a pocket of gas in the upper atmosphere."

"Aye, ma'am." Well, that was the most exciting thing he'd seen in weeks. A month, probably. Ellis's boots retreated behind him. Jacobs waited until the coast was clear.

Iyer glanced at him, corkscrewing her finger near her temple. Yeah, yeah... He put his fingers to the tab key, but right before he changed applications, another pulse went out.

And his whole display lit up.

It looked like a shotgun blast. A dozen bright, hot contacts simultaneously dropped out of Z-space in attack formation.

Oh shit.

"Radar contact!" Jacobs practically shouted, fingers frantically tapping at his keys. A whole damn fleet had just appeared. "Multiple skunks, fresh from Z-space, coming in from Euphrates's horizon!"

"Confirmed," said Iyer, her voice charged. "Designating skunks Alpha through November. They're squawking IFF. Firing interrogation..." She practically spat the words. "Nothing, dammit. I'm detecting IFF transponders, but they're not any configuration I've ever seen. It could be a new Chinese system."

Could very well be. The United States and the Chinese had been at peace for nearly twenty years...plenty of time to adopt a new system of transponders.

"Action stations, action stations," said Ellis, the station-wide address radio in her hand. "This is not a drill." She turned to Jacobs. "Give me a firing solution on the nearest skunk. Sparkle them with infrared lasers. Make sure they know we're giving them the stink-eye."

"Aye, ma'am," he said, flicking the plastic cover off the master-arm button and thumping it with his fist. The faint hum of energy grew around him as the station's weapons systems, too long inert, came to full power. Time to blast those red bastards into the cold vacuum of space. He fed the coordinates for the closest contact, Skunk Alpha, into the computer. "Targets highlighted, ready to engage."

"Hold steady," said Ellis, leaning forward behind his chair. "Iyer, establish inter-system communications. Get Fleet Command on the horn. Tell them we are"—the slightest hesitation—"under attack. Updates to follow."

"Aye aye," said Iyer. "Transmitting."

Silence, save Iyer's frantic typing. The hostile ships closed in on them.

"Sent." Iyer twisted around in her chair. "Lieutenant, are we sure—"

A deafening blast stole the rest of her words, joined with the roaring of splintering metal. A pressure wave blew Jacobs forward, onto his console, smashing his nose into the screen.

Air howled all around him. Dazed, confused, his nose a smashed wreck, Jacobs instinctively reached up to pinch it, to staunch the flow of blood.

His hand was covered in the stuff before he even touched his face.

"Iyer," he said, his voice strangely muffled, having to shout over the sound of air rushing past, the wind throwing debris all around. "Hey, I think I'm bleeding."

Her headless body drifted upward, past his chair, into a massive hole in the hull and out into space.

How had a single shot penetrated so far into the armored core of the ship?

"Evacuate!" roared Ellis over the rushing air and wailing klaxons. "Operations is breached! Get to the escape pods!"

Jacobs clambered over his chair, frantically trying to get to the rear of the room, to the armored door that led to the eight escape pods.

Another round blew through Operations, crumpling a bulkhead and blasting debris everywhere. The screaming fragments of metal whizzed past his ears like a swarm of hornets. Ellis collapsed, dozens of red flowers blooming on her body, and then she too was sucked out.

Jacobs felt the howling air tear at his legs, yanking him off his feet. He climbed forward with his hands, pulling himself from chair to chair. Three meters. Two. One.

The door hissed open. He hauled himself into an escape pod the size and shape of a coffin, gasping with lungs that barely had any air to fill them. He pulled a safety belt around his body, clipped it securely, and then tugged the pod's lid closed, sealing himself in the armored sarcophagus with only a tiny window the size of his fist in front of his eyes.

"Wait!" shouted one of the other operations crewmen, his voice muffled. The ensign moved into view, bashing his fist on the lid. "Let me in!"

There were seven other pods. "Take another one!" yelled Jacobs, right as a third round blew through the room. The crewman's blood splattered against the pod's window, painting it crimson.

Nothing he could do. Jacobs drove his bloody fist into the *launch* button.

The pod shook as it blasted free of the doomed station, the porthole instantly replaced with empty space. The howling disappeared, replaced with ominous silence.

With its minimal fuel exhausted, the pod drifted through space, maneuvering for an orbit around Euphrates. Finally, he saw Station 43, atmosphere pouring from multiple breaches, the sparkle of debris drifting away.

From Euphrates's horizon, a massive ball of ice and rock, leaving a trail like a comet, swung around toward the station. Helpless, Jacobs could only watch as the object, almost moving quicker than he could comprehend, barreled into the side of Station 43 and blasted it into a billion pieces. The debris scattered into the void.

Jacobs's pod would be transmitting a distress signal in the open. His enemies would certainly pick him up. Being a Chinese prisoner couldn't be too bad though. Hopefully they would acknowledge *admin* was a real word.

Jacobs sat curled up in the pod, waiting for one of the enemy ships to make an approach to capture him. But as he watched the distant ships, they suddenly disappeared with a flash, one by one, until the whole fleet had departed as quickly as it had arrived.

Then he was alone.

Chapter One

Shuttlecraft "Hestia"
Cor Caroli System, 27 light years from Earth
Meanwhile

Admiral Jack Mattis had seen a lot in his day, but laying eyes on the massive steel space station through the window of the forward section of the shuttle left a taste in his mouth more sour than the cigar still perched between his teeth.

Friendship Station. A massive ring perched in the asteroid belt of the Cor Caroli system, bristling with docking clamps, passenger umbilicals and radio antennas, it resembled a colossal crown floating in space; jutting out above it all was the American flag, flying beside the Chinese one, two massive cloth banners on twin flagpoles, motionless in space. A red floodlight illuminated the Chinese flag and a white one the Americans, while the light of Cor Caroli's twin blue stars cast the remainder of the whole station in a pale cyan light that seemed cold. Foreboding.

Red, white, and blue hues. Interesting patriotic statement for a station that stood for the biggest betrayal of the American people since the war.

Mattis inhaled, sucking smoke into his lungs. The cigar tip flared. Now they were all friends, of course. The Americans and the Chinese. Oh, sure, they had shot at each other for almost a year, killed and died in equal measure…but now they were friends.

He'd thought the nicotine might help. It didn't. Never did.

"You shouldn't smoke in here," said a voice from across the shuttle, its tone like sandpaper to his sanity. It moved, swaggered like the person who owned it, dripping with self-righteous smugness. Senator Peter Pitt.

Pit. An empty hole in the ground. Pitt. An empty head in the black of space. The guy was tiny—barely five foot two—and dressed in a suit that seemed at once obnoxiously expensive and embarrassingly cheap. A pale little weasel, nearly sixty, someone far too old to be leading this delicate diplomatic mission, despite his freshly dyed yet receding black hair, a pathetic protest against age's encroachment.

"They say," said Mattis, drawing in another lungful of ash and then blowing the smoke out into the shuttle's atmosphere, "that smoking's bad for me. They ain't cured the kind of cancer these things cause. They say they *can't*. That there's just something filthy in them that burrows into the cell walls of the lungs and nestles in there real good, like some kind of varmint digging its nest, and once it does, it can't be dug out for nothing."

Pitt laughed—a noise high pitched and annoying—and slid over to him. "Right, right. So how about you put that thing out, hey, Grandpa?"

Grandpa? Funny words coming from someone his own age. Mattis turned with slow, careful deliberation toward the man, the cigar tip flaring an angry red.

Pitt held up his hands. "Easy now, big fella. I'm just sayin'."

Mattis stared him down, casually puffing on the cigar. The shuttle adjusted its course. Blue light crept up Pitt's body as the craft tilted to one side. Mattis imagined the blue line was the shadow of some great hand crushing this tiny bug of a man.

"Look," said Pitt, all pretense of faux-humor fading away, his craggy face becoming an angry sneer. He jabbed his finger at Mattis's chest. "You're only here because the military big-shits want you here. I didn't. *They* did. Some kind of show of trust or…whatever. Okay? Listen: you're here to show these damn reds that we're here in peace, and that even a bitter old dog like you can be brought to heel. That there won't be any more plausibly denied, state-sponsored insurrections on their worlds. You're here to say *nothing*, do *nothing*, and let me do my fucking job. I do the talking. You just stand there and don't screw this up for me. Okay, Mattis? You get that? Huh?"

Mattis glared down at him, a silent tower, smoke trailing from his cigar.

"Say something."

Oh, you probably don't want me to do that. Mattis bit back ten thousand bitter words and focused entirely on the practical. "It's *Admiral* Mattis."

"Whatever." Pitt snatched the cigar and crushed it underneath his slightly too cheap shoe. "And no more *goddamn* smoking, or I'll ship you back to the States to live out your life giving speeches to kindergarteners and complaining about the neighbors, you senile old fuck. Capiche?"

Senile. What a hypocrite. "Right," said Mattis, his eyes two narrow slits. "No more smoking."

Pitt pinched the bridge of his nose. "Why are you giving me such trouble, Mattis? After I got you that promotion and all. I did you a favor."

Yes. The promotion. Promoted away from the command of the USS *Midway*, promoted to a desk, promoted away from the best job he'd ever had. Because, as Pitt had put it, it was 'better politically.' Whatever *that* was supposed to mean.

Pitt had pissed on him and was now standing there telling him it was rain.

A faint hiss echoed through the shuttle, and the pilot's voice echoed from speakers placed throughout the forward section. "Please be advised we've docked with *Friendship Station*. All passengers to disembark through the forward docking ring."

"Just remember," said Pitt, waggling a finger at him, "this is my operation. I'm in charge. Got it?"

"Of course."

Pitt took a deep breath, and seemingly put his mask back on. "C'mon," he said, flashing the biggest, cheesiest, fakest smile Mattis had ever seen. "Let's go meet the Chinese delegation."

He tried to move, genuinely, but for some reason, his feet remained rooted to the ground. As though some invisible force was keeping him anchored there, in the shuttle.

"You okay?" asked Pitt, the barest hint of real compassion in his voice.

Cor Caroli System. The system that had seen the bloodiest battle of the entire war. The battle where Phillip had died. No, not died. Been *killed*. Killed by the damn Chinese…

The past was in the past. "After you," said Mattis, gesturing with his hand.

Pitt gave him a weird look, but then together, with Mattis taking up the rear, the two men headed out of the shuttle and crossed the threshold into the docking umbilical, a long tunnel dotted with windows. As they walked, a light shining through one of the windows caught his attention and held it. Like the face of an old friend, docked next to the tiny shuttlecraft, he saw…*her*.

The *Midway*, her mighty guns silent, her superstructure draped in scaffolding and dotted with yellow-suited workmen, welding and fixing. Must have been here for her refit. She still had fighters aboard, so she was probably responsible for the station's CAP.

They had brought him barely a hundred meters away from his ship. Probably just to mess with him.

"Come on," hissed Pitt, breaking the trance. "Don't dawdle. We can't keep the Chinese waiting."

Mattis ground his teeth together, forcing his lips to make something he hoped resembled a smile. "I suppose not," he said, barely able to contain his growing frustration. "We wouldn't want to hurt their feelings, would we?"

"Right," said Pitt.

With gritted teeth, Mattis walked down the long corridor toward the waiting delegation.

Chapter Two

Lt. Patricia "Guano" Corrick's Warbird
Midway *Fighter Bay*
Docked at Friendship Station

"I'm telling you," said Lieutenant Patricia "Guano" Corrick, her fingers tapping on her F-113 Warbird's throttle assembly, "the reds can't fly for shit."

The fighter bay's doors remained closed. She waited impatiently for them to open.

Her gunner, Junior Lieutenant Deshawn "Flatline" Wiley, didn't seem amused. "You're higher than the national debt. You realize that the PLANAF are some of the best pilots in the galaxy, yeah?" *The People's Liberation Army Naval Air Force.* What a name. "The best engines. The best ships. The best missiles."

Guano adjusted her heavy ejection suit. "Sure, but nothing beats good ole' American know-how. Good ole' American freedom missiles."

"Pretty sure," said Flatline, "that the turn radius on those

Chengdu J-84's beats good ole' American freedom missiles."

J-84s. Basically flying cigars with stubby little thrusters on them. They could barely fight in atmosphere, it was true, but they were quite deadly out in space. "A poor workman blames his tools," she said. "I can fly rings around them."

"Don't forget about me," Flatline said. "I'm in here too, you know."

"What," she teased, "you think you'll have another heart attack?"

The origin's of Flatline's callsign was a sore point. He'd passed out during flight school and had a heart attack. They'd gotten him back, naturally, and cleared him for duty—but only as a gunner. He'd never be a pilot. "Hey," he said, "screw you."

"You wish," said Guano. She loaded up for more teasing—something about how she'd be there to give him mouth-to-mouth if he needed it—but the *Midway*'s hangar bay doors jerked and began to open. "Let's show these chumps why we're the best there is."

"One of these days," said Flatline, "you're going to be the death of me. You're a madwoman."

"And yet you agreed to fly with me," she said, slamming the throttle to the wall. Her Warbird leapt forward, soaring out of the *Midway*'s hangar bay and into open space, leaving behind it a silver trail of exhaust. "Ultimately, this is all your fault."

Ahh, powered flight. Guano eased off the juice, flying her ship in a lazy circle around *Friendship Station*, her engine leaving a silver half-halo around the outer ring. As they reached the far side, they saw the Chinese ship.

The *Fuqing*, the warship that was there to meet *Midway*. A massive teardrop bristling with missile launch tubes, guns, and open mouths ready to disgorge fighters. Predatory, sleek, and their…friends.

"What a fu-king pile of shit," said Flatline.

Guano sniggered, angling her craft in a little closer for a better look. "How long've you been waiting to use that line, eh?"

"Since we got here," confessed Flatline. "Stole the joke off the pilot's ready room. Some guy thinks he's funnier than me. Good jokers borrow, great jokers steal."

It was probably Yukon. Or Gumball. Those wankers always had a stupid joke on their lips. "I guess that makes you a God of comedy."

"Damn straight," said Flatline, and then his voice changed slightly, becoming more professional. "Hey, it looks like they're launching a patrol too."

She craned her head and spotted them too. Three fighters, bright gleaming silver ships, flew out from one of the open hangar bays, moving as one, drifting toward them. J-84's.

"Wonder what frequency they're using," said Guano, flipping her ship around and decelerating, the equivalent of giving a playful wave.

"Wonder if they want to race," said Flatline, an edge to his tone that suggested he might have been, just a little, serious. "A friendly race. Between friends. Because we're friends now. And that's what friends do."

Their assigned task was to implement perimeter patrols, and staying on their assigned path was important…but, if she recalled the mission briefing correctly, no explicit limits were placed on the speed of their ships. Guano flipped her ship around again and, once more, opened her throttle.

The three Chinese fighters flared their engines, pulling out behind them.

"The race is on," she said, her little fighter whipping around the station, the g-forces pushing her into her seat.

A glance in the rearview mirror showed the Chinese fighters falling behind. Her fingers ached as she tried to force the throttle forward. Farther and farther ahead…until finally the Chinese craft slipped behind the station.

"Woo," she said, exhaling and releasing a breath she didn't know she'd been holding. "Dragged their asses."

"Glad I didn't have any money on the Chinese," said Flatline.

"Good," said Guano, slumping back in her seat. "Keep your money. Its value only increases over time anyway."

"W-Wait, what?"

She tapped her microphone. "You ever heard of inflation, idiot?"

Flatline didn't reply, a silence she could only attribute to her stunning economic brilliance.

Beating the Chinese pilots had been too easy… She barely felt the rush she wanted. To be the best, baddest ass fighter jock in the whole galaxy. One didn't earn that by simply having a slightly faster ship.

She flipped her ship around and floored it, the inertia crushing her back into her seat. Her own silver trail fell over the cockpit like rain.

"What the hell?" shouted Flatline, gasping for air. "What are you doing?"

Time to prove themselves once and for all. The Warbird came to a complete stop, then leapt forward, beginning the long journey around *Friendship Station* in reverse.

"Let's see how brave they are," said Guano, flying down the trail she had left, retracing her ship's steps. Just as the Chinese would be.

Flatline's silence gave her everything she needed, but she ignored his sulking. His earlier praise of the Chinese would be his undoing this time.

Around they went, the silver exhaust splattering on the cockpit, a decent amount of it water vapor. Ahead, she could barely see the Chinese ships come around *Friendship Station*, their engines white hot. "Enjoying the rain?" she asked, gently touching the rudder pedal, keeping her ship within the slowly dissipating silver stream.

"Break away," said Flatline, his tone humorless. "You've proved your point. C'mon now. This is dangerous."

Nope. She adjusted her course, steering along the silver path she had left.

"C'mon," said Flatline, voice pitching up. "Guano, this shit is dangerous. If we head on, they won't be able to tell which parts of you are you and which parts are me."

Won't happen. The Chinese ships drew closer, closer, closer…a three-ship arrow with a tiny gap in the middle. Just big enough for a Warbird to fit. Probably.

"Oh no. Oh *hell no*. Break! Break, damn it!" His voice became shrill. "Jesus, they can't see us in the exhaust trail, Corrick!"

Nope! Guano laughed like a maniac, rolling her ship so one Chinese fighter would pass over her port wing, and one under her starboard.

They passed so close she swore she could see through the

cockpit, to the startled Chinese pilots within. The lead pilot had a red helmet emblazoned with flames. She yanked back on the stick, the ship pulling up and around into a huge loop, drifting through space.

"Holy shit, that was awesome!" She squirmed around in her chair, looking over her shoulder at Flatline, her face hurting from smiling so much. "Say that was awesome. *Say it.*"

Flatline glared at her, huffing down oxygen like he might, actually, be about to have another heart attack. He glared at her, eyes as rough as stones, and then slowly a smile crept back. "Yeah, okay, that was awesome."

She turned back to her instruments, settling into her seat, taking a breath through her breathing mask. The Chinese ships scattered and turned toward her. Probably real pissed off. Ahh, well…

Then a yellow light flashed on her cockpit dash and a high-pitched alarm wailed. Her blood froze in her veins.

A missile tracking radar was locked onto her ship.

"Holy shit," she said, barely able to believe it. "They're… They're going to shoot!"

Chapter Three

Docking Umbilical
Friendship Station

Mattis forced one boot in front of the other. He'd been on twenty-kilometer marches, he'd waded through swamps and rainforests and deserts, but the empty ten-meter corridor to *Friendship Station* was the hardest stretch he could remember.

A crowd of people were waiting for them, their hands politely folded behind their backs, a mixture of uniforms, American and Chinese. The US forces stood to the left, the Chinese to the right.

Even on *Friendship Station*, there was an uncomfortable gap between them.

"Senator Pitt," said one of the faces, and immediately, Mattis felt a little better about it all. Martha Ramirez. Reporter for GBC News, obviously a part of the party, the press representative. Fancy seeing her here. She extended her hand to Pitt. "It's a genuine pleasure to have you aboard."

Of course she had brought herself out here to tell a story. Of course she had. Martha… Oh, it had been years. Too many years. Martha's kindness and a soft voice belied a mighty power, the strength of someone who took no prisoners and always fought to get the truth. There had been something between them—something they both knew would interfere with their careers and which couldn't be pursued—but her presence brought an easy smile to his face.

Well, maybe this wouldn't be so bad after all.

"Thanks," said Pitt, flashing a cheesy grin. "It's great to be here, Martha."

Pitt was almost blocking access to Mattis with his body, but Ramirez stepped around him, extending her hand to Mattis as well. He looked right into those gentle brown eyes. "Admiral," she said.

So brief and short, but that was good. She had flattered Pitt—using his civilian title, spinning words about how it was a *genuine pleasure*, all that garbage. That was diplomacy. The art of telling someone to go to hell and having them enjoy the journey.

It was like his grandmother had always said. Beware the nice ones.

"Thank you," said Mattis, shaking her hand firmly. "I'm very glad to be here." Ninety percent lies, ten percent truth. Martha being that ten percent.

Something flickered across Ramirez's face, the briefest flash of emotion, and he understood. She knew he was just keeping the peace; he didn't really support this. "Of course." She released his hand and gestured to the side. "Admiral, this is the delegation from the People's Republic of China, led by—"

Pitt slid in, smiling that wide, fake smile of his. "Miss Ramirez, *I'd* love to meet the delegation. Mattis is only here as an observer."

A moment's pause. Although not a word was said, and neither of the two people's expressions changed, Mattis sensed some kind of subtle power play here. Who would fold first?

"Of course," said Ramirez, with that perfect, practiced smile of hers. "But it's impolite to not introduce our whole group. Everyone, this is Senator Pitt." Then, ever so delicately, ever so deliberately, she put her hand on Pitt's arm and eased him aside. "Friends, this is Admiral Mattis, representative of the United States Space Navy."

"Mister Mattis," said one of the Chinese delegates, extending her gloved hand. "It's a pleasure to meet you. I am Captain Shao."

The woman's name, her voice, was so familiar. Shao had a narrow face, and she spoke with a slight British accent, as though she were from a rich family, or foreign educated, or from their prestigious military academies. Why did it sound so elusively, tantalizingly familiar? Then the truth blasted into his mind.

"Ahh, Captain Shao," said Mattis, taking the hand and squeezing it. Tightly. "We've met before."

"We…have?" asked the woman, inclining her head, eyes flicking down to the joined hands. "I don't recall."

"I remember perfectly." Mattis held the grip. "At the Battle of Euphrates. The *Midway* engaged the *Changsha* at standoff range. The *Changsha*, that was your command, wasn't it?" Mattis chuckled softly. "You got us good with those ten-inch guns. Couldn't penetrate our hull, but they damaged almost every system we had. *Midway* limped back to space dock on sublight power. A lot of superstructure damage. See, the first salvo struck the upper superstructure, and then the second salvo hit the same spot…so the majority of our casualties were damage control teams. Poor bastards didn't even see the rounds that killed them."

A tense silence. The two officers locked gazes, the tight handshake frozen. "The *Changsha* lost crew as well," said Shao, her hand squeezing his back. "I don't know what your intelligence corps told you, but we only managed two salvos. The first counter-battery hit us on the armored hull. However, an engineering flaw meant that what we thought was our strongest part was actually the weakest. Eighteen crewmen died and the ship was scrapped."

Finally, Mattis released Shao's hand, and the two stood in silence. If he had hurt her hand in any way, she didn't show it.

Pitt glared at him, and Ramirez in turn, then stepped in between them. "Well," he said, "as you know, we all have so much to discuss. No sense in bringing up the past. On either side."

"No," said Shao, clicking her tongue. "Merely observing a historical curiosity."

Mattis inclined his head in agreement.

"Admiral Mattis," said Ramirez, "let's go and meet the base commander. Senator Pitt can show the People's Republic delegation around and get them settled." Her gentle voice carried with it the hint that her suggestion was something more. "We can reconvene later for dinner."

"Of course," said Pitt, putting his hand on Shao's shoulder and pulling her away. "I'll take these ladies and gentlemen on a grand tour."

Physically separated by Ramirez and Pitt, Mattis followed Ramirez away from the Chinese delegates.

"Well," she said, once they were out of earshot, "that could have gone better."

"Are you talking about the conversation, or the war?" asked Mattis.

She stepped in front of him. "When did you become like this, Jack?" she asked pointedly. "Grabbing some Chinese officer's hand, bringing up old battles like the Chinese never lost a soul in combat... Do you *want* me to send you home?"

A smirk slowly crept across Mattis's face as he regarded her. "Honestly, you're the only reason I'm staying around." He paused. "And *Midway*."

"Two of your old girls in the same place. Must feel like old times."

Like old times. Everyone always said that like it was a good thing. "Definitely, Martha. Definitely."

They stood there, in the corridor, enjoying a moment of quiet, until Mattis realized just how close they were. He coughed politely and stepped back.

She did the same thing, but her obvious happiness remained. "Well," she said, leading him onward, her professional voice in place again. "Let's meet the station commander. The People's Republic have their turn now; in a year's time, we'll take over. One year each...that's how it works."

That seemed fair. They headed toward the core of the station, Operations and the CO's ready room.

"So," he asked, "what flinty old warrior have the Chinese

dragged out to man this... *Friendship Station?*"

She opened her mouth to answer, and right as she did so, Admiral Yim stepped out of the CO's ready room, a steaming cup of coffee in his hand and a tablet in the other.

Mattis froze, hardly able to believe it. The man had barely changed in twenty years; he still had the same stubble on his chin, baby fluff, the same round face, the same tall and broad frame. The only difference was the gray that had crept in around his hairline.

"Ah! Here he is," said Ramirez. "Admiral Mattis, it's my pleasure to introduce you to your counterpart, the CO of this station, Admiral Yim."

Admiral Yim.

The man who'd killed his brother.

Chapter Four

Lt. Patricia "Guano" Corrick's Warbird

Guano stared at the flashing amber light on her fighter's console in disbelief, half expecting it to disappear, like the whole thing had been a bad dream.

Then she realized Flatline was screaming at her.

"Hey! We need to get the fuck out of here! Wake up! Corrick, wake up!"

Her hands wouldn't move. Her feet wouldn't move. All she could do was look at the blinking yellow light and the approaching green dots on her radar.

Then, all of a sudden, everything started moving again.

Guano opened the throttle with one hand, jamming the stick into her gut with the other. "Flares!" she shouted as the g-forces pressed her into her seat. "Chaff! Decoy them!"

Flatline's fingers thumped on the keys in the background. "Working. Break right! Turn and burn!"

She yanked the stick to the right, the inertia tugging at her skin. She thumbed the radio button. "CAP 1-1 transmitting in the blind guard, we are buddy-spiked. Bearing 113 mark 201 from station. Abort, abort, abort. I say again: abort, abort, abort."

The Chinese said nothing. The amber light continued to flash. The three craft split up, like an opening hand getting ready to grab them. Crush them.

What was she supposed to do? Fire back? The thought flashed into her head, her eyes falling on the master-arm switch that would move her missiles from *safe* to *live*.

"CAP 1-1 transmitting in the blind guard, I say again, buddy-spike, buddy-spike. You are engaging a friendly craft. Acknowledge!"

They didn't.

They couldn't keep turning like this. Flatline was right; the Chinese fighters were able to accelerate better. She had to do something…

She dumped another load of chaff and flipped her ship, drifting backward, her nose pointed to the closest Chinese vessel. She fishtailed, swinging her ship left and right, and flicked the master-arm switch. The hum of her weapons-lock radar filled her ears. Positive target on the main bird. But there were three of them. If she shot, the survivors would shoot back. That was no good.

The Chinese could accelerate faster than she could, but her side-thrusters were more maneuverable. She could turn better. She needed to play to her strengths.

Jamming her throttle to one side, she flung her ship perpendicular to them and accelerated, a maneuver called a reverse hook-stop. The spacecraft's frame shook around them as the lateral forces strained the Warbird.

Come on, hold together…

The Chinese tried to turn with them, but their great acceleration was their undoing. They overshot, and in seconds, Guano's nose was pointing toward their engines, the infrared-guided system locked on all three of them, humming eagerly.

"Light them up," said Flatline, gasping for air from the turning. "Shoot those motherfuckers!"

She almost did. Her finger hovered over the fire button, but instead, she chose the radio. "*Midway*, CAP 1-1, be advised. We have been radar-locked by Chinese fighters. Have secured an advantageous firing position. Request permission to engage."

"Shoot them!" said Flatline urgently. Already the Chinese fighters were beginning to maneuver out of their perfect firing position. "Do 'em!"

The voice of Major Muhammad "Roadie" Yousuf, the Commander of the Air Group, her boss, came through on the line. "CAP 1-1, *Midway*: Priority alert, weapons safe, do not engage. I say again, you are not authorized to fire on any Chinese vessel at this time."

"Shit!" she spat. The Chinese fighters turned, repeating her maneuver exactly. Now they faced each other once again. "*Midway*, they're still maneuvering for a shot. CAP 1-1 once again requests permission to engage."

"Hard pass on that engagement, CAP 1-1. Do *not* fire."

She ran her thumb over the fire button. So close. She could almost feel the missiles begging to leap off their racks and fly toward their targets…

"This is bullshit," said Flatline, and she couldn't help but, at least a little, agree. So tempting.

"CAP 1-1," came Roadie's voice, suddenly much more stern. "Make immediate heading to *Midway* and RTB. Switch master-arm to safe. Acknowledge, over."

The Chinese were right there, and she had a perfect shot, but…orders were orders. "Acknowledged, *Midway*, CAP 1-1 is RTB." She tapped her master-arm switch, flicking it to safe, and broke off the attack. If the Chinese were going to shoot, they had ample opportunity, but as her craft pulled away, she could almost hear the three of them laughing at her back.

Flatline let out a loud sigh that came across as more of a crackle over his microphone. "What the hell?"

"Yeah," said Guano, "how did a playful race come to that?"

"Everyone's on edge," said Flatline.

No kidding. Guano made the final turn through the black, the edge of the *Midway* appearing from behind the station.

"CAP 1-1", said Roadie. He sounded *pissed*. "You are clear to dock in the main fighter bay. Once complete, power down, and you and your gunner are to report to my ready room *immediately*."

"Shit," said Flatline, his tone bitter. "Well, I hope *you* weren't considering a long and proud career in the military either."

Chapter Five

Friendship Station

Mattis could barely feel the breath moving in his lungs. Time seemed to slow down. Yim, standing right there, coffee in hand, heading to a duty shift as though it was just an ordinary day. His chest was littered with a wall of medals.

Yim smiled professionally and turned to face him. "Good evening, Admiral Mattis. Welcome to *Friendship Station*."

Bastard probably slept like a baby. Guilt free.

Mattis's mother had come home to two uniformed officers asking to come in, with a US Military car parked outside. As a military woman herself, she knew what that meant. The woman was gray, ancient, and had to be held up as she heard the news her firstborn son had been slaughtered in a meaningless death light years away from home.

They never even had any remains to bury.

"Admiral Mattis?" said Yim, his face scrunching up in confusion, eyes briefly flicking to Ramirez and then back to him. "Are you okay?"

Mattis couldn't look at him with anything other than hardness. Anger. Yim had been the commanding officer, and as always with the military, the buck stopped with the CO. This was his fault.

Mattis forced words out. "My apologies," he said, barely able to pass the sounds through his lips. "I was…thinking of something else."

"Happens to the best of us," said Yim, somewhat unconvincingly. He turned to Ramirez. "What can I do for you both?"

"Actually," said Mattis, stealing the conversation back, "you did quite enough during the war."

"Jack!" hissed Ramirez.

"Is that so?" asked Yim, sporting a slight, cold grin. "Have we met?"

"No," said Mattis, "not us. My brother knew you though. Lieutenant Commander Phillip Mattis. XO of the *Saragossa*." He leaned forward, stressing the words. "*Saragossa*. You know that ship, don't you? I wonder which medal she earned you, huh?"

"This one, since you asked specifically." Yim pointed at his chest, to one of the medals. "Medal of Naval Achievement. Awarded for contributions in combat. The sinking of an American ship absolutely counted—the medal is difficult to earn—but truth be told, I'm not sure if it was the *Saragossa* that pushed me over the line." Yim's smile widened. "There were just so many."

"Who could ever truly know?" said Mattis, but he knew the truth. Yim's cruiser had broken the *Saragossa*'s back, her reactors igniting in the cold depths of space. No survivors.

"Your own breast is adorned with much metal," said Yim. "I wonder how many Chinese widows you made, how many families you destroyed, how many graves your own hands have dug."

Mattis conjured the darkest glare he could. "Not enough."

Ramirez audibly gasped beside him. "Admiral Yim," she said, a diplomatic air coming through like molten cheese. When the diplomat voice came out, she was always *pissed.* "Please accept my *unreserved* apologies for Admiral Mattis's words. The truth is, the war is still fresh in the mind of our people, as I'm sure it is with your own." She gestured around her, a faint, angry twitch to her fingers, the only emotion slipping through her mask. "This, after all, is the purpose of this station, to mend those old wounds. It is the ancient Chinese who said, *A true warrior, like tea, shows his strength in hot water.*"

An interesting attempt to salvage a situation Mattis had no desire or intention to save. "Hot tea, is that what you were in when our ships had yours dead to rights, Admiral? You should thank your tea, or whatever it is that you Chinese do, that that ceasefire was called when it was, because the US forces were about to wipe you out of the sky."

Yim considered what he'd said, casually sipping his coffee. "Thank you for coming aboard, Admiral. I doubt we will ever speak again." He turned his back on them both and headed toward the Operations room.

"Prick," muttered Mattis, too low for Yim to hear. Probably. Hopefully.

Ramirez wheeled on him, all diplomatic pretense gone. She grabbed his arm and practically dragged him into a nearby room. "What the hell, Jack? Are you *trying* to start a war?"

Guilt stabbed at him, but he squelched the feelings beneath a steel facade. "Sorry," he said, unconvincing even to his ears.

"Sorry doesn't exactly cut it when there's just so much at stake," hissed Ramirez. "What's wrong with you?"

"It's...my fault." The confession alone hurt his chest to say. "I remember it like it was yesterday. The delivering personnel did the right thing. Professional. They skipped the euphemisms, just like they're supposed to." His tone turned blithe. "The manual is quite good. It tells you to be direct. Such things comfort nobody except the one delivering the news."

Ramirez's hard expression softened a little. "Dammit, Jack. I know this is hard for you—"

"No," he said, a little harsher than he intended. "You *don't* know."

A moment's silence, and he knew he'd really hurt her.

"Sorry," he said, more genuinely. "Martha…"

"It's fine."

Fine. He hated that word. It was a word people said when something wasn't *fine*. More silence.

"Talk to me, Jack," said Ramirez, softly closing the door.

Where to start? What to say? He took a breath. "The… Casualty Notification Officer did a good job, you know. And that's the absolute worst job in the military next to minesweeper. These poor bastards…they know their job is hopeless. They can't make it better, but an untrained operator sure can make it worse, so they do what they can."

Ramirez managed a little smile. "It's…interesting to me that you speak more about the procedures, the protocols, of this than the actual events."

"It's just how I deal with things."

She crossed her arms. "Well, deal with it better."

There was the Martha he admired. Strong. He smiled back. "Yeah. I will."

"You sure?"

"Sure. Still, Yim's lucky I didn't put a round in his gut."

"This is *his* station."

"*Sic Semper Tyrannis*," said Mattis.

Ramirez glared at him, and then leaned forward, putting her forehead on his shoulder. "One of these days," she said. "One of these days…"

He wasn't sure exactly what to do. The way she was standing, it just confused things. Made everything all fuzzy.

A knock on the door broke the tension. "Hey," came Senator Pitt's voice from the other side. "Mattis? You in there?"

Ugh. The two of them in a dark room… This was going to look weird. How to cover this up? How to pretend they were…?

Almost immediately, Ramirez straightened her back, adjusted her hair, and pulled out her phone. "Sorry," she called out to Pitt. "It's me. Just taking an important call."

Not bad. Mattis raised a curious eyebrow.

"Well," said Pitt, "Mattis has one, too."

He was in no mood to talk to whoever Yim had tattled to. "Don't care," he said.

"It's from someone called Chuck," said Pitt, sarcasm painting his every word. "Chuck Mattis. Ring a bell?"

His son.

"Okay, okay." Mattis stepped over to the door and, with a groan, pulled it open a crack.

Pitt, Shao, and the whole group were standing clustered around a phone with a blinking red light. Intersystem communications. Mattis pulled the door all the way open and took the phone.

"Jack speaking," he said.

"Dad," said Chuck's voice, a slight tremor in it. "Thank god. I thought you were dead."

Why was everyone harping on about his age like this? He glared at Pitt momentarily. "I'm old, Chuck, but believe me, they will send someone to tell you when I finally bite it."

"Huh?"

"Son, talk straight. What's wrong?"

The line distorted slightly. "Dad, turn on the news and see for yourself."

Chapter Six

CAG's Ready Room
USS Midway

The printer in the CAG's ready room spat out paper nonstop, forming a massive pile of reports on Roadie's desk. Guano wasn't sure it was ever going to stop.

"Now," said Roadie, taking a deep breath and leaning over his desk, "perhaps you two irradiated, dopey, inbred, defective, bowlegged, ugly, clusterfucked, soup-sandwich, mutated, kitten-shitting, half-baked, slack-jawed, pathetic, muppet-faced worthless hunks of weak-minded, indiscreet, shit-dicked, nut-sucking, dimwitted, completely ass-backward, messed-up, sister-kissing, defective, similac-chugging, piddlyshit, senseless, ass-dragging, malformed, penguin-fucking, subnormal, numbskulled, imbecilic excuses for utterly useless space garbage will be so kind as to explain to me what the *fuck* got into those tiny hunks of gristle you call brains, or should I just shoot myself in the dick because the pain of hearing you speak will be less painful than trying to magic up the brainpower to comprehend whatever fuck-fuck game you shitbreathers were trying to play with our Chinese friends?"

"No excuse, sir," said Guano.

He jammed a finger at her. "Do you *want* to start a war, dummy-number-one?"

"Sir, no sir," said Guano.

The finger turned to her gunner. "What about you, dummy-number-two?"

"Sir, no sir," said Flatline.

"So, neither of you drooling morons want a war," said Yousuf, leaning so far forward she thought he might fall over. "Either of you got *anything* to say for yourself?"

For a moment, neither of them said anything.

Then Flatline finally spoke up. "You said defective twice, sir."

"Damn right I did! You know why? Because you two are the biggest pieces of absolutely stupid, dumb, empty-headed, flat-chested, dirt-eating—"

"I'm sorry, sir," said Guano, although some part of her was curious just how long he might have gone on. "It was my idea. We wanted to engage the Chinese fighters in a friendly…" *Race* would be a bad word to use. "Impromptu test of our spacecraft's acceleration parameters when compared to our new allies' craft, under battlefield conditions. And it got out of hand."

"Out of hand?" Roadie slammed his hand down on a stack of printouts, his fingers quickly buried under newly arriving paper. "Look at this shit! I have complaints pouring in from eight sectors. All official. Theirs and ours. You won't *believe* who is signing these. The goddamn *President* is going to have her eyes on these reports, dumbo. Do you understand me? I have to write a letter about this to the *President. Of. The. United. States.*"

It had gone that far? Guano risked a glance to Flatline. His jaw was hanging open.

"Close your goddamn mouth, Wiley!" roared Roadie. "It's not raining dicks!"

"S-Sorry, sir."

"You will be." Roadie took another long, deep breath, but instead of another torrent of abuse, his words came out much calmer, more measured. "You two legitimate fuckups will be assuming the duties of the cleaning staff of this good vessel with regard to the pilot's ready room for a *year*, specifically by making sure that every single inch of this pig sty is clean enough for me to eat my breakfast on each and every duty shift, which you better believe I fully intend to do. Am I in any way unclear, wankers?"

"No, sir," they said in unison.

"Good," said Roadie. He closed his eyes for a moment, took another calming breath, and then, when he opened his eyes, his voice was back to normal. "They can really burn fast, can't they?"

"Yes, sir," said Guano. "Fast. Faster than us. And they're brave...fearless, really. They locked us up like they were saying, *come get some.*"

Roadie seemed to digest that. "They were pushing the boundaries, but...that's the behavior of someone who's hurting. Scared. Frightened. Those who speak the loudest fear the most." He tapped his finger on his desk. "Means they aren't trying to start shit… They're afraid we will."

Interesting observation. "Maybe," said Guano. "In my opinion—"

"Shut your damn mouth, pilot! If I wanted your opinion, then I'd have asked for it!"

"Yes, sir, Lieutenant Yousuf."

Roadie let out an exhausted sigh. "Time will tell. In the meantime, I also want a full write-up from both of you on your take on the J-84's capabilities. *Especially* any kind of weaknesses you observed."

"Yes, sir," said Guano. Right as she said it, her personal comm beeped.

"Turn that shit off," said Roadie, eyes practically bulging out of his head. "Before I make it *two years*."

"It is off, sir," she said, unclipping the device and holding it out to show him. "That's the emergency signal."

Suddenly, Flatline's started beeping, and Roadie's right behind it, all of them flashing an angry red.

Chapter Seven

Friendship Station

"Turn on the…news?" Mattis balked at the request coming from the tiny handheld comm. The diplomats gathered outside, especially Shao and Pitt, were watching him. He moved farther into the room, cupping the tiny speaker with his hand. "Are you crazy, son? I'm a little busy out here."

"Capella Station's gone, Dad," said Chuck. So simply stated. "They found the debris earlier this morning. It's on every channel. Looks like it went down with all hands."

Shao's eyes told him she had overheard. The mild panic and confusion. Mattis studied her. Was this the panic of someone who didn't know what was going on…or the panic of someone who *did*?

He lowered his voice to a whisper. "What happened?"

"No idea," said Chuck. "They haven't said."

He moved into the corner of the room, cupping the communications device with his hand. "It's got to be the

Chinese. Who else could it be? No other nation state could pull that kind of action, nor would they want to. They're the only ones who would—"

"Dad," said Chuck, a weariness in his voice. "Stop. Just stop."

"Who else could it possibly be? You tell me, Chuck. Who?"

A short silence. "I don't know," he said. "We don't know anything right now. Things are just happening. Don't leap to conclusions."

Despite the immediate dopamine rush of someone who'd had every single one of their suspicions verified, that feeling of being *right*, all those years of military training gnawed at the back of his mind. Why would the Chinese go to all the effort of setting up this very station, so-called *Friendship Station*, on the border of the Sino-American lines…and then attack some other distant border station of no strategic or military value whatsoever?

Why would they tip their hand like that? *Follow the money*, he always said. *Who stands to gain from this?*

Perhaps the Chinese plan hadn't been properly exposed yet.

"Where the hell are you anyway, Dad?" asked Chuck.

"I'm at work," he said evasively.

"With Pitt?"

"Yeah," said Mattis.

"You know," said Chuck, bitterness creeping into his voice, "that I've been working for him for a *year*, right? I'm only not there right now because he's angry at you. I want to speak to him."

Mattis's eyes met Pitt's, then he looked away. "He's not here."

The brief eye contact was enough for the rest of the group to jump in. "Admiral," asked Shao, her tone carrying a slight tremor, "is something wrong?"

"It's fine," he said, raising his voice to be heard and straightening his back. "Don't worry about it."

"Dad?" asked Chuck. "Is someone there?"

The awkwardness of this was getting to him. "Work colleague," he said, putting his voice back to the comm device. "I'm out here with Pitt, remember?"

"Wait," asked Chuck, "you just said he wasn't there. Now you're saying he is. Are you with him or not?"

"It's complicated."

"She sounded Chinese," said Chuck. "The person I heard."

"Only because she's Chinese."

Chuck was silent for a moment, and Mattis could almost feel his son's anger rising on the other side of the line. "Seriously," said Chuck finally, "what the hell are you doing out there, Dad? You need to get over it. The Chinese wouldn't have done this. The war is over. It's been over forever."

Another quick glance to Shao, who looked even more nervous. "We'll see," he whispered.

"Right," said Chuck. "I guess I'll leave you to it. By the way, Javier is good, thanks for asking."

He spoke without thinking. "Is that your"—the word got stuck in his throat before he forced it out—"boyfriend?"

Chuck sighed bitterly. "No, Dad," he said, and then the line clicked off.

Decorum be damned, Mattis nearly hurled the

communicator across the room, when it started beeping. Another incoming communication, but this one on the emergency line.

And on Pitt's belt, too.

And on Shao's. And Ramirez's.

"What the hell?" asked Ramirez, and the room exchanged a series of confused glances.

Chapter Eight

Friendship Station

Everyone answered their communicators at once. Mattis put his to his ear. In the background, he could hear the Chinese delegation receiving a similar message.

"Attention all personnel," it began, a synthetic, robotic text-to-speech playback. "All leave passes for all personnel are cancelled. All personnel on shore leave are to report to their vessels. This is not a drill."

Well, given that he arrived in a shuttle, that was going to pose a problem. The delegation looked at each other in silence, and then, as though some spell had broken, the Chinese delegation started yammering to each other in their own language.

"We should get to the *Midway*," said Mattis, to Pitt and Ramirez. "I know that girl like the back of my hand."

Pitt scrunched up his face, as though physically straining to find the right argument to use.

"You should remain on the station," said Yim. When did *he* get here? Was he always here? Mattis berated himself silently. "This station is well defended."

And in the command of a Chinese officer. This was hostile ground. "No," said Mattis, "I saw fighters launching from the *Midway* as I came in. If we need to get out, we can. If whatever"—he stole a quick glare at Yim—"or whoever took out Capella Station attacks here, we'll want to be mobile."

Yim's visage darkened. "Capella is a long way from *Friendship Station*," he said, an edge of caution creeping into his voice. "Whatever attacked that outpost is unlikely to strike here next…if, indeed, there is an outside force at all."

All eyes fell on Yim.

"What are you implying?" asked Mattis, glaring at him through narrowed eyes. "You think we sank our own station?"

"The PLAN have not received any information as to the identity of the attackers," said Yim, "nor seen firsthand confirmation that the station, indeed, has been destroyed at all. It could have been moved out of its orbit, or deliberately scuttled."

Mattis felt his voice creep up in volume. "Why the hell would we do that? Blow our own station to bits?"

"The enemies of China will stop at nothing to harm her," said Yim.

"Oh," spat Mattis, "so now we're enemies."

Yim said nothing.

"None of this is productive." Pitt held his hands up, as though calling for peace. "All we know, at this time, is that active duty personnel have been recalled to their ships. As none of the American diplomatic mission," he said, casting a deliberate glare Mattis's way, "are active duty personnel, it stands to reason that we should remain aboard *Friendship Station*, as a gesture of solidarity with our Chinese friends, in the face of this obvious shared threat."

Obvious shared threat. What utter garbage. Mattis's voice snapped as he spoke. "If you think for one second I'm staying on a station administrated by the PRC, you're joking."

Shao, surprisingly, nodded along. "I feel it's best," she said, "given the potential risk that the Americans pose to this station and its People's Republic administrators, that they tactfully retire to their own ship until the situation is resolved."

That was diplomatic speak for *piss off*, which he was more than happy to do. "C'mon, Pitt, let's go."

Pitt's upper lip curled back. "This is my operation," he said. "And I'm telling you we are remaining where we're put."

Mattis drew himself up to his full height and summoned forth the best glare he could. "You ever been in a war, Senator?"

Pitt glowered. "No, but—"

"A battle in space is like a thunderstorm. It's distant rumbling, and cool pleasant breezes, and dark clouds on the horizon. Before it's *all* over you at once, and then it's over with. Sometimes you end up where you started. Sometimes you're swept out into the ocean, and if that happens, you want to be with someone who can swim.

"We don't know what's happening, because in war, nobody knows what's happening. Our best bet of getting the facts is by talking directly to Fleet Command on the *Midway*. Maybe our friends over yonder blew up Capella, maybe they didn't. Either way, you won't find the truth here, only what they're willing to tell you."

Shao started to talk, but Mattis cut her off. "Senator Pitt, I'm sure you can agree that maybe, just maybe, this is a situation where your"—the very implication almost made him scowl harder—"particular talent with words and diplomacy might be needed very shortly. If that is the case, fortunately for us all, they can be conjured forth from wherever we happen to be...including a mobile battleship getting the hell out of here. You can't help our allies defend this station, Senator, but you can get out of their way."

Mattis could see the gears grinding away inside Pitt's empty, stupid head.

"Clock's ticking, Senator."

"Fine," said Pitt, the bitterness in the admission dripping from the air. "In this case, you're...right. This is an unusual situation not covered by the general orders. Let's head to the *Midway*, speak to Fleet Command, and await further instructions."

Mattis nodded his approval. "Good choice, Senator."

Pitt turned around to talk to the Chinese. Mattis stepped over to Ramirez.

"What's going on?" she asked. In her hand was an audio recorder, but she hadn't switched it on.

He glanced to the device. "Not now, Martha. This could be serious."

"*Could* be." She considered that. "So it could *not* be, too."

"More likely the former than the latter. Stations don't just vanish. The debris from the last war with the Chinese left a ring in that system that's still there. Maybe they got a signal out, maybe not, but I'm guessing a resupply ship came along and saw that there was a bunch of new debris and no station, and called it in. If the station managed to get out word they were under attack, it might have been another warship, but the Chinese—" He caught himself. "Whoever did this, they did it fast and they did it clean. No time for a general rally of the fleet. This isn't good news for us."

She nodded firmly. "Where to, then?"

"Come with us. To the *Midway.*"

"Right." A smile, ghostly and small, formed on her lips. "You haven't changed a bit."

"Neither have you."

The same *feeling* came over him, the same hesitance as when he'd first stepped into this room, been close to her. Alone. Just the two of them.

Then Pitt coughed loudly. "We're ready to go."

"Right." Mattis moved out of the room and fell into step with the rest of the diplomatic team, directly ahead of Pitt, who took up the rear.

After a moment, Pitt turned and gestured for him to wait. Obligingly, he did so, letting the others walk ten paces or so ahead.

Pitt leaned close to him, his face an entirely unamused mask.

"I warned you," said Pitt, his tone ice cold. "This is my operation. My decisions. The moment we get back to the *Midway*, you're going to request quarters, go to those quarters, and wait there until you have a shuttle back to Earth. You're *finished*, Admiral. Your career is officially done. Dead. Gone."

Mattis said nothing, but slowly reached for his breast pocket, withdrew a cigar, lit it, and puffed on it. He glared at

Pitt until the other man was forced to look away.

And then, holding the cigar between his teeth, Mattis jogged slightly to catch up with the others.

Chapter Nine

Docking Umbilical
USS Midway

Mattis puffed on his cigar the whole way to the forward docking ring, until the group found itself outside the thin steel tube that led to the *Midway.*

The marines manning the station stiffened as the three of them approached. "This ship is closed to civilians," said the closest.

Mattis stepped up. "Admiral Mattis, US Navy. You're Petty Officer Bird, yes?"

"Sir?" Bird tilted his head. "I haven't seen you in years, sir. What the hell are you doing here?"

"Here on a diplomatic mission," he said, casually puffing on his cigar. "Orders came through to report to our duty posts. Figured I'd be more use here than on this blasted station."

"Of course, Admiral," said Bird. "You'll want to report to the captain."

"Right," said Mattis, and he gestured for everyone to follow him. As Pitt passed, he gave a cheeky smile. "See, Senator, I'm still useful for something."

Then it was Pitt's turn to say nothing and scowl.

Being aboard the *Midway* was like coming back to his hometown. Everything was exactly as he remembered it, as though he'd never left; the docking umbilical led to the superstructure, and the tunnels—narrow and claustrophobic—led deeper into the ship in every direction, a narrow stairwell leading up and down. Even the scuffing on the deck was familiar, where boots had worn down the deck plating.

The ship was eternal, an unchanging creature, the crew merely guests upon it.

"You're staring," said Ramirez, good-naturedly. "Should I be worried? You and me and the other woman, all in one place? What if we fight?"

Mattis couldn't help but smile. A thousand comebacks drifted into his head—how could someone have another woman if there wasn't a first woman?—but they all felt secondary to the sense that, for a brief moment, he could enjoy the idea. The idea that, had their careers not gotten in the way, there could very well have been something there.

The Admiral and the Reporter. It sounded like a terrible romance novel found on the floor of a space station bathroom.

But it was a nice thought.

"C'mon," he said, "I'll show you to the old girl's heart."

The way to the bridge was clearly marked, but Mattis didn't need to follow the signs. He made his way down the stairwell, toward the ship's middle decks, leading all the others toward the ship's armored core. The farther they got, the busier the corridors became, but Mattis flowed through them like water. The others attracted stares, odd looks, but he passed through almost unnoticed.

The bridge. Technically the CIC, the thickly armored core of the ship, surrounded by steel and the ship itself. His office, workplace, and home for so many years.

Mattis stepped onto the bridge and, as though it were a muscle reflex, addressed the room. "Someone give me a sitrep and coffee."

A young man wearing captain's epaulettes, leaning over a monitor, straightened up and looked at him. He had a neatly trimmed dark beard, with a thick head of hair, barely a hint of gray in it at all. Right away, Mattis realized he had made a serious mistake.

"Admiral," said the man, deferentially but firmly, "welcome aboard the *Midway*. I'm Captain Malmsteen, sir." He put the slightest stress on *Captain*, just to articulate his point. "Given your experience with this ship, and the extraordinary circumstances of your arrival, I instructed our marines to give you access, including bridge access. But, with respect Admiral, you're an observer here. The *Midway* is my command."

Firm but polite. Pitt could take notes. Mattis took the cigar out of his mouth. "Of course. I'm just...making sure you're taking care of the old girl."

"She's in good hands," said Malmsteen. He went back to his work.

Dammit man, he thought, *pull it together. Back in the day, you would have hated some old fossil dragging himself onto your bridge, barking orders like he owns the place. Pretty sure there'd be a cell in the brig with his name on it in seconds.*

"Mister Pitt," said Malmsteen, "status report on that number two reactor coupling issue."

What the hell would Pitt know about reactor couplings? Mattis twisted around to glare curiously at him, but Pitt was talking with Shao over a communicator.

Instead, it was another officer, a somehow even younger man—was Mattis ever that young?—who spoke up. "All fixed, Captain. The reactor is at full power."

"Thank you, Mister Pitt," said Malmsteen.

The resemblance between the officer and the senator was uncanny. They had the same angled face, the same receding hairline. Far too similar to be a coincidence. "Wait," said Mattis to Senator Pitt, "is that your son?"

"Yes," said Senator Pitt, a ghost of a smile on his lips.

And now…*now* it all made sense. That's why he had been promoted away from the *Midway*. To make room for Pitt Junior. Like spring cleaning, out with the old, in with the new.

Well. If that wasn't piss in his cornflakes, nothing was. So much for *I did you a favor*…

Mattis wasn't angry, and he non-angrily ground his teeth together, his fists non-angrily balling at his sides as he glared at Pitt Junior, Lieutenant Commander and XO of *his* ship, strutting around on *his* bridge that he stole. That his father stole.

Ramirez touched his forearm. "Hey," she said, nice and quiet. "Easy."

Right. Easy.

Apparently she wasn't the only one who noticed. Senator Pitt slid up to his other side. "You don't like me, do you?" he asked plaintively.

"I don't think about you at all," said Mattis.

That seemed to make Senior Pitt angrier, but putting the guy in his place sure helped calm Mattis down a bit.

Senator Pitt stormed away, tiny feet thumping on the metal deck. He grabbed Commander Pitt's shoulder and hurriedly whispered something to him that Mattis couldn't hear.

Malmsteen, fortunately, spoke loud enough to include them all. "We don't have any more information than you do. I'm sorry, Senator."

One of the junior Comm officers twisted around in his seat, his console flashing. "Captain, Flash traffic from Fleet HQ."

A printer began working, decrypting the communication and preparing it to be read. Mattis fought down the urge to walk over and look.

Malmsteen picked up the printout, touching the side of it so that it could be decrypted and read. His eyes scanned over the lines of text, then jumped back to the beginning and read it again, then jumped back to the beginning and read it a third time.

Must be serious. Out of respect, Mattis extinguished his cigar between pinched fingers and returned it to his breast pocket.

Malmsteen touched the ship-wide communicator at his neck. "All senior staff report to the briefing room," he said and glanced Mattis's way. "And you as well, sir. And you, Senator."

"I'll wait here," said Ramirez.

Malmsteen laid down the printout and, for a brief moment, Mattis could see something within him being brutally

suppressed. A concern. Worry. Fear.
Serious indeed.

Chapter Ten

Briefing Room
USS Midway

Mattis always liked being in the briefing room. It meant trouble. It meant danger. But it also meant a chance to do his damn job.

The senior officers of the *Midway* filtered into the cramped room, taking seats around the central, raised wooden table. Those from the bridge came quickly, and the remainder filed in over the next few minutes. He swam in memories in this place…his first deployment with her, his first real mission. His first military action.

Damage reports and casualty assessments. That memory brought him back down. Every time there was a shooting war, someone died. Shao's ship had lost crew too, and apparently, many more than his own…

Wow, concerned for the Chinese now, are you, old man? What was wrong with him? *Focus on the present.*

Malmsteen stood at the head of the table. "Thank you all for attending so promptly. It'll come as little surprise that the first order of business is to confirm what many of you already suspect: At 0544 Zulu-Earth time, the medical ship USS *Keelaghan* detected a relayed distress call from Capella Station, reporting that they were under attack. The strength, composition, nationality and nature of their assailant or assailants are unknown at this time. However, reconnaissance by automated probes has confirmed that the station has been destroyed, seemingly with all hands." He paused, and Mattis digested the news he expected to hear. "A search is currently underway, led by the *Keelaghan*, to locate any potential survivors, but based on the support capacity of the Mark V escape pods, any recovery efforts will, in a matter of approximately sixteen hours, transition from rescue to body retrieval."

It was unlikely anyone got out alive, if the only transmission from the station was a single status report. What had *happened?* Those things were armored fortresses bristling with weapons. In peacetime, certainly, they would have been more cautious about bringing their full power to bear, but... still.

"It's particularly worrisome to me," said Mattis, "that whatever destroyed Capella either silenced all transmissions from a military-grade relay, without even static getting through, or wiped them out before they could even identify their attackers. This represents a shift in the balance of power we haven't seen since—"

Senator Pitt coughed loudly. "I'm sure you have lots to bring to the table, Admiral, but let's hear the captain out."

Mattis almost reflexively touched the still-warm cigar in his breast pocket, but let the insult slide.

"Either possibility is troubling," said Malmsteen, resuming his seat, "but the latter is downright terrifying. Either way, we have no further information to go on, so until until that point, I'm keeping the ship at Condition II."

"I concur, Captain," said Mattis. "The crew will grumble about the increased readiness, but we'll be needed soon... I can feel it."

That raised just a little smile from Malmsteen. "We Are The Fulcrum," he answered.

"What?" asked Senator Pitt, squinting in confusion.

Time to educate the son of a bitch. "It's the ship's motto," said Mattis. "The *Midway* is named for The Battle of Midway, the turning point in the Pacific theatre. Imperial Japan had the US Navy on the back foot; we were still bleeding from Pearl Harbor. The Zero ruled the skies. Their ships were faster, bigger, better. But then...the American forces intercepted and decoded a series of Japanese transmissions before their attack on Midway, reconstructing their battle plans in significant detail. The result was a hard battle—it wasn't a rout or a massacre, by any stretch, merely an even battle. Fortunately, the Japanese were surprised, their carriers in a vulnerable position refueling their aircraft, and their losses were heavy. Imperial Japan already struggled to replace lost ships, planes and pilots, whereas the US could.

"After Midway, the US had the initiative, and rode it all the way to Tokyo. Midway was the turning point, the most stunning and decisive blow in the history of naval warfare. Accordingly this ship, too, is the turning point. The fulcrum upon which battles and wars turn."

"This ship," said Senator Pitt, the venom in his voice barely disguised, "is the relic of a past war, of battles with a people who are now our friends, a needless provocation. There is *no evidence* that Capella was destroyed by anything more than an industrial accident which they mistook, in their paranoia, for an attack by some kind of outside entity. For all we know, they might have just been, I don't fucking know, hit by a comet or something, because some Junior Lieutenant was snoozing in front of their radar."

"Comets don't jam military comm relays." Malmsteen drew himself out of his seat, slowly and deliberately. "Thank you for your tactical input, Senator Pitt," he said, and then looked deliberately to his XO.

Commander Pitt stood as well. "Senator, we have a lot to discuss, and today's been a very stressful day for all of us. Perhaps you'd consider retiring to our VIP guest quarters."

The way it was phrased implied this was not a request. To Senator Pitt's credit, he stood up, scowled at his son, and stomped out of the briefing room without saying a word.

"The VIP quarters seem a bit ostentatious for someone like him," Mattis remarked. In his day, they had been reserved for visiting signatories and political figures, such as Pitt, and were spacious and lavishly decorated—especially for a military vessel. The office was full of potted plants that were actually real, set against wooden panelling and floors, filling the room with vivid hues of greens and natural browns. It was like a Bob Ross painting come to life.

"The VIP quarters," said Commander Pitt, "are currently unoccupied due to a *minor* issue. Last I heard there was a small leak—tiny, really—in the nearby sewage pipe." There was a slight crack in the facade of the officer. "Old bastard should learn to shut his face."

Sometimes the apple did fall far from the tree. The brief moment of satisfaction was stolen from him, when he recalled his own son hanging up on him. Chuck and Commander Pitt…were they so different? Was Mattis on the right side of this one?

Malmsteen tilted his head, looking away for a moment, as though listening to a noise none of the others could hear. He touched his throat. "Acknowledged. I'm on my way." Then he turned back to the rest of them. "I'm sorry, all, but duty calls. Long-range sensors have detected an incoming contact."

"A contact?" Mattis didn't like it. Not one bit. "What kind of contact?"

Malmsteen hesitated before answering. "We don't know. But it's big."

Chapter Eleven

Fighter Hangar
USS Midway

Guano walked out of the CAG's office, her gut aching as though she'd been sucker punched. Capella…gone. She'd almost been deployed to that station. But for the whim of some fleet bureaucrat, the medical ships would be picking up the pieces of her body and trying to vaguely guess what went where.

A US space station destroyed out of the blue. What the hell was happening?

"Hey," said Flatline, jogging to catch up. "What the hell, right?"

"Yeah." What else was there to say? "What the hell?"

One of the *Midway*'s other pilots, Mohinder "Longjohn" Silver, was waiting for them. "I heard you two in there," he said, grinning like the Cheshire cat, "trying to give Major Yousuf an aneurysm. Apparently it was, uh, raining dicks."

Flatline glared at him.

"Yup," said Guano, waggling her fingers in the air. "Apparently I'm *trying to start a war*, or something. Ugh." She couldn't fully stifle a laugh, not even smothering it in a massive grin. "It was all Flatline's fault," she said. "He was all like, hey, we should totally race those Chinese fighters. He basically forced me."

Flatline choked. His eyes nearly bugged out. "It wasn't me! It was her—she was all like—and then, and then…"

"It's true," said Guano, straight faced. "All his fault."

"You were racing Chinese fighters?" asked Longjohn, his eyebrows leaping toward the ceiling. "Oh shit, were they J-84's? Please tell me they were J-84's."

"Yup."

The guy was like a ten-year-old talking about a girl he had a crush on. "How…how close did you get?"

"Close enough to look into their cockpits with Mark I eyeballs."

"Holy shit! You *saw* the pilots with your own eyes?" Longjohn grabbed her shoulders. "Tell me literally everything that happened, immediately."

"I don't kiss and tell," said Guano, casually peeling his hands off her.

Undeterred, Longjohn similarly grabbed Flatline. "Tell me literally everything that happened, immediately."

"Uhh," said Flatline. "No? It's classified, dude."

"Careful," said Guano, "you'll give him another heart attack. He's delicate. Fragile. Especially after Roadie smoked him like a fine cigar."

"Never heard that one before," muttered Flatline. "Hah,

hah, hah…"

Longjohn scrutinized them carefully. "Wait, Chinese fighters… Is this because of Capella? Did they attack you?"

"They locked us up, but I don't think they *really* wanted to shoot." Guano stuck out her tongue, scrunching up her face. The memory hurt. "But dammit, they—"

"Scared the shit out of us," said Flatline.

"They did *not*." She folded her arms. "They just… concerned me."

"*Concerned* the shit out of us," said Flatline.

Right. Same difference, right?

"So," asked Longjohn, "you're still on the flight roster after all that?"

"Yeah," said Guano, taking a short breath. "Roadie had me swear to every God that I could name that I wouldn't be so, uhh, 'damn fool clusterfucked idiotic' ever again, which I was more than happy to do—"

"Likely because you'll be doing worse," said Flatline.

"Likely because I'll be doing worse." No sense denying it. She was the best pilot in the fleet, despite being nearly posted to a station out in the sticks—obviously a mistake on Fleet's behalf—and when someone was that good, they had to take some risks. "I thought he was about to blow a gasket."

"Eh," said Flatline, "if he wanted us off the flight roster, he would have just done it instead of spending twenty minutes abusing us. Roadie's a good CO in that way; he wants us to learn and do better. He's trying to teach us, not punish us."

Guano grumbled. "Cleaning the ready room for a year sure feels like punishment."

Longjohn blew out a low, long whistle. "A whole year?" He

grinned at Flatline. "You done fucked *up*, brother!"

"I told you, it was her!"

Guano guffawed. "Nah, nah. I tell you what, though, I came *this* close to shooting them…"

"That would have been bad," said Longjohn.

"Yeah, no shit!" She laughed. "Man, I would have loved to bag me a couple of J-84's, though. First kills in the *galaxy*, my friend! We would have lined them up like ducks and—"

A klaxon cut her off. The whole hangar bay flooded with red light and Yousuf's voice came over a crackling speaker.

"All hands to action stations, all hands to action stations. Alert-five craft prepare to launch and intercept bogeys at two-two-eight mark six-nine. All pilots to their craft."

"Shit," said Guano, and then all three of them ran for their ships.

"You might still get a chance," said Flatline as he pulled ahead of her, sprinting toward their Warbird.

Smartass.

Chapter Twelve

Bridge
USS Midway

Mattis led the senior staff out of the briefing room, with Captain Malmsteen and the rest trailing behind. Ramirez was right where he'd left her, arms folded in front of her.

Despite everything, despite the chaos that was seemingly sweeping through the ship and carrying all sense and logic away with it, Ramirez was there like a rock. Was she always this tough?

Of course she was. It was stupid to think otherwise—

"Admiral Mattis?" Malmsteen's voice shook him out of his trance. Damn it. How long had he been staring?

"Uhh," said Mattis unhelpfully. "Sorry, I was thinking of something else. Say again?"

"I was just asking," said Malmsteen as he slid into his command chair, every bit the pompous captain, "if you had any thoughts on the signal we've detected. Commander

Lynch?"

"I'm bringing it up now," said their comm officer. Commander Lynch, presumably.

*The signal...*yes. Mattis strode over to Lynch's tactical seat.

"This is the damnedest thing I've ever seen," said Lynch, seemingly half to him, half to Malmsteen. "It looks likes a fleet signature, it vanishes for fifteen seconds, and then it reappears. And it keeps repeating that pattern. Here, look."

"Never seen anything like it," said Mattis. "Must be a glitch."

"With such regularity, Admiral? That's a hell of a glitch."

Mattis squinted, curling back his upper lip. The guy was right. Lynch's instincts aligned with his; he just didn't like the way it *smelled*. A career captain's instinct nagged at him. Didn't feel right. "We should get our alert-five craft out there," he said finally. "Get eyes on that thing. And I don't mean radar and fancy sensors. Human eyes. See what we can see. If there's something there, then we can engage it at standoff distance. If there's nothing there...well, the fighter jocks get a little bit of excitement to break up the endless patrols and drills, don't they?"

Malmsteen smiled a proud, ever-so-slightly smug smile. "Commander Lynch?"

Lynch twisted around in his seat. "Alert-five craft have already been ordered to launch, with the rest currently either refueling or on standby."

Well, good. Mattis couldn't help but return just a little of that smile. "Nice work. I'd also move the old girl out, get away from this station—or should I say big fat target? Again, if it's nothing, no harm no foul. We get to stretch the old girl's legs.

But if there's something out there, the last place we want to be is tethered to a massive space station under Chinese command."

Malmsteen seemed less enamored by that suggestion. "I'm afraid," he said, "that moving the ship away from the Chinese station might be taken in a very poor light, especially given that the nature and intentions of this mysterious contact— whatever it may be—haven't yet been made clear."

That, thought Mattis, *was a fancy way of saying: we don't know if they're Chinese or not.*

Fair call.

"We could at least power up all our systems to alert footing," said Mattis, carefully phrasing it as a suggestion rather than a command.

Again, Malmsteen considered. "Let's wait until the picture clears, or our fighters have eyes on the contact. I don't want to risk antagonizing our Chinese friends."

Well, he tried. Malmsteen's command, Malmsteen's orders get followed. Mattis had to accept that.

"Alert fighters are away," said Commander Lynch, "designated Wing Alpha. They're vectoring toward the contact now. Another wave of fighters is being scrambled. Estimated time till launch: three minutes."

Good. Nice, even dispersion.

"Sir," said Lynch, "the signal is…it's evening out."

"Good," said Mattis and Malmsteen in chorus.

Mattis inclined his head respectfully, signaling for Malmsteen to continue.

"Analyze it," said Malmsteen, "and get a clear picture up —"

"Sir!" Commander Pitt cut over the top. "Z-space contact!"

Another ship? "Did the damn reds call in one of their friends?" asked Mattis, letting a little more venom escape than intended.

"Unclear," said Commander Pitt, reading the radar screen with frantic eyes. "Another contact, and another, and another… I'm reading a dozen ships, sir. They're not any configuration I've ever seen."

"Bring all systems to alert power," said Malmsteen, drumming his fingers on the armrests of his chair. "And recall our marines. Sound the decompression alarm until our crew are aboard. Then seal the outer hull, cross check, and detach the docking umbilical. Execute emergency disembark and move away from the space station."

"But, sir," asked Lynch, "what if there are people still in the forward docking ring? Tourists, sightseers? They won't have much time to get to the station before we open it to space."

The captain's face displayed no emotion. "Then they will have a very bad day indeed."

Sometimes being a CO meant making the hard calls. Mattis wouldn't have done it any differently, except he might not have wasted time with the alarm.

"Aye, sir," said Commander Pitt. "It will take some time to unhitch the scaffolding."

Twelve scaffolds, each tethering the ship to the station. Each would have to be unhitched manually. That would take time…too much time. Maybe the engines could pull away, breaking the scaffolds off, or maybe their hull would peel back like a banana.

Bad news.

"Very good, Commander. Start working on that scaffolding."

A thought wormed its way through his brain. Something he hadn't considered yet and, in a flash of frustration, realized he should have. "Are there any Chinese ships currently docked with *Friendship Station*?"

"Aye, sir," said Commander Pitt, "The *Fuqing*. They've been here for almost a week."

"What are *they* doing?"

Commander Pitt consulted his systems. "Emergency disembarking," he said. "Just like us."

Mattis ground his teeth together, both liking and not liking that answer. "They wouldn't do that if they were expecting a fleet's worth of reinforcements… No way they'd risk it. These new ships aren't their friends."

"And they're not ours," said Malmsteen, his tone full of guarded curiosity, "so who the hell are they?"

Chapter Thirteen

Lt. Patricia "Guano" Corrick's Warbird
Midway Fighter Bay
Docked at Friendship Station

"Whoa!" Guano felt a shudder run through the *Midway* and into her Warbird, the tremor vibrating her seat. "What the hell was that?"

"We blew the docking umbilical," said Flatline, his voice tight. "Check your external camera."

She did so, piping the feed through to her main screen, then immediately wished she hadn't.

Two bodies, spinning in space, surrounded by puffs of gas and the wiggling worm of the docking umbilical, broken.

"That's cold," she said, shutting off the feed. "Poor bastards…what a way to go."

Flatline said nothing. She took a deep breath and refocused herself. No time to think about it. They were still attached by the scaffolding, anyway, so… it was a moot point.

Why was she so jumpy? Flatline, by far the most chicken-shit of the two of them, hadn't even been rattled—he knew where to look. Like he'd sensed it.

Instinct. That's what she needed. She needed her pilot's instinct.

Roadie's voice crackled into her ear. "Guano, you are clear to launch. I'll come out with you as Wing Bravo."

Of course. Dammit—all her instruments were green! She was sitting there with her thumb up her ass with Major Yousuf looking on. "Roger, Roadie." Why hadn't she been paying attention? What the hell? "Guano launching."

With a shaking hand, she opened the throttle and her ship leapt away from the *Midway*'s hangar bay, leaving a thin stream of expanding silver behind it as it soared through space. They were the second wave. The alert five were already way ahead of them.

"All wings, this is Roadie." Yousuf sounded stressed. *Join the club.* "We're going to be racing to catch up to the alert fighters. *Midway* says there's some kind of contact out there, an intermittent one, and we're tracking it down. Stretch your legs, people, we are *moving*."

For the second time today, Guano opened her throttle, pushing it right against the redline. Roadie was just behind her on her port. Her radar painted four fighters up ahead, friendlies.

"Roger," said Longjohn in her ears. "This is Wing Alpha. Can't see anything out here. Just empty space."

Her hand was trembling, holding the throttle. Too much adrenaline in one day. She should focus…keep it under cool and in control. Fighter pilots only had two settings: cool and ice cold.

"Keep looking, numbskull," said Roadie. "We're vectoring to your position, ETA six minutes."

"Don't know why you're running so hard," said Longjohn. "What? Jealous of Guano?"

"Ain't like that," said Flatline over the radio. "Believe me, the way she flies…"

The slightest bit of dead air. Everyone was waiting for her. *Banter,* she thought to herself. *Say something. Show you're not cracking up.*

"Yeah," said Guano. "I'm just a regular grade-A lunatic, but really, I'm shaking in my panties over here." The joke fell flat. Nobody laughed. Perhaps there was something in her tone that suggested sincerity. She tried again. "See, the thing is, if Flatline's ticker gives up again, I can probably claim a month's stress leave, so you know…the more I push him, the better."

That got a titter. From Longjohn in particular. "Yeah, well, I wish my gunner was known for *dying* on the job. Would really make my leave situation a little easier. Francine, you disappoint me." Playful laughter. "Whatcha reckon, Caboose? How's your gunner?"

"That *ain't* my callsign," said the woman, which was probably the *worst* thing anyone could say. Howls struck up over the radio.

"Rules of callsigns," said Roadie, talking over the laughter. "Number one: If you don't already have one, you will be assigned one by us, your *bestest* buddies. Number two: You probably won't like it. Number three: If you complain, well, you'll be assigned an even—"

A huge white flash turned the communication into static,

searing her eyes. The computer snapped up various filters and tried to block it out, but the skin on her face and neck tingled.

Instantly, Roadie's voice was all work, no play. "All craft, check in by the numbers! Bravo-1, check!"

Check in! Check in or people will think you're hit! Panic reared up within her, but she fought it down, squinting to see. The black afterimage began to fade and she, burned and half-blind, fumbled for the radio key. "Bravo-2, check."

"Wing Alpha," said Roadie, "report."

Her vision came back. That flash…a Z-jump aftermath. There were ships around. She looked at her radar.

A dozen capital ships saturated her radar. They were right in front of her, each one of them a towering wall of metal, huge, pushing past even the *Midway*. They were black and featureless, with glowing red navigation lights, ominous, blocky, dark beasts.

Nothing was left of Wing Alpha. Two silver trails ran dead into one of the ships, two blackened scorch marks marring the front of its hull. Shit. So much for Longjohn and Caboose. Gone.

"They're gone," said Guano simply, entranced. They were just so big…

"Corrick!" said Flatline behind her. "Pull up!"

Oh shit! She was blindly following the others to their fate. Guano yanked the throttle to one side, steering her craft away from the strange, alien vessels and back toward open space.

Roadie swung around above her, inverted, looking down at her. "USS *Midway*, priority alert, this is the CAG: We have a dozen skunks out here. I say again: twelve contacts, all capital ships. Alert fighters have been destroyed. Commence SAR procedures and route distress beacons to our computers."

Search-And-Rescue was a procedure, at this point, barely worth considering. The ships had gone straight in. Nobody had ejected.

"Look," said Flatline, "the capital ships are launching strike craft!"

They were, too. The center mouths of the flat, boxy ships had opened like a maw, and from them, three craft had emerged, their engines leaving a dark red trail behind them, a bloody mirror of their own silver exhaust. Then another three came behind those fighters. From *all* the ships… Scores of them, a dark swarm bearing down on them at impossible speed.

"I count forty bogeys," said Guano, trying to keep the tremor out of her voice. "More."

"They're coming in fast," said Roadie. "We can't outrun them. Designating those craft as bandits. Tally, Bravo-2, get ready to turn and engage."

Fight them. Two US fighters versus almost fifty craft of unknown alien origin.

"This is Wing Charlie," said a voice in her ear. "We are ETA your position, tally in six minutes."

Six minutes. There was no way they were going to last that long.

Chapter Fourteen

Bridge
USS Midway

The whole bridge leapt to life, instantly turning the small, cramped room into a hubbub. Fingers clicking on keyboards. Beeping systems and alarms. Voices calling out reports.

"Contacts designated Skunk Alpha through Lima, painting with targeting lasers."

"All weapons coming online. Guns are loading and coming around. Prepared to lay down fire."

"Still no response from Wing Alpha. Craft aren't squawking transponders."

"Damage control teams report the umbilical has detached, and they've been able to remove scaffold one. Scaffolds two through twelve are still attached."

"Captain, Wing Beta reports capital ships are launching strike craft."

That last report caught both his and Malmsteen's attention,

both heads swiveling.

"Play their report," said Malmsteen.

The voice of an Arabic-sounding pilot was difficult to hear over the noise. Mattis strained to make out his exact words. *Twelve contacts, all capital ships… Alert fighters…destroyed… SAR procedures…*

"We should dispatch the SAR bird," said Lynch. "It's possible they ejected."

Mattis had been in enough fights to know that when people said things like *possibly ejected*, that was more of a prayer than a legitimate tactical assessment. "Do it, but keep the SAR bird close," he said. "Don't let it stray into weapons fire. Wait until we clear space first."

Lynch hesitated. His eyes flicked to Malmsteen, struggling to catch his attention, looking for approval. Delay, delay…

"Yes, Lynch?" asked Malmsteen. Great. Now Lynch had to repeat the whole order.

"Captain, the Admiral suggested that we keep our SAR bird at standoff distance."

Malmsteen considered. "If our pilots are out there, they'll need extraction. Belay that, Commander. Order the rescue craft in close."

"Aye sir, SAR bird away."

Mattis took a breath, letting it out slowly. It wasn't that Malmsteen overrode him, it was…the delay. The inefficiency.

Once again, Mattis had to tell himself, a little more forcefully than he had before, that the *Midway* wasn't his ship. Not anymore. And it couldn't be, not if his every order was to be cross checked. That kind of overhead would destroy their combat effectiveness.

"Captain," said Commander Pitt, "I have Admiral Yim on the line. He reports that the station is coming to combat effectiveness, and they're forming a defensible posture with the *Fuqing*. Heavy torpedo launchers are being loaded now. There's some delay priming their warheads, but they report they'll have that fixed, uh, soon."

In combat, *immediately* was just in time, *momentarily* was too long, and *soon* was an eternity.

"Tell him to step on it," said Malmsteen. "We're going to need the station's firepower if we want to take on a dozen contacts with just us and the *Fuqing*."

"Aye, sir." Commander Pitt repeated his request into the line.

"Also Commander," said Malmsteen, "if Yim can't get his precious torpedoes loaded fast enough, spin up the Z-drive."

"We're rabbiting?" asked Mattis incredulously. The intruders had just killed two Warbirds. Two people in each of those… American blood had been shed. To retreat without firing a shot seemed an unconscionable insult.

"I'm keeping my options open," said Malmsteen.

But it was more than that. To power the Z-drive would take critical power away from defenses and weapons. It was fighting with one hand tied behind their back. Wasn't twelve to one already enough for the bastard?

Commander Pitt touched his earpiece. "Sir, I also have the *Fuqing* actual on the line. They've detected our Z-drive spinup. She wants to know our…" His tone grew confused and bitter. "Intentions."

Malmsteen ignored the request, instead choosing to deal with something Mattis didn't much care to deconstruct. It was the *Midway*, the *Fuqing* and *Friendship Station* against an unknown, powerful enemy. This was no time for politics.

Mattis walked over to Commander Pitt, picked the earpiece off his ear, and put it on. "Captain Chao. This is Admiral Mattis."

"It's *Shao*," came the frosty voice on the other line. "You're not abandoning us, are you, Americans?"

Shao. Not *Chao*. Dammit. Mattis silently glowered at his own error. "Listen. Captain. Those ships aren't American. But they aren't Chinese either. And they aren't looking friendly to *either* of us."

"Tell me something I don't know," she said.

"I know you're a good captain." The words kind of tumbled out. "We... When we spoke, your only concern was for the loss of your crew. Well, those bastards—whoever the hell they are—just killed four of my pilots, and they're closing in on all of us pretty damn quickly. Whatever disagreements we have, Captain Shao, I'm sure you'll agree: the *Midway* cannot stand against twelve ships, but neither can you and your station."

"So you're just going to run?" She practically spat the words, but there was something else there, too. "I expected you to be made of sterner stuff, Admiral!"

"It's—it's not my decision," he said, far weaker than he meant to. "The *Midway* is Malmsteen's command."

"Don't give me that. He's a captain. You're an admiral. Perhaps my knowledge of American ranks is somewhat out of date, but you *should* outrank him."

It was more complicated than that... Excuses flowed through his head like a gushing torrent over a waterfall, all grinding together into a word-salad that just ultimately sounded like a string of excuses.

Mattis ground his teeth together. He needed to do something.

He needed to do something *very* stupid. "Standby," said Mattis, and muted the line.

With that dark, churning feeling deep in his gut, Mattis turned to Malmsteen. "Captain," he said, raising his voice loud enough to be heard over the din, "The *Fuqing* reports that they will fire on us if we do not power down our Z-drive and divert that energy to our weapons systems."

Malmsteen, then, did the absolute worst thing he could do: hesitate.

He sat there, in his fancy chair, doing nothing.

"To be blunt, Captain," said Mattis, trying to jolt the guy into action. "They have a good point. We can either die separately or we can fight together and stand a chance. Best decide now. These skunks are looking a mite ornery."

Silence. Nothing.

So Mattis reached over Lynch's console and casually hit the emergency shutdown on the Z-drive.

The system whined, and with a pathetic whimper, shut down. The energy flooded their weapons systems, and the tactical console lit up.

"Sir!" shouted Lynch.

"Admiral," said Commander Pitt, "are you out of your fucking *mind?*"

Malmsteen remained frozen, staring wide eyed at Lynch's console, at the blinking red display that counted down the time until they could jump again. 19 minutes, 59 seconds. Essentially forever.

All the noise died. In the stunned silence, Mattis, with a careful, deliberate action, touched his stolen earpiece.

"I fixed it," he said. "Z-drive powering down."

The line lost its distinctive hiss. Shao had muted the line, presumably to talk to someone else on her end. At least she hadn't hung up… That was a small mercy, but he'd take whatever he could at the moment.

Nobody said anything. Mattis matched their stares, eyes narrowed, daring anyone to say anything or do anything.

The hiss came back. "You don't get a cookie for doing the right thing," said Shao. "We're not friends."

"We don't have to be," said Mattis. "Just keep your guns pointed at those skunks, and we'll do the same."

"That's enough for now," said Shao, to his significant relief. "Stand by for shared firing solutions and engagement plans."

Malmsteen suddenly seemed to realize what Mattis had done. "Open a communication," he said, his voice stunned and small. "All channels, all frequencies. Tell them we surrender. Mister Pitt, tell the Chinese to stand down. Lay down arms. We can't fight—"

"We're already fighting!" roared Mattis, any semblance of pretending Malmsteen was in command now gone. "We just don't know it yet!"

"Sir," said Lynch. Mattis wheeled on him, about ready to have another argument, but Lynch's finger was pointed at the radar screen. "Look, sensors have detected some kind of… mass. The lead skunk is towing something. Something *big*."

"A mass?" asked Mattis. "How big?"

"Approximately four hundred meters across," said Lynch. "Spectrometric analysis suggests it's…it's rock and ice, Admiral. Just mass."

No way the hostile ship would be just, coincidentally, towing that thing. They wouldn't need the water. They wouldn't need the raw materials. It was something else. Not a shield, it was too brittle… Not anything. What value was in a huge chunk of frozen rock?

Then it came to him. "That ship," he asked, dreading the question. "Does it have a very large power signature?"

"Yes," said Lynch. "More than the others."

"It's a mass driver," said Mattis. He'd seen them before. During the war, Chinese stations had them—they were the only things big enough to use them. They could use almost *anything* as ammunition. A purpose-built hunk of iron, or just any old massive object…an asteroid, a comet, or even a ship hulk. They required tremendous amounts of energy and were generally considered impractical and unwieldy when compared to smaller, more precise railguns. "Their lead ship…that whole ship is a *gun.*"

"And it's aiming at us," said Commander Pitt.

Chapter Fifteen

Bridge
USS Midway

"We need to get out of here right *now*," said Mattis. "Mister Lynch, status on that scaffold?"

"Sir," said Lynch, "we're still attached. Damage control teams report that they've successfully uncoupled scaffold two and are making their way over to scaffold three."

They'd unhooked two in a few minutes. That was far, far too slow. "No," said Mattis. "Have our teams return to the ship immediately. We'll do this the quick way. Helm, ready all engines ahead."

"Uhh," said the helmsman, a fresh-faced kid who couldn't possibly be any more than a year or two out of the academy. "Sir?"

Nobody moved. Mattis's anger swelled. "Do it!" he roared.

"C-Charging engines, sir!"

"Belay that," said Malmsteen, seeming to find his voice at

exactly the *wrong* time. "I'm in command here, not Admiral Mattis. And we haven't exhausted our diplomatic options. Commander Lynch, hail those ships again. We can talk our way out of this."

No. No, they couldn't.

Malmsteen's in charge, Malmsteen's in charge, Malmsteen's in charge… The more he said it to himself, the less credible it sounded in his mind's ear. *Malmsteen's an idiot.*

Commander Pitt moved beside him, dropping his voice so that only Mattis could hear. "Admiral, look…this is Malmsteen's first real battle. Mine too. You're doing it right, but…I know what you're thinking, and the helmsman knows it too. We can't just force ourselves away from the moorings. They're dug in deep in the ship's hull. We'll tear ourselves apart."

Was there a problem in human history firepower couldn't solve? "Open fire with our main guns," said Mattis. "Blast that crap off. Don't have to get all of it, just enough that we can pull away."

"We can't," said Pitt, shaking his head. "Those guns don't have the depression to hit our own hull. By design, Admiral."

Good point. Fortunately, they had smaller weapons. "Engage point-defense on the scaffold, then. The autocannons should take care of it nicely."

"We *can't*," said Lynch, again, his tone exasperated, still trying to keep his voice down. "The ship's computers won't let us fire on our own hull."

When had they made *that* change? Probably part of the refit, bringing the *Midway* up to modern standards. Modern ships. Always too cautious. "So," said Mattis, feeling like he was talking to a child. "Override them!"

"That'll take hours," said Pitt. "Our systems are just not designed for—"

"Strike craft? Can they hit it?"

"The next wave isn't out for four minutes, and then they'll need to land and rearm…assuming, of course, they can even get their missiles to lock on the scaffolding, which, given that it isn't a hot target, isn't guaranteed. Their guns aren't powerful enough, and the missiles's warheads won't detonate that close to the hull."

Nothing would work.

"Captain," said Lynch, turning to Malmsteen. "I'm reading a massive buildup of energy around the lead ship, and they're pulling in the mass closer to their hull."

"They're loading their gun," said Mattis. "We *have* to get out of here. Right now."

"Hail them again," said Malmsteen.

It hadn't worked the first three times, it wouldn't work now.

Options. There had to be a way… None of their own guns would work; they were all too smart, too new. They needed something either old school, too old to care if it was being shot at by itself, or they needed some other kind of gun. Guns that wouldn't care about shooting their hull.

Lightbulb. Mattis touched his ear. "Shao, you still on the line?"

"Yes, Admiral."

"I'm about to make your day." He picked the cigar out of his breast pocket and chomped down on it. "You still carrying those ten-inch cannons? The ones that couldn't penetrate our hull during the battle, but heavily damaged all our outsides?"

"If you're here to remind me of past defeats, Admiral, this is *not* a good time—"

"Believe me, I'm not." Mattis ran his tongue over the back of the cigar. "Captain Shao, hear this: Our undocking procedure is fucked up. We're stuck on the scaffolding. On my authority, I need you to open fire on the USS *Midway* with your ten inches, targeting the scaffolds until we're free. How copy?"

"Oh, that'll be my pleasure," said Shao, a little too quickly, and he could sense that, perhaps, it really was. "You know how to make a woman happy, Admiral." She switched languages to Chinese, which, strangely, his earpiece translated almost instantly. "Bring the guns online, target the scaffolding pinning the USS *Midway*! Free our comrades!"

The ship began to shake, a pounding reverberating through the bridge like distant rain on a tin roof. Every monitor linked to external cameras lit up, glowing an angry yellow. The *Fuqing* rained fire down on them, blasting away the scaffolding, each shell a fiery streak leaping through space that burst against the hull in a way that was both familiar and, strangely, more terrifying.

The barrage ceased. "*Midway*," said Shao in his ear, "you are now clear. I hope it was good for you, too."

Flirting? In the middle of a pitched battle? "Seems like your shells stung a bit more than I remember," said Mattis. "Have you been giving them upgrades on the sly?"

"Oh," said Shao, "of *course*. I just assumed you would have upgraded your hull to match."

Well, no time to consider it. They were scorched, cooked, but they were free. The tangled, blasted remains of the scaffolding hung limply in space.

"The lead ship is preparing to fire," said Lynch, staring at his monitor. "The mass has been fully loaded within the ship!"

"Clear moorings!" shouted Mattis. "All engines full ahead! Now!"

And then, with a white flash, the hostile ship fired.

Chapter Sixteen

Lt. Patricia "Guano" Corrick's Warbird
44km from Friendship Station

Two versus forty. There was just no way…but in the heat of the moment, Guano had nothing to think about but the next second ahead of her.

All they had to do was last for six minutes. Three hundred sixty seconds. No worries.

Spinning and turning, like a swarm of angry hornets, the hostile craft descended. They were thin and angular, covered in sharp spines and protrusions, asymmetrical and oddly shaped as though grown from crystals.

"Bravo-2," said Roadie in her ear, "break on my mark. Three, two, one… Mark."

She cut her engines and yanked back on the stick. The Warbird pitched upward, spinning on its axis, the g-forces crushing her into her seat. She heard Flatline grunting, gasping behind her until the craft leveled out, its nose pointed to the enemies. Silver engine wash streamed over their craft.

"Weapons free," said Roadie. "Engage at will. Light 'em up."

She thumbed the master-arm switch to *live*. The hum of her weapons-lock radar filled the cockpit, but there were so many fighters. "Which one do I shoot?" she asked, eyes flicking between dozens of identical craft.

"Doesn't matter!" shouted Flatline. "Just fire!"

Good tone, solid lock. She squeezed the trigger, her Warbird's airframe shuddering briefly as the missile leapt off its railings and darted toward the enemy, a white plume behind it. "Fox three," she said, almost a fraction of a second too late. "Missile away."

"Fox three," said Roadie, as a single missile flew away from his craft.

She switched targets and shot again, loosing another missile on her right side. "Fox three," she called, "missiles away. They're going in, they're going in…"

Her twin missiles continued to accelerate, each a little yellow dot on their radar. Silver engine exhaust splattered against their canopy, and through the mist, she saw an angry golden flash as her first missile detonated against the hull of the enemy fighter. The strange craft, its surface splintered like shattered glass, broke into a dozen fractured pieces, spilling atmosphere as secondary explosions engulfed it, blasting the fragile-seeming craft into millions of pieces. Barely a second later, her second missile hit home, blasting another bandit into shards.

"Splash one," she said, a sudden surge of excitement rushing through her. "Splash two."

"Good hits, good hits," said Roadie. "Swing and a miss for me, no joy." One miss for him, and two hits for her. Good.

The swarm of ships, undeterred by the loss of two of their kin, descended on them. Red streaks of fire leapt from the spines on their front and sides, bursts of hyper-accelerated mass. Guano kicked out with her left foot, flooring the rudder and opening the throttle, pulling out of her own engine wash and into clear space.

Something struck the rear of her ship, screaming as it tore through her hull and out the side.

"We're hit," said Flatline, his voice tight. "Dammit, they clipped the starboard side of the hull."

The craft still maneuvered. Still flew. "I'm good in the front," said Guano.

"Looks like it missed everything," said Flatline. "Good in the back. ECM active, guns are ready."

Guano alternated her feet, fishtailing the ship back and forth as red streaks zipped past her cockpit. There were so many. "Ready for another couple of shots?" she asked.

"Damn straight," said Flatline. "When we're winchester on long-range weapons, bring them into guns range. I wanna punch them on the nose."

Guano spun again, and pointed her nose toward two more fighters. Flatline locked them up and she squeezed the trigger. "Fox three." Once again a missile leapt out, but this time, the engine spluttered out after barely a second, the missile tumbling end over end uselessly. She saw a smoking hole on one side as it fell; the missile had been damaged when her ship had been raked by enemy fire. They were lucky it hadn't exploded.

One left. This would be the last of their radar-guided missiles. After that, they would have to close to dogfight range. "Fox three," she said, "winchester on long-range missiles."

"Acknowledged," said Roadie, "fox three, fox three, fox three." A ripple-fire; he was dumping all his remaining long-ranged missiles at once, obviously confident.

Or desperate.

The missiles streaked out, all four of them, but this time, the hostile craft were not easy prey. They fired their red streaks, high-velocity masses clipping the missiles, defeating each of them in turn. They burst into yellow flashes, too far away from their targets, each futilely spraying shrapnel in every direction, too little, too far away.

Well, shit, she thought.

"Well, shit," said Flatline.

"That's what I was thinking," said Roadie. There was the briefest pause, then he spoke again. "Bravo-2, close to dogfighting range. Engage, engage, engage."

"Tally," said Guano, hoping it wasn't the last radio transmission she ever sent. "Going in."

She opened her fighter's throttle and roared toward the hostile ships, Roadie on her wing, and in the back seat, she could hear Flatline's breathing pick up.

"You okay back there?" she asked tepidly.

"Yeah," said Flatline, his voice shaky. "L-Let's do this. Let's go."

The red streams of the enemy fighters spun in a corkscrew as they drew closer and closer.

Chapter Seventeen

Bridge
USS Midway

The lead hostile ship fired and, almost faster than the human eye could see, its massive payload streaked across open space, splintering and breaking apart from the forces exerted on it, forming thousands of tinier missiles that bombarded *Friendship Station* all at once.

A deafening howl stole every sound, tonnes of metal dragging on tonnes of metal as *Friendship Station* came apart, millions of pieces of debris scraping across the *Midway*'s hull. The blast wave of her erupting reactors tilted the ship on its side, and everyone was flung into the far wall.

Mattis landed on something softer than he expected—something squishy and human, not hard steel like a bulkhead—and then Ramirez landed on top of him, blasting the air from his lungs. Entirely by instinct, he wrapped his arms around her, holding her tight.

The lights went out, plunging the entire room into utter darkness for a terrifying second, blacker than space outside, and then slowly, flickering, groaning, emergency power came on.

Artificial gravity reasserted itself over inertia and everyone slid off the wall, down to the ground.

"You okay?" asked Mattis, forcing air into his lungs. He was too old for those kinds of maneuvers, far too old… The wheeze in his lungs was unbecoming.

"Yeah," said Ramirez. She was white as a sheet, her hands shaking, and blood ran freely from her crown, framing her face in red. "I think. I feel kind of dizzy. What happened?"

"We got blown up," said Mattis simply.

"Damage report," groaned Commander Pitt, but nobody was close enough to their stations to comply.

Mattis, harnessing the stubbornness that had carried him this far in his career, dragged himself up to his feet. As he did, Ramirez looked past him, to whatever he'd hit on the way down.

Captain Malmsteen, his neck twisted at a horrid angle, almost completely around on his shoulders, the skin broken, blood pouring from the tears and forming a pool on the corner of the bulkhead.

"Don't look," said Mattis. He offered his hand to Ramirez, an offer he retracted when he saw it was covered in blood. So was his back. Wet. Damp. The other hand was clean. He offered her that instead.

Shakily, Ramirez pulled herself up. For a civilian, she was doing very well.

"Back to your posts," said Mattis, addressing the bridge

with as much strength as he could muster, far less than he wanted and needed. "I want a damage report, just something. Doesn't have to be perfect." He stumbled over to Lynch's console, grabbed it, and touched the ship's intercom. "Corpsman to the bridge. Multiple casualties."

Nobody responded. They were probably inundated with casualty reports.

Lynch dragged himself up to his console, and Mattis stepped aside. The guy's arm was clearly broken. It hung at a twisted angle, giving him a second elbow. His skin was white as a ghost. Shock.

"We've lost hull integrity in several sections," said Lynch, his words slurring together. "Damage repair crews are… dealing with it."

"*Friendship Station*?" asked Mattis, although he knew the answer.

"Gone." Lynch shook his head, dazed, and kept reading. "The, uh…the outer docking arm detached and hit the rear of the ship. We're down to maneuvering thrusters only, no sublight propulsion. One of our long-range radars is out, but the other's fine. We'll lose some target fidelity, but we're not blind."

Without engines, they were stuck here—but if he hadn't powered down the Z-drive, the whole thing might have gone critical. Probably would have. "Okay," he said, taking stock of their options. "So we're boxing. We can't shift our feet. One eye's swollen shut. We can dodge, a little, but… we're bleeding. Backed into the corner of the ring. Can we hit back?"

"Weapons are operational," said Lynch. "More or less. Some of our point defense cannons are damaged, but the screen will hold. Guns, missiles, torpedoes…all good to go, Admiral."

He hated stressing an injured man, but he had to. "Commander Lynch, select a target and open up on them. Everything we got, don't be shy."

"Very good, sir," said Lynch, obviously struggling. "Punching in the targets now. They're…all around us."

"Good," said Mattis. "That simplifies things." He took a deep breath. There was a certain advantage in being outnumbered: the ability to fire freely without hitting their allies. "Mister Pitt, status on the *Fuqing*?"

"They're engaging, sir," said Commander Pitt, "but they, too, have suffered damage. They are transmitting firing solutions for us."

"Good. Use them."

"Weapons ready, sir," said Lynch.

Beaten, bloody, but still standing, the *Midway* wasn't out of this fight yet. "Fire."

Chapter Eighteen

Lt. Patricia "Guano" Corrick's Warbird
39 km from Friendship Station

The hostile fighters descended on her, their weapons flashing angrily, sending red streaks across space, each one a piercing lance trying to blow her to pieces.

Not today. "Guns, guns, guns!" She squeezed the trigger, strafing one of the fighters, her cannon rounds blasting huge holes in its upper structure. The craft belched smoke, drifting lazily past her cockpit.

Behind her, Flatline opened up, his rear quad-cannon sending shells streaking across space, finishing the craft in a fiery explosion. Her ship's computer played a generic explosion sound behind her as a situational awareness cue.

"Got him," said Flatline, energy surging into his voice. "I nailed him!"

Three down in just a few minutes. "Nice shot," said Guano, pulling the ship around. Debris plinked off the hull, deflected by the thick plating.

"Yeah," said Flatline. "But we got hit before. Cost a missile, and there's damage to the hull."

He needed to stop complaining. "I know," she said, swinging her nose around. She pulled to the starboard, a nimble enemy fighter pulling out of her guns arc just in time.

"We've used our long-range missiles," said Flatline. He *really* needed to stop complaining. "And we've got less than a thousand rounds of ammunition for two sets of guns. Even with a computer guiding the rounds, and the short-range missiles we have left, there isn't enough ammo to go around."

"Right," said Guano, just as a pair of fighters darted in front of her. "Looks like they'll have to share!"

She squeezed the trigger, but her burst went between the two enemies, the rounds flying off into the black.

Damn. That would have been so cool if I'd hit both of them. Typical.

Flatline fired behind her. Three of the hostile ships split away in a multi-pronged star, their engine exhausts shimmering in the refracted light of his weapons fire. One round clipped one of the enemies, a flash on its port side, but it continued to fly, turning back to them.

Eight hundred rounds left. Really only a few bursts. They needed to put more ammo in these things. In order to "get some," you gotta "bring some."

Guano dove her ship as the hostile fighters screamed overhead, their red exhaust creating a striped curtain over her cockpit. She rolled her ship, pulling the stick back into her gut and opening the throttle.

G-forces crushed her into her seat, and for a second, spots

swam in front of her eyes. She kept turning, silver exhaust spraying out as she desperately tried to avoid being killed.

The ship appeared in front of her, right as Roadie flew up from below, blasting it into a thousand pieces with a heat seeker. "Fox two!"

Debris sprayed over their cockpit, tiny shards of spaceship smashing against the hardened transparent cockpit. It cracked, blossoming into a spiderweb, her HUD flickering weakly.

Guano nearly choked. "You're supposed to say that *before you fire*, you goddamn idiot!"

"Too many G's," said Roadie. "Sorry."

Sorry? Right. She took a deep breath, eyes cautiously examining the cracks. They seemed intact, but... "Hey Flatline," she asked, "you have your ejection suit on right?"

"Yeah?"

"It's sealed?" she asked.

"Of course it is, why?"

"… No reason." She whacked the side of her HUD display, and the flickering stopped. It was difficult to see out through the cracked glass, but she couldn't fix it.

Then a searing white flash lit up space, turning the hostile fighters half white, half black. Flatline shouted incoherently behind her.

"What? What?" she asked, twisting around in her seat to look.

Friendship Station had broken in half, the white flash her reactors going up. From it, a massive shockwave was heading their way.

"Oh shit."

Roadie barked in her ear. "We gotta outrun that blast

wave," he said. "The capital ships can survive it, but we can't. You wanted to race, Corrick, now's your chance!"

She didn't need to be told twice. Guano opened the throttle, angling her exhaust toward the ruins of *Friendship Station*. Her ship leapt forward, crushing her into her seat. The hostile fighters pulled ahead of her, outrunning the blast too. Faster and faster she went. Two kilometers a second. Three. Four.

It wasn't going to be enough. The shockwave was gaining on them. They needed cover, something to shield them from it. Something to hide behind.

Out of the corner of her eye, a reflection in the shattered cockpit glass. A glint. Something she couldn't possibly have seen if the glass was intact.

A capital ship. A small one. Destroyer class, probably a little bigger. But they were going too fast; she'd overshoot if she didn't...

"Follow me!" she shouted, pulling back the throttle, feeling the forces push her toward the glass. "Come on, Roadie, there's a ship we can hide behind!"

"Are you fucking crazy?" said Flatline, practically screeching. "We have to get out of here! Faster, faster, not slower, slower!"

No time to argue. "Roadie, form up on me, this way." She swung her craft around, sliding into the shadow of the ship, braking and coming to a dead stop.

"Hope you're right about this," said Roadie.

Three, two, one... Roadie slid in just behind her, and then the shockwave passed overhead. The force shook her ship, tumbling it over and over like a rodeo ride, and she eyed the glass with a skeptical eye.

It held. Amazingly. She waggled the stick, aligning herself to galactic central point.

"Okay," she said, taking in a deep breath through her oxygen mask. "We're good back here. Roadie?"

"Yeah," he said, "I'm good. Where are those fighters?"

She craned her neck, looking for them, but her radar had no signals. Only debris. Despite being ahead of her, they hadn't outrun the blast.

No time to feel smug and superior. The hostile cap ship was moving away from them, toward the cloud of debris that, only moments ago, had been *Friendship Station*.

"What are they doing?" she asked. "They're moving in to attack?"

Her computer plotted the course. She saw where they were going and immediately understood.

They were heading to the *Midway*. To finish off their mothership.

"Come on," she said. "We have to follow them!"

"Hey?" said Flatline, his voice a little…vague. Distant.

"What?" she asked.

He didn't answer straight away. Guano took off after the ship, weaving from side to side, just in case they decided to shoot. She pitched the nose downward, and little red droplets floated up, splattering on the broken cockpit glass.

She could hear his breathing behind her, growing a little more labored. "Flatline?"

"Corrick, I…I think I'm bleeding."

Chapter Nineteen

Bridge
USS Midway

Cannons spoke silently in the depths of space, torpedoes flew out from the ship in waves, and her point defense cannons fired a seemingly endless stream of shells out toward the attacking ships.

Mattis hadn't felt so alive in years. "Bring the number four gun up," he said. "Get it firing with the others. We have to hit them in a barrage. Transfer all the heat to one section of the hull, soften it, so the next barrage can punch through."

"The gunnery crew know how to shoot," said Commander Pitt, glaring at him. At that moment, he seemed his father's son, the spitting image of a jackass.

"Doesn't hurt to be reminded every now and then." Mattis looked over to Lynch. The guy was getting worse, sweaty and pale, but right now—especially since the corpsman hadn't arrived—everyone was needed. Commander Lynch was doing good work. "We need every advantage we can get."

"No question," said Commander Pitt. To his credit, he didn't argue the point any further. "Number four gun is up again. Adding it to the barrage."

All that was good, but they needed engines. "How are those damage control teams faring? Any chance we can move sometime soon?"

"The docking ring debris messed the engines up pretty good," said Commander Pitt. "Teams are in place, but work is slow. There are just too many sections that are holed, too many casualties. Preliminary reports suggest we won't be able to get away for some time. "

Some time was a euphemism for *never for the duration of this battle*, which, given their present situation, might as well be forever. "We'll just have to make do," said Mattis. A sinking feeling in his gut almost squashed his next question flat but, after a quick glance to Ramirez and then back to Pitt, he forced it out. "ETA on the Z-drive recharge?"

"Oh, so *now* we wanna get out of here?" The anger in his voice was understandable. "Eleven minutes, Admiral. Assuming our Z-drive doesn't take any damage from now until then, which is a bit of a definite maybe. Regardless, we won't be able to get out of here for some time yet."

More of the *some time* same-same. "Noted," said Mattis. "Pitt, do me a favor. Keep me posted on that—we might have to get out of here real quick."

"How could I refuse," said Commander Pitt, "after all you've done to try and kill me with spontaneous, poorly thought through attempts to secure the cooperation of the Chinese flagship?"

A fair barb, and one he didn't answer. Eleven minutes. He could do this. "Status on our strike craft?"

"They're heavily engaged, but we lost some when the station went up. The remainder are damaged or non-combat effective. We're trying to rally them now, but...they're heavily engaged."

"Captain," said Lynch, the urgency in his voice seeming to cut through the haze of his injuries, "the lead ship. I'm detecting a massive power signature coming from it. They're loading another mass—something smaller, but still big enough to crush even a cap ship."

Either they were going to fire on the Chinese ship or on them. No prizes for guessing which one. The attackers would have realized that their engines were out.

"Lynch," said Mattis, "how many shots of that thing do they have?"

"No more masses," said Lynch. "This is their last one. I think it's their emergency reserve. One for the station, one to mop up."

Made sense. Probably too damn heavy to carry more than that. "Okay," said Mattis. "They got one shot to hit us, and we can't move. Analysis: When they fired last time, when did the energy reading reach its peak? How long did it take?"

"Uhh, uncertain, Admiral. About two minutes. But this mass is smaller. It might not be the same."

"Can you speculate?"

Lynch considered. "It's possible. I'd have to talk to Modi in Engineering. There isn't a reading that man can't find a pattern to."

"Do it," said Mattis. "We need to be able to pinpoint, to a

couple of seconds, the moment they're about to fire."

"Why?" asked Commander Pitt, sarcasm dripping from every word. "Want to know the exact moment we're going to die?"

"Just find out," said Mattis to Lynch, then he turned to fully regard Commander Pitt. "So. The Z-drive is getting close to charged."

"That's right," said Commander Pitt, quickly checking his instruments and then looking back up. "The lead skunk's still loading. No way we'll be ready in time."

"That's fine," said Mattis.

The confusion on his face was profound. "What's the play here, Admiral?"

"Plan is," said Mattis, "to cancel the Z-drive jump again."

Slowly, carefully, Pitt reached up and pinched the bridge of his nose. "In God's name, why?"

"Because," said Mattis, "this time, instead of shutting down safely, I'm going to blow the energy out the emergency vents."

Commander Pitt's eyes widened. "That'll tear the aft section apart."

"Yes, it will," said Mattis. "The aft section that's already heavily damaged and almost completely evacuated."

A warning light flashed on Lynch's console. "They're nearly finished loading," said Lynch. "Modi reports the energy signature suggests an imminent firing."

"Got a better idea?" asked Mattis, his hand hovering over the *emergency Z-drive vent* button.

Commander Pitt's eyes told him everything he needed to know. He pressed down on the button, holding it as he readied to shutdown their Z-drive yet again.

"Loading complete," said Lynch, a slight tremor in his voice. "They'll be firing any second now."

"They'll wait to aim." Steady. Steady. He had to time it perfectly. Three, two, one… "All hands, brace for impact. Brace, brace, brace!" They couldn't wait any longer.

Mattis slammed his fist down right as the white flash of the firing filled every screen. The *Midway* lurched violently to port, forced into a spin, and all around him was the straining of metal. Fortunately, this time, he held his footing, but debris —including the bodies of the living and the dead, and broken computer equipment—flew through the air like shrapnel. Once again, the *Midway* was thrown around, but she was a tough girl. She bent, cracked, warped, but she didn't break. At least not in any way that would kill them all.

Their maneuvering thrusters pulled the ship out of its spin. His stomach kept up the gyrations, but through some strange mix of stubbornness and pride, Mattis managed to keep down his breakfast. A quick glance at his commander's console told him the damage was extensive, but ragged, as one might expect from an emergency blow.

"They missed," he said, scarcely believing it himself. "Hah."

"Great," said Commander Pitt, his eyes fixed on the radar screen, and the huge array of hostile ships still out there. "But now what?"

Chapter Twenty

Bridge
USS Midway

What now, indeed. Mattis had blown his load, twice, and didn't have any more tricks up his sleeve. The alien ships—he assumed they were alien—kept pounding at them, and they kept firing back, but there were just so many. The stench of acrid burning filtered through the bridge, smothering all other smells.

The bridge was the *Midway*'s armored heart. If it was that bad here, elsewhere would be hellish. But he had other concerns as well.

"Mister Pitt," he asked, "how's the *Fuqing* holding up?"

"According to sensors, they have sustained heavy damage, Admiral, especially on their forward superstructure, but they're still in this fight. Their heavy railguns are firing at about two rounds a minute, to good effect."

That was good. Maybe there was something they could do.

"Any chance we can use our maneuvering thrusters to get…" The defeated look on Commander Pitt's face showed him there was no point in finishing that sentence. "Okay, what about *Friendship Station*? Can we use what's left of it as cover?"

"Not enough of it is left to even provide a distraction," said Commander Pitt. "Our options are very limited." Yeah. No shit.

"Son?" a voice cut through the chatter. Senator Pitt. "Jeremy, what's going on?"

This was not the time. "You. *Out*." Mattis jabbed a finger at him. "Back to your quarters. This is a ship's bridge and—" The vibration of a significant weapons impact shook the room, accenting his point. "We're a little busy."

"The rear of the ship's on fire," protested Senator Pitt, turning his attention to Commander Pitt. "You've got to do something. Where's Malmsteen?"

"I'm in charge here," said Mattis, jabbing his finger, now, at the far wall, smeared with blood, where Malmsteen still lay. "Like I said. Busy."

"But son, aren't you the XO here? Isn't this your command?"

Another external explosion rocked the ship. Was he serious? Was this really happening? Mattis affixed the stink-eye on the senator. "Senator Pitt, under the US Space Navy Regulations, Chapter 10, article 1081, if a commanding officer is killed in battle, the next ranking officer takes command. Guess who? You may be the cat's ass back home, but out here, you don't mean shit. We are on a war footing, Senator, and you are *in my goddamn way*. I am in command of this vessel at this time. Now get off my bridge, or I'll have you thrown in the brig."

Commander Pitt didn't look happy, his face a sour mask, and the surviving bridge crew looked nervous and bewildered.

"I believe, Senator," said Lynch, his speech still slurred but his intention quite clear, "you were given a direct order."

Senator Pitt turned on his heel and, like an angry badger, stormed out of the bridge. Pitt Junior looked pissed, but another wave of incoming enemy fire seemed to snap him out of that.

"Right," said Mattis. "With that little idiotic distraction out of the way...options. How do we get ourselves out of here?"

"I'm not sure we can," said Lynch, his tone light but filled with honesty. "We just lost gun four. The crew say it's jammed. Well, I told 'em to get in there and fix it, but we've lost hull integrity in several sections, and our damage control teams are swamped."

One gun down. Severe hull damage, surrounded by enemies on all sides and at a significant tactical disadvantage. The *Midway* was a mighty beast, but even she had her limits.

Well, then, I guess we go down fighting was the only thought that popped into his head as he slid into the captain's chair.

And finally felt at home.

"Get me Shao," he said, clipping the earpiece back on. "I wanna have a chat with her."

Chapter Twenty-One

Lt. Patricia "Guano" Corrick's Warbird
33km from the wreckage of Friendship Station

They were gaining on the cruiser. Guano kept the throttle open and her nose pointed toward it, locking up the massive ship.

"Come on," said Roadie. "Ready to roll in?"

"Damn straight," she said. And then the engine spluttered, coughed, and died. All her electronics went out, everything except emergency power, and the ship began to drift.

The damage had caught up to them.

"Dammit." She initiated the emergency restart, jamming her thumb on the big red button. Working through the process. The ship coughed, spluttered, but didn't start. "C'mon, baby, don't leave Momma here all alone in the dark…"

"Contact!" shouted Flatline, some energy coming back into his voice. "I see flashes. Glints reflected off metal, two o'clock high. Three contacts. They're fighters!"

Without power, without weapons, they had no real hope. "Get ready to eject," she said, grasping hold of the yellow and black striped handle.

"No!" said Flatline. "Dammit, Corrick, I'm shot, remember? My suit's holed. There's no way I'll survive ejection into vacuum!"

Crap. That was true. She gingerly let go of the handle. Dammit… *Dammit*. "Maybe they won't see us."

"They see us," said Flatline. "They're coming around, they're coming around…"

Guano almost didn't want to look at the machines that would kill her, but she forced herself, twisting around in her seat. The ship's drift made it easier, putting her nose toward the fighters, their silver jet exhaust three dots in the distance, closing fast.

Silver.

"Wait," she said. "Those are friendlies!"

Three J-84's roared past her, banking around and forming up on her wing. She looked through the cockpits and saw a familiar helmet, red, emblazoned with flames.

"Holy shit," she said, breaking into a wild, manic laugh. "It's them! It's the ones we raced!" She punched the air. "How'd they get here so fast, all the way from the *Fuqing*?"

"Wow," said Flatline, "guess they were holding back."

She tried the engine restart and, mercifully, this time her ship sprang to life. Her electronics came back, her HUD outlining the ships in green. Allies.

"Hey, Guano, you there?" Roadie seemed panicked. "We got company."

"I'm okay," she said. "Ship's back up, power's back…and

yeah, we got some allies to help us shoot this bastard." She turned the ship around, back toward the enemy cruiser. "Assuming we can talk to them."

"Already on it," said Flatline, but she didn't like how his voice sounded. Listless. Hollow. "I'm picking up chatter on 194.44, standby…"

Suddenly, her helmet was full of Chinese.

"Hey," she said. "You guys out there?"

"Hello?" The pilot's English was thickly accented but clear. "American pilot?" Laughter. "Hey, she's awake."

"Yeah," said Guano. "Lovely to have you boys with us."

The Chinese fighters scooted closer to her wing, and her computer flashed as it interfaced with their new allies. "We're in a dangerous situation here," said her counterpart. "Why didn't you eject? Your ship is badly damaged."

"Haven't finished the fight yet," she said. "That cruiser is heading for the *Midway*. You boys wanna help me take it out?"

"That's what we're here for." The Chinese ships moved along with her. "Try to keep up."

Fighter jocks throughout the galaxy were all the same. She laughed and leapt back into the action, her ship racing toward the enemy cruiser, but the levity quickly faded. Flatline hadn't said anything for a while. "Hey, buddy, stay with me, okay?"

"I'm fine," he said, in a tone of voice that suggested he was not fine. Airy and distant. "I can't find where I'm hit. That's good, right?"

More blood drifted up in front of her, floating in the microgravity. She swatted the droplets away angrily, smearing her gloves with the stuff. "Yeah, that's good. Definitely good."

"Maybe it's my foot," said Flatline. "I can't see anything in this seat. It's too cramped."

"Maybe it's your dick," said Guano. "Explains why you might not be able to find it."

He didn't laugh, which was a bad sign. "I'll keep looking," he said. "Talk to me later."

"Is now later?" Guano adjusted her weapons console. Her ship was in worse shape than the national debt, but it would fight. "Because if you die in my ship, I don't want your nasty-ass ghost floating around haunting me, like, *woooooo, wooooooooo...* Get the fuck out of here."

He still didn't laugh. He was breathing in a pained rasp, wheezing with every inward breath, and occasionally little spherical rubies would drift in front of her vision.

She couldn't think about all of that right now. They had to save the *Midway*. She reopened the channel to the Chinese fighters. "So hey, guys, I forgot; I'm Lieutenant Patricia Corrick, but please, call me Guano."

"My name is Sub-lieutenant Shen Fong," said the lead Chinese pilot, just a little more formally than he needed to.

"Great," said Guano. "What's your *real* name?"

She could practically hear his smile over the line. "My callsign is *Dúshé*."

"His name is douche?" slurred Flatline worryingly. "Hah hah, hah, haaahhh..."

She quickly checked her instruments. The ship's computer had translated it. "It means Viper."

"Viper, huh," said Flatline. "Funny how... *F*unny how we all have the same ideas, like, you know...about pilots and things. With callsigns."

"Yeah," said Guano, the enemy ship looming larger in her

gun sights. The ship's computers painted the cap ship with their missiles. "A'right, Viper, Viper's buddies, get ready to blow this ship."

"Thoughts on how to engage it?" asked Viper. "Our 20mm cannons are unlikely to pierce even the rear armor. Our missiles are HE, not AP… They won't even scratch the surface. We need torpedoes and nukes to get through that armor."

They studied the large ship on her readout monitors. Viper was right. The hostile ship was clad in heavy armor that her systems couldn't penetrate, and it was the size of a small cruiser, just under one hundred forty meters, its hull comprised of six ovular sections stuck together, bristling with guns and weapons. Six engines were clustered together from the rear, red exhaust streams leaving a trail across space. Fins protruded like those of a fish, handfuls of lights glowing an ominous red. Sleek and fancy.

Time to turn it into scrap. Her radar reflections showed that the hull was thick and well layered, but the RCS was warped toward the rear of the ship. The farther they got away from the front, the thinner the armor was, and then she saw it.

"The engines," she said, looking directly at them from behind, "that's the key. The rear is armored, but they don't seem to have any protection at all in the exhausts." Which made sense. "Normally they'd be too small to target, for capital ships, but us little fighters? If we lob whatever we have into there, it *might* piss them off a little bit. Our heat-seekers have the best armor penetration… Let's keep our semi-active medium-ranged missiles in reserve."

"Sounds good," said Viper. "Hitting the exhausts will be

difficult. They're not much bigger than two meters."

She felt like calling the guy Red Five, especially since he was Chinese, but she controlled herself. "Great," she said. "Lock S-foils for attack run."

"What's an S-foil?" asked Viper, confused.

"Never mind," she said. "Just a line from some old movie." She swung her ship around, aligning her craft with one of the engines, plunging into the red stream behind them. It was like flying through a bloody mist, dark red glinting stream of particles scratching across her cockpit, thousands of them becoming lodged in the cracks of the damaged glass. Her ship shook and trembled as the stream buffered her around.

Time to do this before they discovered her. She turned on the forward-looking infrared; the FLIR glowed white hot. At least aiming would be simple.

"Ready to shoot this shit?" asked Roadie.

"I am ready," said Viper.

"Guano's a go," she said, and dumped all her heat-seeking missiles, not even worrying about brevity calls. Four white streaks, one after the other, cut through the red exhaust stream. Before they even hit, she switched over to guns, and turned ammo into noise. She squeezed the trigger, sending a twin stream of high-explosive shells along the exhaust trail. She switched over to using Flatline's ammo supply as well, emptying that in just a few seconds.

And then her guns were dry and her missile racks empty. The only sound was the distant grinding of some logistics officer's teeth.

She pulled out of the crimson exhaust stream, flecks of it coming away with her ship, like a battered dolphin cresting out of the ocean. Roadie and the J-84's emerged similarly. She watched, waiting, to see if it had all been for nothing.

For a second, the ship seemed to jerk, a ripple running from its stem to its stern. The exhaust cut out from all engines and it began to turn. Slowly, inexorably, as though to crush them.

Then, with a blinding white flash that seared her retinas, the ship jumped away.

"Wow," said Guano. "I guess we got 'em."

"Don't crow too soon," said Roadie.

But in her radar, she could see the other hostile ships around them, similarly, begin to turn.

"What the blue hell is going on?"

Chapter Twenty-Two

Bridge
USS Midway

Mattis touched the earpiece. "Shao, are you there?"

The voice that came through the line was harried but full of energy. "This is *Fuqing* actual. Send it."

"It seems we're outnumbered," said Mattis. "I was hoping you'd have some advice regarding ways we can remedy this predicament."

"We're firing as fast and as hard as we can, and we're taking the brunt of enemy fire in return. Not sure what else you want from me, Admiral." A slight pause. "Although, you know, if you let me shoot you again…I'm all ears."

"I'm sure you are," he said, unable to keep back a small smile. No matter what else he'd thought of asking his old enemies to give them a broadside, it had been pretty awesome. "But I meant more with regard to our enemies. Any particular hints you might be willing to drop?"

"I'm afraid *keep shooting at them 'till they die* is the best we have at this stage, Admiral."

That was all they had as well.

"Actually," said Shao, slightly distracted as though listening to a report that barely carried over the din of her bridge, "we're receiving a report from some of our strike craft that a preliminary examination of the hostile ships reveals that their engines are a notable weak point—this might explain why they're all taking great care to angle their frontal armor toward us."

"Makes sense," mused Mattis. "This fleet's obviously designed to attack… They have guns and frontal armor, and a mass-driver system, but their capital ships are built to attack strike craft and smaller ships. That means…they probably weren't expecting two capital ships here, and they weren't expecting one of those ships to lose engine power and continue to fight against such overwhelming odds."

"Okay," said Shao. "So if they're built to attack, what should we do?"

"Well," said Mattis, "when the ball's on your ten-yard line, you don't wanna block, you wanna get it to your running back and take the game to them."

Shao didn't answer right away. "Sorry," she said, "I don't follow. I thought my English was actually okay, but none of that makes *any* sense."

Right. The Chinese didn't play football. "You're doing great. I'm suggesting we go on the attack. We need to get close to them, right up close, and hit them with our torpedoes, old-fashioned broadside style, at point-blank range so they can't dodge. Punch through their hulls with nuclear fire."

"Sounds good," said Shao, the notion seeming to agree with her. "I'm sick of trading jabs. Let's snap-kick them in the throat."

Now they were talking. "Get your nukes ready," he said. "We're going to want a full barrage from both ships. Target one hostile, flank it, bombard from both sides. And Shao—don't miss. These things *will* hurt us, and you."

"My gunners never miss," said Shao. "Let us know when you're able to move and we'll do it."

"Status on those engines," barked Mattis. "Good news, if you please, Mister Pitt."

"Damage control reports that engine three is functioning at one-quarter capacity," said Commander Pitt. "That's all they can give us at this stage."

He'd asked for good news but hadn't actually expected to receive it. Still, it was welcome. Mattis knew his ship like the back of his hand; one-quarter of one-third of their engines wasn't much power, but it was something. "Good. Bring it up, slowly now, gently. One-eighth engine power. We don't want to stress it. Just navigate straight toward the nearest ship. It's not much, but it'll make it harder to coordinate fire on any weak points they detect. Get us away from the wreckage of *Friendship Station*."

"Aye aye, sir, one-eighth ahead." The command was relayed throughout the bridge.

It felt good to be moving. The repaired engine gave them a whisker of mobility, and a little bit of movement could go a very long way indeed.

"Shao," said Mattis, "follow our lead."

"Right."

"We're pulling away, sir," said Commander Pitt. "All guns maintaining fire for effect on targets of opportunity."

Commander Pitt, despite everything, had performed admirably. If they survived this, he'd be commended in some way. Mattis would make sure of it. "Very good," he said. "Continue to hammer those skunks, and coordinate with the *Fuqing*. We want to hit them at the same time, if we can. I know it's difficult with our wings clipped, but we gotta make it happen."

The door to the bridge opened and a pair of corpsmen arrived. Finally. Two women in uniforms adorned with red crosses in white circles. They seemed drawn, instinctively, toward Malmsteen, but the moment they saw him, they moved on. Mattis wordlessly pointed to Lynch and then turned his attention back to the outer view.

Glowing yellow lines of cannon fire leapt out from all sides of the *Midway*, streaking toward the enemy fleet. Red lines of their return fire darted back, absorbed by the hull and ricocheting off into space, or sinking into the thick metal. For the most part, that fire seemed ineffective; the overwhelming majority of their damage had come from the mass-driver strike on *Friendship Station*.

"Status on torpedoes?" asked Mattis.

"Standby." Commander Pitt consulted his console. "All tubes loaded, sir."

About time. "Get ready to fire a volley, full spread, targeting the closest ship, the same one the *Fuqing* has targeted. Use their firing solution on the opposite side and concentrate on weak points. See if we can punch right through its weaker side armor."

"Got it, sir," said Commander Pitt. "We're moving into position."

They were, but it was agonizingly slow. At minimal engine power, the *Midway* crept forward.

Lynch, with the medics still tending him, seemed drawn to his console. "Admiral?"

"Yes?"

"It's the attacking ships," said Lynch, disbelief in his tone. "They're all turning and jumping away. Six, seven, eight…and that's the last of them."

It took him looking at the radar output to believe it, to watch the beam sweep space and find only strike craft and debris, but it was true. The attackers had left behind their strike craft, but all the capital ships had jumped away.

"The alien fleet is bugging out," said Commander Pitt. "The AO is clear of anything bigger than a fighter, and debris."

But the *Midway* had barely hit them.

Chapter Twenty-Three

Bridge
USS Midway

The guns were quiet and, unbelievably, almost all noise on the bridge ceased. Pitt's words echoed around the room.

The alien fleet.

It was true. The ships were not from Earth. They weren't Chinese or American or Indian—they were… something else. From somewhere else.

Mattis slumped back in his chair, taking in a long, slow breath and letting it out. The stench of burning electronics filled his nose, pungent and acrid, and he could smell other things. Chemicals. Metal. Blood.

These things always lingered in the wake of battle. It had been so long that he barely remembered.

Ramirez appeared beside him, her hands on her hips. She was bloody, scorched, but defiant. "Okay," she said, clearly being as patient as she could. "I'm going to tell one amazing

story about this when we get out of here. But aliens…
seriously. Are they aliens? That can't be." She paused, regarding
him. "Ready to tell me just what the hell is going on, Jack?"

He couldn't have her doing that. Talking to him like that,
on the bridge. Calling him *Jack*. His command was tenuous as it
was, with the body of the former captain in the corner covered
in a sheet, and he couldn't have anyone undermining it. Not a
civilian, someone from the press. Not…her.

"You'll be briefed in time," he said, a little more curtly than
he truly meant. "A statement will be made to the press, when
we have more information, and I'll make sure it gets passed
along to you."

Passed along… The moment the words left his mouth, he
regretted them. He didn't mean it, but it would be improper to
countermand himself in such a way. He'd committed.

Martha looked at him impassively, with that practiced
reporter's face, and then turned curtly and left.

It was always worse when she said nothing.

But there were a million things he *should* be focusing on,
not watching her leave the bridge, slipping out through the
narrow door. It wasn't his fault. He was just doing his duty…

So he'd told himself for so long he almost believed it.

"Admiral?" asked Commander Pitt, his tone suggesting it
was the second or third time. "Are you okay?"

"I'm fine," he said, shaking his head to clear away the
doubts. "I was just…thinking."

"Thinking," echoed Commander Pitt. The guy had a
calming vibe to his voice. "About the aliens?"

He grimaced. The whole idea was cringeworthy to him.
"There's no evidence that the ships that attacked us were

crewed by extraterrestrials," he said, a little more condescending than he probably should have been. "For all we know, this was some kind of attack by…" He couldn't finish that sentence in a way that didn't sound very silly in his mind.

"I understand," said Commander Pitt. "But the level of technology, the composition of the ships—it *does* seem very alien, in the literal sense of the world. Otherworldly. Different. I think we can all agree that the use of the word *alien* is justified in this case, at the very least, until we learn more."

He couldn't contest that. "Very well. But more importantly, Commander, the *present*… How's my ship?"

Commander Pitt drummed his fingers on his arm. "Well, sir, the *Midway* is badly damaged and not combat effective. Now that we're not being shot at, we can start to seal up the breached bulkheads and try to restart some of our damaged secondary systems, but the rear of the ship took one hell of a beating, sir. I'm not sure we'll be able to coax much more out of the engines, but we're going to do our best. If anyone can do it, Modi can."

"Right," said Mattis, cupping his chin in his hands. "We'll need all the help we can get. Dock with the *Fuqing*. Get Shao on the horn. I want her best damage control teams and engineers over here. And don't take no for an answer. Extend that offer to anyone else who can reach us in time, regardless of flag." Gotta give a little carrot to go with that stick, though… "Tell anyone who agrees to help that no part of the ship is off limits. They have an all-access pass to the *Midway*, and tell our marines to cut the workmen some slack. I know they're going to want to pick apart this ship for intel and, to be perfectly frank with you, I'm going to let them. After that battle, they've earned it."

Commander Pitt's skepticism was clear. "We could keep the reactor room under lockdown," he said. "That's where the ship's biggest secrets are, and where our biggest advantage over the Chinese is."

Lynch shook his head vigorously, his eyes on Mattis. "Hell no, sir. If they figure out how our heart beats…"

"Then," said Mattis, "it'll be better for us when we go toe-to-toe with these bastards again." He wasn't sure if Commander Pitt was on board with this plan, so he reiterated. "On my authority, Commander."

Commander Pitt straightened his back. "Yes, sir. I'll send word."

Lynch looked distinctly unimpressed, but he had no time to deal with that. His earpiece chirped. He expected Shao to be on the line, but instead it was another voice. Clipped and proper and Indian-British.

"Admiral Mattis," he said, "this is Commander Oliver Modi from Engineering, sir. I have been asked to give you my report."

Mattis waited for him to do so. He didn't. "Proceed," he said finally.

"Very good, sir. Report is as follows: Engine one has sustained critical damage and is inoperable. Engine two has sustained critical damage and is inoperable. Engine three has —"

"Sustained critical damage and is inoperable?" guessed Mattis, slightly sarcastically.

"Incorrect, sir. Engine three has sustained severe damage and is functioning at one-quarter capacity." He paused. "Sir, I imagined you would be aware of this by now."

"I was, I just…" Mild frustration crept in, some of it genuine and justified, while another part was really thinking of Ramirez walking off the bridge. "Well, you kept saying the same damn thing over and over."

"People say I am repetitive, sir. I simply prefer the terms 'accurate' and 'comprehensive.'" Another slight pause. "Are you ready for me to continue?"

"Yes," he said.

"Engine four has sustained critical damage and is inoperable."

"Great." Mattis rubbed his temples. "Got anything else for me, Commander Modi?"

"No."

Well that was a waste of time. He went to close the connection, but Commander Lynch leaned over his own console and patched himself into the call.

"The Admiral really needs these engines working," said Lynch. "Crack the whip. Work faster, Modi."

"Good idea. I hadn't considered that option."

"Don't get smart with us," said Commander Lynch, leaning so far over his console it was like he was going to bite it. "You goddamn robot. Just fix the damn ship."

If Modi was in any way offended, his tone didn't convey it. "Physically repairing the ship is the purvey of damage control teams. I am simply the chief of engineering. However, given that there exists some capacity within engineering, I am happy to allocate resources to accommodate your request."

"Great. Get to it. This is important," said Pitt, waving a calming hand down toward Lynch.

"I concur," said Modi.

"Bridge out." Pitt closed the connection and, seemingly frustrated, shook his head. "Hey, Lynch. Go easy on him, okay?"

"Hell no," said Lynch, scrunching up his face in frustration. "That damn man. Like four hats short of a rodeo."

"Everything okay?" asked Mattis cautiously. "This isn't going to be a problem, is it?"

"Oh, no," said Lynch, his formal visage slipping. "Modi's great, when he's not driving me up the damn wall. He's smart —no, better than that. Smart doesn't even begin to describe how genius this guy is. But, *ugh*. It's always 'I concur, I concur.' Ain't nobody told him to say just plain ole' yes? I tell you what, what he got in book smarts, he took from people smarts. Damn fool's half machine. No wonder he loves them so much."

Mattis smiled. "You know, the more you get annoyed at him, the more your inner Texan really starts to come out."

"If that ain't a fact, God's a possum, sir," said Lynch. "You can hang your hat on it."

The phrase took some time to process. "O…kay."

"That's nothing, sir," said Commander Pitt, making an obvious effort to maintain a professional air. "You should see him when he *really* gets started. Nobody can understand his jabbering. They're like words being put in a blender. Malmsteen used to say that's why I was here: to interpret."

"I'm fine," said Lynch. "It's Modi who's the problem. Bright as a new penny, but trying to get him to *get to the point* is like hugging a rose bush." He rolled up his sleeve, the grogginess in his voice completely gone. Whatever the medics had done to him had done its work well. "Also, Admiral, I wanted to show you something."

"Go ahead."

"I was looking at the pulsing signal before the attack," said Lynch. "Remember that?"

"Yeah," said Mattis, the flickering signal almost forgotten in the rush of battle. "What you got for me, Lynch?"

"Well, it just kind of hit me, Admiral. I think I figured out what the signal was."

Chapter Twenty-Four

Lt. Patricia "Guano" Corrick's Warbird
31 km from the wreckage of Friendship Station

The enemy fleet had jumped away, leaving the impromptu fighter wing surrounded by empty space.

"Are they all gone?" asked Guano.

"Scopes are clear of capital ships," said Viper. "I'm only seeing scattered wings of strike craft remaining, in twos and threes."

"We didn't hit them that badly," said Roadie, his confusion shared by her. "We put a few missiles up their tailpipe, emptied our guns… The ship barely seemed to slow down."

Coincidence? She didn't think so. "Let's press our advantage," she said, resting her hand on her throttle. "I'm winchester on guns, radar-guided and heat-seekers, but I still have my semi-active missiles left. We can mop up these strike craft and go home for tea and medals."

"Negative," said Roadie. "Pull back to the *Midway*. I can

see your busted canopy from here. Your ship is badly banged up. We can't afford to lose you."

Her blood was up. Five kills would make her an ace, a coveted title, one nobody had been able to win since the war with the Chinese. "Those strike fighters are without their cap-ship support craft, without any kind of help. They should be easy to wipe up. I can help."

"Not without any guns and a couple of small missiles, you can't."

"I can handle it," she said, thumping her foot against the floor of her ship. "C'mon, Roadie, cut me loose. I got two missiles left. I'm still in this fight."

Roadie's voice grew incredulous. "Bravo-2, I am ordering you to immediately make your heading 111 by 31 and RTB. Those missiles are a last-ditch only and the *Midway* will require fighter escort until we sort out what the hell is going on. May I remind you your craft lost power for nearly half a minute only moments ago? Now hear this: you are not to attack any craft without an explicit call for weapons free. How copy?"

She wanted to resist, to argue, but she knew that it was pointless. A war zone wasn't the right place to undermine the CAG's authority on any matter, especially not one so serious as tactical decisions. "Solid copy on all," she said, completely unable to keep the bitterness down in her throat, the words practically choking her. "Bravo-2 is RTB."

Guano swung the nose of her fighter back toward the *Midway*, thumping her fist on the side of the cockpit wall. This was bullshit! Roadie was being too cautious.

Another red drop of blood drifted up in front of her visor. When was the last time she'd checked in on her backseater?

"Hey, buddy," she said, twisting around in her seat, trying to get a glance at him. "How're you traveling back there?"

Flatline was slumped forward in his seat. She could only see the rear of his helmet.

"Hey. Hey!" Nothing.

Her gut clenched and she touched her radio. "Mayday, mayday, mayday. This is Bravo-2 transmitting in the blind guard, declaring an emergency."

For a brief second, there were no transmissions, as per protocol, then the *Midway*'s comm officer came on the line. "Bravo-2, this is *Midway*, roger emergency. State the nature of your distress."

"It's Flatline," she said, struggling to keep her tone professional. "He was hit during the battle. I didn't think it was bad—I didn't think it was *this* bad, but he's not moving. There's blood in the cockpit. Over."

Roadie's voice cut over the transmission. "Dammit, Corrick, you should have said something—"

The *Midway* spoke over him. "Clear the air." A pause. "Bravo-2, adjust your transponder and switch to 7700 so we can track you. Proceed directly to the *Midway* hangar bay and prepare for emergency landing. Medical crews are standing by."

Adjust her transponder? What in the hell—why would she do that? She flew with one hand, looking over her shoulder. "Negative on the transponder adjust, I can't reach the switch here. I'm burning toward the *Midway* at maximum acceleration. Prepare mag-brakes, I'm going to be coming in hot."

"Acknowledged," said *Midway*. "Grav-nets deployed. You are clear to land on any strip."

"Oh," she said. "It has to be on a strip, does it? Picky, picky."

The radio operator on the other end was dead calm. "Confirmed, any strip."

A moment's quiet, and then Roadie's voice came through. "Corrick, listen to me. Were you in a coma for flight school? You know—you *know* you're supposed to report damage, especially anything that could jeopardize the safety of your crew. You're the pilot. Flatline is under *your* command in this situation."

"I'm aware," she said, still trying to catch a glimpse of Flatline's face. She couldn't. "I know."

"Can you still fly this thing?"

"Fly it?" Stupid question. "Of course. We're in space. Flying is easy. Landing on the other hand…"

"Can you land?" asked Roadie, his tone ice cold.

"Of course!" She twisted back to her front, flicking the switch to extend the landing gear. The starboard and center struts came down nicely, their indicator lights glowing a healthy green, but the port-side strut flashed red. She tried again to extend it, but the console flashed red once more. "Landing *safely*, however, might be a bit of a stretch. My gear won't deploy. I'm going to have to rely on the grav-nets."

This was not a good idea. The forces involved in a grav-net capture could tear a fighter to shreds if they came in at the wrong angle. Given how damaged their craft was, it was a risk even if her approach was perfect.

"Corrick, if you survive this, I will kill you," said Roadie.

He sounded like he meant it to.

The *Midway* operator came back. "Bravo-2, remain VFR if

you can, remain straight and level. There's a lot of debris out here, and it's too difficult to see with the naked eye. Use your instruments. Trust me, you don't want to get struck by this stuff."

Debris? She finally looked up from her instruments.

The light of the star Cor Caroli glinted off large flat panels that spun, slowly, as they spread out from the wreckage of *Friendship Station*, the location of which was marked by a slowly expanding gas cloud—the internal atmosphere of the facility—diffusing into the surrounding space. Millions of tiny sparkles, pulverized station components, caught the light and reflected it everywhere, a dazzling display enveloping everything, bathed in the blue glare of the stars. Mixed in amongst the debris were smaller clouds, wreckage from the attacking ships, destroyed fighters—friendly and otherwise— and the lingering glow from nuclear torpedoes.

It was a beautiful splash of color across the void, but she couldn't admire it. Her radar was useless, the energy reflected off infinite surfaces and scattering in all directions. Her screens showed a soup of light, color, and sharp pieces of metal silently drifting through the emptiness, a picturesque testament to a colossal battle she had barely seen, full of objects big and small, all deadly to a fighter that was coming apart at the seams.

And she would have to fly through it.

Chapter Twenty-Five

Bridge
USS Midway

Mattis beckoned Commander Pitt over, and Lynch, too. He took off his earpiece and put it on the armrest of his chair, reaching over and calling Shao, patching Modi into the call as well.

"Shao here," she said, the sound of welding in the background.

Time for a team huddle.

"So," said Mattis. "One of my bridge officers informs me that the signal we detected before the battle has been identified. You're on speaker, everyone, so try not to talk all at once. Tell me what you have, Lynch."

The man suddenly seemed less confident of his assertion. "It's just a theory," he cautioned.

"Facts are better than theories," said Mattis, "but I'll take a theory over a wild guess any day of the week."

Shao interjected. "You called me away from fixing my ship to navel gaze about a sensor glitch? Admiral, tsk tsk tsk. I had thought so highly of you."

"Just hear him out," Mattis said, forcing a diplomatic tone past his lips. "It could be useful."

"So could fixing my ship."

Mattis gestured for Lynch to speak up.

"Well," said Lynch, "I was examining the RCS returns from our primary long-range radar. Normally when we're analyzing an intermittent signal, it's either something so small and non-reflective that we can barely see it—it keeps crossing over the threshold between signal and noise based on speed, rotation, etc.—but this one was different. The signal was either there, strongly, or it wasn't there at all. Which means we were either detecting an object similar in design to a massive spinning sheet of paper a mile wide…or they were doing something to hide their RCS profile."

"The simple explanation," asked Mattis, "if you would."

"It's cloaking technology," said Lynch, a not insignificant amount of pride in his voice. "A theoretical construct in our lab, back in the day. It's been theoretically discussed for nearly a century, but interest in it picked up after the war. Despite this, it's cutting-edge stuff; the idea is to essentially fold space around an area like a blanket, so that when the radar pulses arrive, there's nothing to detect. The catch is this: it takes enormous amounts of energy to do this. We were unable to fold areas of more than a few centimeters, for more than a few microseconds, and that took most of a cap ship's reactor running at emergency power. It was possible, and well understood, just not feasible."

Modi spoke up, his tone betraying just the barest hints of excitement. "You never indicated to me you were involved in experimental research after the war, Commander Lynch."

"Well you never asked."

"I would dearly love to read your notes, Commander Lynch, if you could just—"

"Sorry," said Lynch. "Classified."

Modi said nothing, but Mattis could practically *feel* his frustration.

"So," said Shao, her voice small and tinny through the too-small speaker, "obviously this isn't *too* classified, or you boys wouldn't be talking about it in front of me."

"Obviously," said Commander Pitt, "you know something about it, too, or you wouldn't draw attention to this fact."

Everyone exchanged a knowing look, and Shao's silence told them all they needed to know.

"If you know something about this technology," said Mattis, "we'd appreciate a little reciprocity when it comes to openness and trust."

"Trust has to be earned," said Shao, somewhat unconvincingly.

"I think we've done our part."

She hesitated again. "You realize that if The People's Fleet Command has *any* reason to suspect I am sharing this information with you, I will be lucky if it simply costs me my command, yes? The PRC still practices capital punishment, and their needles are sharp."

"That's odd," said Mattis. "My superiors are bound to be thrilled when I file my report and inform them how we fought alongside each other without verifying the identity of our attackers, how we risked an American asset to defend a nominally Chinese space station, and how I had your engineers tromping all over my ship with an all-access pass to see her inner workings. They'll probably promote me. What rank comes after Admiral?"

"Point well taken," said Shao. "Stand by." He could hear the tapping of keys in the background, followed shortly after by the rustling and shuffling of papers. Paper archives? How *old* was this stuff? Or was it a security measure against electronic theft? No modem could hack into a locked safe. "According to these reports," she said, "our scientists couldn't bring the quantum field regulator's temperature down below minus two hundred and twenty two point two degrees Celsius."

Lynch looked like he might explode. "Two two two, point two? Precisely? Just confirming that."

"That's what it says here," said Shao.

"You son of a bitch!" Lynch's face screwed up like he'd swallowed a peeled lemon. He leaned right over the tiny earpiece like he was going to swallow that, too. "That's not what your scientists said. That's what *I* said! I wrote that damn report. I hadn't slept for four days, we were way over budget, and I—well, I nodded off. My elbow hit the 2 key, the computer filled in the decimal point, and then when my chin hit the enter key, it got logged as an official report!" His upper lip curled back. "I got smoked by my CO, because it's not meant to be cooled, it's meant to be *heated*. You damn fools stole our research!"

"Every... Uh, every nation engages in espionage from time to time—"

"Dammit! You red bastards broke into our computer

systems because you couldn't do your own legwork and—"

"A'right!" said Mattis, holding up his hands. "A'right, a'right. We get it. We get it. We're going to move on." He took a long, slow breath. "Captain Shao, do you have any information that wasn't…uhh, *borrowed* from us, as it were?"

"Yes," said Shao, flicking through the pages. "Our scientists noted several incorrectly set parameters on the quantum waveform emitter, which we suspected was because it made no sense to cool it rather than heat it, buuuuut…there's one thing here. One theoretical application of this was to, instead of cloaking an object for a duration of time, analyze incoming radar pulses and cloak only when a pulse was expected. Since the device could be turned off and on rapidly, this was considered an acceptable compromise, especially when performing reconnaissance against long-range radar, where pulses were regular and infrequent."

"Sounds like that's what they were doing," said Mattis, musing over it. "They were trying to save power, but they messed up. They didn't know our systems as well as they thought they did." He turned to Lynch. "Can we exploit this to find a weakness?"

"You bet," said Lynch, nodding emphatically. "In fact, I can do one better."

"What's that?"

Lynch grinned. "I can track these bastards."

Chapter Twenty-Six

Bridge
USS Midway

The huddle broke up. Shao closed the connection, presumably to supervise the repairs on her own ship, and Mattis sat in the captain's chair like a big ole' grumpy grandpa, chatting to Lynch about this cloaking device or…whatever it was.

Which meant Commander Pitt was left to deal with managing the flaming, smashed wreckage of their own ship.

Just great. Technically it was Modi's job to organize it, but fixing a vessel of this size wasn't something one man could do, no matter how robotic and brainy they were. It was tempting to go down to Engineering and crack the whip over Modi personally, but too many things on the Bridge demanded his attention, so that pleasure would have to wait.

Malmsteen's body wasn't yet cold, and although the corpsmen had carried it off the bridge on a stretcher, Pitt knew it was too early to be talking about anything like a permanent replacement. The *Midway* needed a CO, and the chain of command was pretty explicit. Authority was passed down from officer to officer, from the most senior to the most junior, as it always had been going back to times of antiquity.

Didn't mean he had to like it.

Pitt had served as the *Midway*'s XO for nearly five years. That was a long time for most positions, and he had expected, in the next year or so, for Malmsteen to be promoted out of the position and assigned to a newer, shinier ship, leaving him in command.

Now, although the circumstances had been remarkably tragic, he couldn't help but feel a little bitter that the clock had been seemingly reset. Would he spend another five years here? Ten? Would another series of unlikely, galaxy-changing events once again rear their heads, and some other circumstance push him out of the captain's chair?

He couldn't help but look at it. He'd often physically sat in it, of course, and had the conn to himself; such were the perks of being the XO. But that was a temporary position. Borrowed. Unreal, in some way, and the key decision making was always in the hands of the captain.

Malmsteen had done a good job. As had Mattis, during his day, or so he'd heard.

But Pitt could do better. Deep down, on some level, he *knew* he was better for the position. He deserved the *Midway*. It was difficult to accept any other conclusion. He should be in the big chair, not the old man.

His communicator chimed. His private one. He quickly plucked it out of his pocket and put it to his ear. "What?" he snapped.

"Wow," said his father defensively. "Rude."

"Dad," said Pitt, his teeth grinding together. "I'm a little busy here."

"Oh, yes," said his father, "I know. Far too busy to even give your old man a text message to let him know what's going on. No, you'd rather he sit in this dark, smelly room all by himself, as the ship rocks and shakes all around him, wondering what the hell is happening because nobody is telling him *anything*."

Was he always this bad, or was there something in the *Midway*'s atmospheric processors that was affecting his father's brain? "Listen, Dad, I understand. I know that information has not been forthcoming from the senior staff, but the truth is: we don't know a lot either."

"Fine," said his dad. "Let me know when I can go back to the station. At least they have the news there."

No reason to sugar coat it. "*Friendship Station* is gone. Blown to pieces. There's some kind of new force at work here that we truly don't understand a great deal about. All we know is that it's hostile, it's aggressive, and we need to focus all our efforts on fixing the ship. I don't have time to talk you through this."

"But—"

"But nothing." The frustration reached a crescendo. At the other end of the bridge, Mattis and Lynch were engaged in some kind of argument. Civil, but firm. Mattis made some kind of decision, and Lynch nodded acceptingly. That was how it was, how it had to be… He had accepted it, and it was time for his father to do the same. "You're stuck here, so you better get damn used to it." He hung up.

Lynch broke away from his conversation and came over to him. "You okay, Commander?"

It was tempting to be honest, to say no, to explain how arguing with his father during this stressful time made things a lot worse, but he, instead, forced a smile. "Everything's fine," he said. "How can I help?"

Lynch stared. "How can *you* help *me*? Ain't that supposed to be the other way around?"

Pitt gave a little half-smile. "My job as the XO is fire extinguisher. I solve the problems so that the captain doesn't have to. But, paradoxically, I'm also a fire *starter*; I'm here to encourage people, get the sparks flying on dry wood, and build up the senior staff so they can do their jobs."

"Modi's brain is dry wood," said Lynch, but the smile on his face told him he'd done his job. His eyes drifted to the captain's chair. "That ain't a…problem for you, Commander?"

"I'm just fine," said Pitt firmly. "I would have liked to sit there, but we have a crisis. Admiral Mattis is handling it as well as I could."

"No better?"

"Time will tell," said Pitt.

Indeed it would.

Chapter Twenty-Seven

Bridge
USS Midway

Mattis dismissed Lynch and sat back in his chair. There would be plenty of time for reflection in the coming days and weeks, time to analyze how the battle could have been played better, but for now, he was happy. They'd come through alive, more or less, and the enemy fleet had pulled back.

That was worth something at least. Snatching a stalemate from the jaws of defeat was as close to winning as anyone could ask. Not an ideal situation, obviously, but for now, it would have to do.

Would Malmsteen have done it better? That little worm of doubt began to creep into his mind, squirming its way through his thoughts. Mattis had been away from the *Midway* for so long. The old girl seemed like an old friend, not a stranger, but time always changed things. Small and large. Staff rotated in and out. Upgrades replaced old hardware and software. Wear and tear wore down the superstructure and mandated repairs. The ship was largely the same as she had been in his day—but not *exactly* the same.

It was also true that no one had asked him to command the ship. In fact, they had kept command from him, but that was no excuse. In battle, the only thing that mattered was results: had he been good enough?

They didn't have a body count yet. How many of his crew had paid the ultimate price today because he hadn't done his homework?

Always time to think about that later. For now, they weren't out of the woods yet. Right on cue, his earpiece chirped.

"Admiral, this is Modi. Status update on the engines."

"Send it," said Mattis.

"An issue was discovered with the primary fuel coupling. This blockage was causing widespread malfunctions on all engines. We've subsequently repaired the blockage. It's not perfect, but you'll get most, if not all, of your power back for most engines."

Good. Being able to move at something approximating their full speed was a welcome change. "So that's all it was? A blocked fuel line?"

"Damage caused by the battle obscured our efforts to diagnose it properly earlier. Although there *is* damage to the engines' exhausts, it's mostly cosmetic, and if we accept a reduction in thermal dispersion capacity and maneuvering ability, we should be able to make good use of them all."

"Excellent work, Mister Modi. This is good news."

"I concur."

Mattis smiled to himself. "With the former or the latter?"

"With both, of course."

He went to give further commands, but his earpiece chirped again, signaling an incoming short-range call. "Standby, I'm adding another person to this call."

He touched the side of his earpiece. "This is *Midway* actual."

"Shao here. We're sitting here with our asses in the wind, Admiral. Any word on when we can get underway?"

"Soon," he said. "Things are going well over here. Our engines are back online. The technical details of the enemy capabilities are still being asserted. Any word on search and rescue from the station?"

"You know as well as I do, Admiral, nobody got out of there alive."

He knew, but it was worth asking. It was difficult to feel sorry for Admiral Yim, especially given the circumstances of their meeting, but he did. Just a little. "Sorry."

"And I too, Admiral. I pity those who finally find revenge."

"Why's that?"

She held the silence for a moment, then said, "Do you feel good? Knowing the man who killed your brother is dead?"

There hadn't really been enough time to process this fact, and Shao's question came suddenly. The only word that found its way to his lips was the pure, unvarnished truth. "No. "

His brother was still dead. It hadn't solved anything.

"And thus," said Shao, "you've lost even the idea that you can get back at Admiral Yim for what happened. The notion of revenge. Accordingly, I pity you, Admiral, for your loss today is more than most."

The growing pain in his gut signaled that it was time to talk about something else. "How go the repairs on your end?"

"Doing well," said Shao, obviously happy to switch topics now that things had gotten awkward. "We're ready to leave when you are."

"Hold on," he said, and turned to Lynch. "Are you sure we can track these bastards?"

"Damn straight," said Lynch. "They all turned the same way before they jumped."

"And we can defeat their cloak?"

"Easy as a coon dog tracking a possum." Lynch must have been confident if such pure, unadulterated Texan was slipping out.

"Hmm. That one's a stretch, even for you, cowboy." Mattis considered. "But if you're confident, I'm confident."

"Aye aye, sir," said Lynch. "I'd stake my life on it."

The exact phrasing of his words put a damp rag over everything. "Hate to break it to you, Commander, but you already have."

Chapter Twenty-Eight

Lt. Patricia "Guano" Corrick's Warbird
22 km from the wreckage of Friendship Station

Guano floored it, racing toward the *Midway*, her ship shaking with the effort. She swung her Warbird left and right, flinging it around debris. Some of the smaller stuff pinged off her hull, screaming as it scraped across the metal, dragging unsightly scars down the small ship's length.

She didn't worry about that. A ship could be fixed. Would be fixed, by some grumbling, annoyed petty officer who would hold a grudge for months. That was usually the way of it.

Come on, come on, come on... She pitched upward to avoid a massive, blackened structural beam, and then had to immediately pitch downward to avoid a blasted hunk of hull armor.

Immediately, she realized her error. Ahead, a thousand tiny shards of glass—one of the station's observation windows, possibly—floated in front of her. She was moving to fast to dodge. Nothing to do but fly through.

Ting ting ting ting ting ting ting. She flew through a hail of shattering fragments.

"Hey, Flatline," she said once they'd cleared it, as much to herself as to him. "Buddy, hey. We are doing a really dangerous thing, so I hope you appreciate this. I really do. You owe me big for this one."

Spinning flat panels, four of them, drifted out to meet her, almost mocking her with their presence. She twisted the ship, flying between them, the corners of each missing her Warbird by meters.

The voice of the *Midway*'s comm officer came through to her again. "Bravo-2, be advised, autodocking offline. It looks like your ILS antenna just took a good hit. We're clearing you for a visual approach."

Landing without machines was fine with her. Even preferable. ILS was too slow, too cautious. She needed to get down onto the deck *fast*. Precision required computers. Speed required humans.

She risked a glance at her onboard auto-doc. Flatline's vitals were fading. "Computer, on my authority, inject my gunner with twenty ccs of adrenaline. Keep his heart rate up."

"Confirmed," said the synthetic male voice. "Injecting."

With a gasp and a disorientated shout, Flatline woke up.

"Welcome back, buddy," she said, risking a quick glance over her shoulder. "Keep it steady. Everything's going to be fine."

She looked back to the front of the ship, and through the cracked cockpit canopy, she saw a body hurtling toward them. American? Chinese? No way to know.

And no way to dodge it in time. She and the corpse collided with a sickening, wet crunch, the cracking of breaking bones transmitted through the fighter's hull into her ears. As damaged and frail as her ship was, it was significantly stronger than a body.

"W-What was that?" stammered Flatline. "Where are we? What am I doing here?"

"Nothing important," she said. Disorientation like this wasn't unexpected. "We're still good. We're still in space, buddy. Still in space. We're going to be skids-down on the *Midway* in a few minutes, so I'm going to need you to not die before then."

She tapped her rudder, swinging the craft out wide, and then, from behind a massive, jagged chunk of debris appeared the *Midway*, with a clear run to the open mouth of the hangar bay.

"How... How far away are we?" Flatline asked. "I'm feeling really shitty."

A side effect of the adrenaline. It wasn't exactly safe. "We're on final approach." She wished they would call it something else. Final approach was a little too morbid for her.

"I won't make it," said Flatline.

"Stop complaining," said Guano, adjusting her course, the white landing lights guiding her in. "I'm doing all I can to save you, so shut up."

"I'm just the gunner," said Flatline, the slurring returning to his voice. The chemical was either wearing off, or his injuries were just too serious. "Couldn't make it as a pilot. So I shoot things. Anyone... Anyone can shoot things. Replaceable. You'll get another one."

"Nope. Not going to happen. You hear me? I'm in

command of this ship, and I am giving you a direct order: Junior Lieutenant Deshawn Wiley, you are not permitted to die on my ship."

"Name's Flatline," he said. "B-Because of the heart attack."

"I know it is."

She had to keep him talking. Had to keep his brain working. "Flatline, buddy, listen. Listen good. When we get outta here, we're going to take some leave, okay? I know where, too. I just gotta take you to this great lesbian bar in Hong Kong. I mean, it's not my thing, but you'd love it. It's perfect for you! You like chicks, they like chicks, you have so much in common. And after that, hookers. So many hookers. We are going to get you *laid*, buddy. Even if it kills me. But if you die out here, I ain't dragging your corpse around. So you better…" A little bit of the facade broke. Just a little. *Keep talking, just keep talking.* She said whatever came to mind. "So you better not. Or at your funeral, I'm going to tell them all about—all about that time we had seventy-six hours of rec-leave in Vladivostok. You know the time! You remember that, you piece of shit. I still have that footage of you dancing to that singer. Um, what was her name? Aviaane. Ayalle? You love that girly crap, you love it! Aw, it's not your fault. When you're drunk, you know, you're dancing to the song in your *heart*, not the one you hear, am I right. Right? Hah. Believe me, your folks won't like that. I won't spare the details either. None. You hear me? Flatline?"

Nothing. The hangar roared up, terrifyingly close, but she didn't slow down.

"Flatline?"

"Lieutenant Corrick, this is *Midway*, you *must* reduce your speed."

Oh shit. The landing. The hangar bay was right there, and she was going *way* too fast.

Guano slammed on the brakes, the tiny ship screaming through the hangar bay doors, shaking as it passed through the artificial gravity field and into the ship. Grav-nets reached out to grab her bird, mighty hands that snatched at her wings and fuselage, pulling and slowing her down. Metal stressed and groaned.

The left wing came off, spilling fuel everywhere in a white mist. The grav-net almost lost its grip, the craft crashing heavily onto the deck, fuel and debris spreading out in a wide arc. The cockpit glass shattered, sucking the air out and stealing all sound.

Silently scraping across the deck, her Warbird came to a stop right at the end of the hangar bay, meters away from the unyielding steel blast wall.

Her head hurt. Her left arm hurt. Everything hurt, more or less. With the cockpit glass out, the only thing keeping her from vacuum was her suit.

Spacesuit-clad medics ran toward her ship, and a pair of medical drones drifted away from their moorings toward the wreckage, their four claws pulling away the metal hull to save the flesh within.

She was okay, but *her* life was the least of her concerns. She pulled up the medical readouts just in time to watch the beating line that was Flatline's heart go dead.

Flatline flatlined.

Chapter Twenty-Nine

VIP Quarters
USS Midway

Senator Pitt stalked the floor of his quarters like a caged animal, a thousand angry thoughts flying through his head at once.

That fucking washed-up has-been had bullied, forced, and shouted his way onto the bridge and into command. How dare that man talk to him, *him*, that way. The ancient, withered bastard was supposed to be a tool, something to ingratiate the Americans to the Chinese and nothing more. Now it seemed Mattis was calling all the shots.

Pitt had gone to great lengths to remind Mattis that this was *his* operation from the beginning. It seemed the man had forgotten that.

And what was that *smell*? Did all the rooms reek like this? It smelled like shit. Had since the moment he stepped through the door. The stench pervaded everything, clung to the furniture, forced its way into his nose, and even drifted out into the corridor. Where did it come from? Did they know?

Of course. They must have known. Even his own son didn't want to talk to him, much less give him the explanation he was owed.

Angrily, Senator Pitt picked up his communicator. He had a number of contacts on his recently used list, various other politicians, lawyers, his doctor. There was one, though, that wasn't labelled. It would be too risky, for them both, if anyone knew who it was. It was for emergencies. Critical matters. Important things.

He pressed it.

The phone dialed, connecting to the subspace relay, routing his call through various Z-space stations and toward Earth.

It connected with a soft click.

"You must be very desperate indeed to call me," said the voice on the other end, obscured by a distortion, as usual. To protect her identity.

"It's not that bad, Spectre," said Pitt, respectfully using the woman's codename. Intelligence spooks were all weird about things like that. "But I do need your help."

"Go ahead," said Spectre. "You know I'm here to help you."

Of course he knew. Senator Pitt knew when someone owed him a debt. That was how politics worked. The currency of government was back-scratching, and he was very wealthy indeed.

But even the richest man had to cash in eventually.

"I have a problem," said Pitt, taking the time to phrase his request carefully. "Admiral Mattis was supposed to accompany me to *Friendship Station* for a diplomatic mission. Things have gone sideways in a *big* way—I'm honestly not sure what to tell you, because it's, well, bloody and dangerous. The point is, this was *my* operation. And he disrespected me."

"Can't have that," said Spectre.

Damn right. "I want him sorted out."

"Sorted out?" Spectre paused, considering. "Do you mean —"

"I mean removed from command." The other thing...that wasn't necessary. "Have someone order him back to the rear. Put him back in whatever museum he crawled out of. Falsify a medical report, issue some order, *whatever* you have to do. I just want him out of my hair."

"So you don't want *him* removed, just the problem he poses removed."

Dealing with Intelligence spooks was always like this. "That's right. Don't do anything...rash."

"Regrettably, there's not a lot I can do about this," said Spectre. "He's the ranking commander in a theater of war. Even with all the tools at my disposal, there are some things even *I* can't arrange."

"Then what fucking use are you?" snapped Pitt.

Spectre was silent, and he realized he'd made a terrible mistake.

"Does working with me displease you, Senator Pitt?" she asked, her tone perfectly innocent, the threat dangling in the air. "If you want to end our mutual arrangement, all you have to do is let me know."

He knew that would be a bad idea. "That won't be

necessary."

"A wise decision."

Pitt tapped his foot on the ground, trying to keep the inertia going. "I'm just trying to do what's best for our species," he said, working a different angle. "We got attacked, and by something quite dangerous. I don't know if they're aliens, or what, but I know that they are hunting us. Hunting for blood. Mattis served well in the Sino-American War, no question. I'm not doubting that. But his time is over. It's time for younger blood—"

"It's time for your son to take command of the USS *Midway*?" asked Spectre.

"I'm not saying that it has to be him."

"But," said Spectre, "he's the next in command, apart from Mattis. There's nobody else it could conceivably go to."

Pitt frowned, slowly easing himself down into a chair. "You sure know a lot about the situation here out at the ass end of nowhere."

"It's my business to know things," said Spectre simply.

He couldn't contest that. "Maybe I'm asking the wrong person," he said, as much to himself as her. "As you said, your skills are"—he deliberately selected a specific word —"specialized."

"Indeed," said Spectre. "Your problem seems to be political. My solutions are practical."

Then he would need a political tool to solve this problem. Someone who owed him a favor from way back. Someone who could use words to accomplish what Spectre's talents could not.

"And I'll be sure to call on you if I need that. Goodbye,

Spectre." He closed the link, finger tapping on his communicator idly. Time to cash in one of his largest chips.

He opened a call to the President of the United States.

Chapter Thirty

Bridge
USS Midway

Mattis watched the green arrows on their radar screen disappear into their hangar bay until they were all swallowed up.

"All fighters have docked, Admiral," said Lynch. "One Warbird crashed on landing. The craft is lost, but it looks like at least the pilot survived. Deck crew are extracting them and removing the debris as we speak."

Mattis nodded approvingly. "And all remaining hostile strike craft have been eliminated?"

"Yes, Admiral. Scopes are clear, but there is a lot of debris around. It's possible some may have survived in a powered-down state."

If so, there was no time to go looking for them. With all their strike craft recovered, more or less, it was time to turn their eyes to the future. "Link our navigation computers with the *Fuqing*'s," he said. "We want to Z-jump with them."

Lynch's confusion was clear. "Wait, they're jumping? *We're* jumping?"

"That's right." Mattis leaned forward, putting his elbows on his knees. "We can break their cloak. They don't have ammo for their mass driver, and best of all, they won't be expecting us to attack. They broke the engagement, Mister Lynch. They were scared of something. Scared of us. I intend to capitalize on and exploit this fear."

"Sir, with respect, we don't know *why* they bugged out. We should wait for more ships."

"Any ship big enough and ugly enough to help us is also going to be slow enough that they're not going to arrive in time to make a difference."

Lynch's skepticism was clear. "We still have repairs to effect," he said. "I can't guarantee that we'll be one hundred percent combat effective when we emerge, or even much more than we are right now."

"We'll have to hammer out the dents on the way." There was no more time for arguing. "Establish the uplink, Mister Lynch, and let's get right after them."

With a polite nod, Lynch went to it, tapping away at his keyboard. His console flashed red. "The *Fuqing* didn't accept our uplink," he said.

Right on cue, his earpiece chirped. "This is Shao. We're experiencing a strange malfunction, Admiral. It seems that our computers believe you're crazy enough to jump away in pursuit of these strange ships, and even stranger, they think you want my ship to come with you."

Typical Chinese cowardice. "That's why you lost the war,

you know? Unwillingness to take risks," said Mattis, a tense edge to his tone. "Are you afraid?"

"Never," said Shao defiantly. "What are you saying? This is merely prudence."

"Is that so crazy?" asked Mattis. "We have the advantage. Let's use it."

"No." Shao's refusal was flat.

Mattis considered that, muting the channel for a second. "Mister Pitt," he asked, "do we have the current course the enemy fleet is taking?"

Pitt nodded. "Of course, sir."

"Are there any Chinese colonies in their path? Or nearby?"

He consulted his instruments for a moment. "They will pass within half a light year of New Guangzhou, assuming they keep up their current trajectory. It's a small research colony at the edge of space. Nothing at all fancy there."

Mattis reopened the line. "Shao, acknowledged. No worries. We'll proceed to New Guangzhou by ourselves and wait for you to catch up."

The faint hiss on the line showed she had taken the bait. "On second thought…" She clicked her tongue over the line, obviously trying to act casual as she changed her mind. "Well, I'm not dead yet, so why the hell not? We can be ready to jump momentarily."

"That's what I like to hear." He motioned to Lynch. "Try again."

Lynch tapped some keys. "Uplink complete, sir."

"Great," said Mattis, settling back into the captain's chair. "As soon as the *Fuqing* signals that they're ready to go, punch it."

He waited, and then the computer chirped.

"Engaging Z-space translation," said Lynch.

From the outside monitors, a field of energy built up. Seeing a Z-space translation from the inside was always a treat. Human eyes perceived the jump as a bright white flash of light, but viewed from within the bubble using a warship's multi-spectral cameras, the sight was something else.

Light in every spectrum of the rainbow flashed in pulses, multicolored sparkles dancing all around them like tiny stars. Each spark grew to be a dot, shimmering and full of energy, then it burst, emitting a flash before fading away to nothing. The color stained the ship's hull like a demented child had gone to town on it with a paintball gun loaded with pellets of every hue.

When the ship was fully painted, it flashed—and reality disappeared.

"We're in pursuit of the attacking fleet," said Lynch. "The Z-drive is holding steady, and the *Fuqing* is just off our starboard bow, in a travel formation. We should be several hours behind our target in Z-space. If they drop out of Z-space, we should have plenty of opportunities to decide our course of action, either to press the attack or sail silently onward."

"Very good, Mister Lynch," he said. "Now, I need a cup of coffee."

"Sir," asked Lynch, obviously uncomfortable. "What happens if the Chinese discover our deception? They're not going to take it kindly. They might even start shooting at us."

He bit his lower lip. "We'll burn that bridge when we come to it. If they get mad, well, I guess we're a little overdue for a rematch."

"I hope it doesn't come to that," said Lynch.

Mattis stared at the colorful display of Z-space, worry creeping in. "Me too."

Chapter Thirty-One

Forward Infirmary
USS Midway

Guano ran alongside Flatline's gurney all the way to the infirmary.

As the medics quickly pushed the gurney through the infirmary doors, one of them said, "Mid-twenties male, crash survivor, found down, unresponsive. Physical trauma to the head, lacerations on the right arm, and a weird-looking gunshot wound to the right leg just above the ankle. Cardiac arrest, restarted with the autodoc. Pulse is forty and thready. Respiration is eight. BP is eighty over sixty. GSC is three."

Shit. Shit. Shit. That was a lot of medical mumbo-jumbo and not a lot of calm, *he's going to be totally fine, don't worry* reassurances.

One of the ship's doctors put down his clipboard and made her way over. "We'll need a transfusion," she said, the words flying out of her mouth. "Intubate. Prep him for surgery. We have to stop that bleed." She jabbed a finger at Guano. "You. Out."

"But—"

"*Out.*"

One of the nurses grabbed her arm and tugged her away from Flatline's gurney. Guano yanked her arm back, but that only resulted in three big burly nurses grabbing her and giving her the old-fashioned Navy heave, dragging her out of the infirmary without a word, and tossing her into the corridor.

"Bastards!" she spat.

"Ma'am," said the nurse, "we'll let you know when he's out of surgery. You can't do anything for him now."

Typical rehearsed speech bullshit. She balled her fist to take a swing, but one of the nurses was talking on an earpiece. She swore she heard a request for marines.

"Fine," said Guano, turning and storming off in a random direction, her feet pounding on the deck.

Stupid nurses and doctors. What the hell did they know about literally anything, ever? Didn't they understand that a flight crew were basically brothers and sisters? She deserved to be in there. She deserved to be watching him, like family, like—

"Lieutenant Corrick," said Roadie, stepping in front of her. She hadn't even seen him there until he was physically blocking her path. "Where the hell do you think you're going?"

"Get out of the way, sir," she said, fists balled at her sides. "Or I might have to punch you."

"You wanna add striking a superior officer to your sheet, Lieutenant?" he asked, but something about the way he said it —firm but understanding, questioning and not demanding— gave her pause.

Silence.

"Not really," said Guano. "But Flatline—"

"I know." Roadie affixed a stern stare on her. "I've been flying fighters for fifteen years. You think Frost's always been my gunner?"

The implication seemed to calm her down a bit. "I guess not."

"Walk with me, Lieutenant." He said it in a way that indicated it was not a suggestion.

Guano fell in step. Still wearing her ejection suit, she trudged along as Roadie led her down corridor after corridor, before stopping outside a small, cramped room labeled *starboard exercise centre*.

"You want me to…lift weights at the gym, sir?" she asked incredulously. "At a time like this?"

"At a time when your partner's in surgery and you can't do anything about it except worry if, maybe, you could have done something differently that would have made this whole mess play out with a better end?" Roadie smiled thinly. "I think that's the perfect time to blow off a little steam. C'mon. Bench is free. Load a pair of twenties and I'll spot you."

"Forty kilos?" Guano rolled her eyes, despite it all. "Lightweight. Literally." She pushed open the door, making a line for the bench press. A steel bar suspended between black-painted stocks. A bench press with no weight on it always looked so sad. She picked up a round twenty-kilo disc, slid it onto one end, and then put another on the opposite end.

"I'll spot the warm up," said Roadie. "Work you up in twenty-kilo increments, see how high you can get." He glanced across the gym at somebody, then grinned. "Hey, Frost."

"Roadie!" The Kenyan woman bounced over to them both, her wide smile almost infectious. Almost. "Hey, Guano!"

Nothing in the world seemed to get Frost down. As Guano slid down onto the bench and wiggled up underneath the bar, she began to suspect the woman's presence was far from an accident.

"A'right," said Roadie, moving above her, hands on the bar. "You ready?"

"To lift forty kilos? Pfft."

"Sixty," said Roadie. "Remember the bar. That's twenty."

"Whatever." Guano lifted it up, lowering the weight down to her chest, then back up. Up. Down. Up. Down. Ten times. The tenseness in her body eased, replaced with the light burn of her arm muscles.

"Easy," said Guano, sitting up.

Roadie nodded understandingly, and then put an extra two disks on each side of the bar. Roadie took his turn, sliding under the bar. Guano bit her lip. If he dropped that, there was no way she could help him.

Still, Roadie hoisted it easily. Ten reps, lifting one hundred forty kilos like it was nothing. Jesus.

Guano kept her face even as Roadie slid out and went to remove the bars.

"Wait," she said. "I want to try it."

No reaction from Roadie, except to silently gesture for her to continue.

"No way," said Frost, her eyes wide. "That's way too heavy. Even for me. C'mon, Guano."

She wouldn't be shown up like this. Guano slid under the bar. Roadie moved above her, ready to spot.

The weight was intense, the bar bending slightly, her arms shaking. She could barely lift it out of the stirrups, but she clenched her teeth, flexed every muscle in her body, and got it over the lip.

Down, down, down… The bar kissed her chest, and it stayed there, her arms shaking with the effort of just keeping it from crushing her.

Roadie didn't help her lift. "How's it feel, Corrick?" he said, tone humorless. "That bar's a hundred and forty kilos. It's enough weight to crush your sternum and wreck your heart if you drop it. This is a do-or-die situation for you, Lieutenant."

Her arms trembled, fingers white. The grip on the bar dug into her flesh, burning. Her arms ached. "Help," she gasped.

"*Hm*, no. You bit off more than you could chew, took on too much, and look where it's landed you."

Frost's voice pitched up. "It's going to crush her. Help her, Yousuf!"

Roadie crouched down, his head right next to hers. "You see, I was a lot like you when I was younger, Corrick. You're reckless. Got a point to prove. But I want you to understand this: it's not just your life you're playing with when you roll the dice out there. If you don't figure this shit out, you are going to burn out, and when that happens, I want you to remember: a Warbird seats two. If you go down in flames, I have to write *two* letters of condolence, and believe me, I hate it. *Hate. It.* And I will not let that happen. Figure it out."

"W-Wait," gasped Guano, her grip weakening.

"Yousuf!" shouted Frost. "What are you *doing*?"

Roadie stood up. "Teaching her a lesson," he said, a hard look on his face. "One that I learned a little too late." He turned his attention back to Guano. "I'm not telling you this again. No more chances. Unfuck yourself at FTL speed, Lieutenant Corrick, because one more slip-up and you are done."

Her breath came in panted gasps. Frost frantically grabbed one of the disks, pulling it off right before her strength gave out. The bar became lopsided, awkward, but it was easier to hold. Frost pulled off another, and then finally the whole thing tipped to one side in a loud clatter.

Roadie walked to the door and closed it, leaving Guano aching, sore, and covered in sweat.

"Are you okay?" asked Frost, her face streaked with panic.

"Yeah," gasped Guano, rubbing her aching arms, staring intently at the closed door. The pain grew worse as the adrenaline, the fear of being crushed to death in a gym, wore off. Numbness spread along her fingers, like a million tiny pins, and thick bruises developed along them.

They might be broken. She couldn't fly.

Chapter Thirty-Two

Captain's Ready Room
USS *Midway*

The hours passed. The alien fleet showed no sign of slowing down on its course toward New Guangzhou, and he authorized a shift change. Which included himself. He retired to the captain's ready room, which was still decorated with Malmsteen's possessions. Pictures. A mug that was probably his favorite. A spent shell casing mounted to a wooden base. It felt invasive to be surrounded with such marks of personhood, but these were no ordinary times. He'd have some junior enlisted crewman remove it all and store it for shipment to his family, but that was a task for the future. They didn't have the manpower to spare right now. Malmsteen wouldn't have begrudged him the use of his facilities.

It'd been so long since he'd seen any action, he'd forgotten how it affected the body. Mattis felt weak all over, as though he'd just run a marathon. Being thrown around on the bridge didn't help, probably, and he knew he had bruises that he couldn't feel—but sleep would bring pain and healing in equal measure.

He stripped out of his uniform, but the moment his head hit the pillow and his eyes closed, he heard a knock on the door.

No rest for the wicked, but even the Devil got some time off. Mattis sat back up with a groan. "Come in."

To his surprise, it wasn't any of his staff but *Martha* who opened the door.

"Well," she said, stepping through the threshold, "you've made yourself at home."

Mattis grimaced. "I was thinking the same thing. Honestly, I didn't want this, Martha. Not like *this*."

"I don't know," she said, her eyes gentle and non-accusing, "I feel like, on some level, you kind of did." She could always see right through him. Those reporter instincts. "A bit more orderly in the transfer of power, perhaps, but I think, in the general sense, you got what you wanted today, Jack."

He couldn't refute what she was saying, so he just sat there on the edge of his borrowed bed in silence.

"How bad was it?" asked Ramirez. "The battle? Did we lose many people?"

"Some," said Mattis, biting his lower lip. "We don't have a full picture of our losses yet, but when all the department heads give their full report, we'll know."

She seemed to take that well. "One thing that I *was* curious about…you and that Shao woman." She smiled. "Should I be worried?"

The teasing caught him off guard. It was the second time

she'd used that line—the first in reference to the ship, and now to his opposite number on the *Fuqing*. "I…I don't know what you mean. You know she tried to kill me back in the day—"

"That's right," said Ramirez. "And now you two are basically flirting like schoolkids."

"We practically argued the whole time!" Mattis squinted at her in confusion. "She shot at me, and it sounded like she was the happiest person in the galaxy. You call that *flirting*?"

Her smile only grew wider. "I think I know you flirting when I see it."

Women. Mattis folded his arms in a way he knew was vaguely petulant. "Well, it's not your business who I flirt with, is it?"

"No, it's not," she said, her tone softening. "Just like we agreed."

"Just like we agreed," said Mattis, a little regret creeping in. Just a little. It was so long ago, and they were younger then. Busier. Trying to make a career out of their jobs. She, on the lowest rung of the ladder at a trashy celebrity gossip channel, and he, a junior officer in the US Navy.

They exchanged a look, a long look, one that was only broken by the chirping of his private communicator. Typical. He'd been allocated some personal, private, necessary rest and relaxation time, and everyone in a thousand suns thought it was the perfect opportunity to get ahold of him.

Ring. Ring. Ring.

"Not going to answer that?" asked Ramirez, raising an eyebrow.

Ring. Ring. Reluctantly, Mattis checked the readout. It was Chuck. He clicked the answer button. "Hello?"

"Dad?" asked Chuck, concern in his tone. "Hey, I've been trying to reach you for hours."

If his communicator had been ringing during the battle, there was no way he'd even noticed it over the noise. "We were a little busy," he said. There was no telling who was listening in on the line—it was, after all, a private phone call to an active conflict zone. "I wasn't able to pick up."

"Right. Well, as busy as you are, I thought you should know: Senator Pitt is calling all over. Everyone he can think of. All about you. A lot of calls, and those people are calling people. This is big, Dad."

"Senator Pitt is an asshole," he said, not even bothering to disguise his anger. "I don't care about what he thinks or what he does. If I had my way, I'd jam his ass into an escape pod and let the Coast Guard pick him up."

"I understand that," said Chuck. "But I mean, Dad, I wouldn't underestimate him. I'm saying this as someone who works with him. I may only be low-level senate staff, but even I know Senator Pitt has his fingers in a lot of pies, and a lot of people owe him favors. He's not the kind of person you should cross trivially."

Mattis could barely stifle a chuckle, giving Ramirez a playful look. "What's he going to do, whine me to death?"

She didn't seem amused, but out of respect—or possibly something else—she didn't comment.

"Anyway," said Chuck. "Javier says hi. Again."

Again with this Javier. It wasn't his boyfriend, apparently—the notion still disturbed Mattis slightly—but it was someone else. A housemate? Friend? *Second* boyfriend? His mind played with the possibilities.

"Tell him hi," said Mattis, sucking up his pride, forcing himself to be polite. "And tell him I don't care what role he has in your life. I don't care. If he's okay with you, he's okay with me. Just make sure he pays his taxes and we'll be fine." Chuck had a habit of letting people couch surf at his place, often for months at a time. "And make sure he gets a job. You know how I feel about freeloaders."

"A…job?" Chuck made a weird noise on the other end of the line, half laugh, half confused groan. "Are you serious?"

"Yes, son." Mattis felt vaguely silly having this conversation with a grown man. "Everyone has to get one, you know. I know it might seem like, over the years, I haven't always been supportive of your…lifestyle, but you know I love you, yes? Whatever you and your friends and your… boyfriends…do, I'll always be there for you, and them." He mustered a smile. "But they have to have a job."

"Dad," said Chuck, his tone saturated with bewilderment. "Javier is a baby."

The revelation hit him like a ton of bricks. "Wait," he said, speaking before even thinking, his brain still in worst-case-scenario mode from the battle, "you stole a baby?"

"*Stole?*" Chuck shouted down the line. "I didn't steal anything! What the hell are you even *saying?*"

"What are *you* even saying?" Mattis scowled. "Is this some kind of joke?"

"Dad, we used a surrogate." Dead silence. "We…we used a surrogate. She's going to give birth any day now. Javier will be your grandson."

The idea of having a grandchild, given Chuck's… preferences…was one he had not ever anticipated. "Oh," he said. It was really all he could say. Anything else would have come out as a stammering mess. "I didn't realize."

"I know you didn't," said Chuck. "But now you know."

This was okay. Good, even. He just needed a minute to process it, a task made more difficult by Ramirez standing awkwardly off to one side, pretending she couldn't hear every word that was being said.

He had some words for Chuck, he had some words for Ramirez, but before he could say anything to either of them, the connection to Chuck dropped. A work transmission was coming through from the bridge. They always overrode personal communications.

"What?" he snapped.

"Sir," said Commander Pitt, "we've located an enemy ship."

Chapter Thirty-Three

Bridge
USS Midway

Mattis dragged himself out of his borrowed captain's ready room. Ramirez beat a hasty, polite retreat, for which he was eternally grateful.

When he arrived on the bridge, the room was a busy hive of activity.

"Admiral," said Lynch, who looked like he desperately needed a nap, but had been surviving on caffeine and adrenaline, "one of the hostile ships has dropped out of Z-space and broken formation with the others."

Mattis slid into the captain's chair, considering that. "Just one?"

"Yes, sir."

He drummed his fingers on the armrest of his chair. "Based on our logs of the initial contact, what was the status of that vessel?"

"It was one of the most damaged, sir. Early reports indicate that one of our strike craft lead an assault on that ship, working in coordination with strike craft from the *Fuqing*." Lynch scrolled through the report. "Apparently, at close range, Lieutenant Corrick's scans were able to find a weakness. The ship's engine exhaust ports were only protected by a cone of armor, so if approached directly from behind, the armor would not protect them. The strike craft dumped their heat-seeking missiles into them, and emptied their guns, right before the ship jumped away."

Mattis turned the information over in his head. It made sense, after all. An exhaust port had to exhaust things, and therefore, had to lead to some other system. And the ship that had been damaged in the *engines* having engine trouble was too much of a coincidence to ignore. "Evaluation of that ship's capabilities, Mister Lynch?"

"Uh, unknown," he said, although sensing that this was not an entirely acceptable answer, he revised it. "The strike craft do not report that they struck any of their weapons systems, only their engines. We can assume that the alien ship is fully functional, both in terms of defensive and offensive systems, but it may lack maneuvering and Z-space capabilities."

There was that word again. Alien. Mattis let it slide. Lynch's conjecture was reasonable. "Good," he said. "Signal the *Fuqing*. Tell them we are to engage and destroy that ship."

"Aye aye, sir." Bright lights once again enveloped the outside of the ship, and in a cascade of color, the Z-space reality disappeared and the real universe reappeared. "Z-space translation complete, Admiral."

The *Fuqing* reappeared moments afterward, and ahead,

Mattis could see the enemy ship. A small cruiser, it appeared almost undamaged on all sides, except for its rear exhaust ports, which belched a mixture of white steam and black smoke, large puffs of the stuff dissipating across space. A minor debris field showed up in radar near the ship, probably the ejected remains of their engines.

Lynch had brought them in close, which was good.

"All guns, target that skunk and fire at will. Launch strike craft. Load torpedoes and fire for effect."

The ship's guns spoke, and at such a close distance, the shells barely had time to be seen before they smashed into the hostile ship.

Or, at least, they *almost* smashed into the hostile ship. Mattis squinted to see. The rounds had exploded about a meter in front of the ship. The areas they had targeted had no scorch marks on them, no damaged armor, no signs of impact at all. Instead, as he watched, another volley streaked in, splashing against some kind of blue energy shield that shimmered faintly as it absorbed the impact.

Damn cheating bastards had shields. Their advanced tech wasn't just limited to weapons. "Lynch, are you seeing this?"

"I was about to ask you the same question, Admiral," he said.

"Dammit," said Commander Pitt. He'd been awfully quiet so far. "That's why we could barely scratch them back at Cor Caroli."

It would certainly explain things. "But how was Lieutenant Corrick able to damage their rear, if they had this technology?"

"Any number of reasons," said Pitt. "It's possible their technology is directional; maybe it can only cover a small area.

Maybe it can't cover their engines because of some technical limitation."

Lots of theories, not a lot of concrete evidence. No time to think about it. The hostile ship seemed to awaken, beginning a slow turn toward them, its hull lighting up as those red beams —hyper-accelerated particles—leapt out for them, raking across the *Midway*'s armored front.

Close range was a double-edged sword. The ship shook as the hostile weapons fire struck them, and alarms rang out across the bridge.

"We're hit," said Lynch. "Absorbed by armor, but their weapons seem a lot more effective at close range."

Well damn. Time to bring their allies into this fight. He touched his earpiece. "Anytime now, Shao."

"We're computing a firing solution," said Shao.

"How hard is it? They're right in front of you!"

She didn't answer, which was probably a good thing. On his monitors, he could see the *Fuqing* firing, her guns blasting against the hostile ship's shields. He stared intently, trying to find some weakness.

One of the *Fuqing*'s shells had slipped through, blasting a chunk out of their shared enemy. It had happened so quickly that he almost missed it. It was almost as though...

"Mister Lynch," he said, energy filling his tone. "Speculation. Do you think that their shields can stand up to repeated, rapid-fire blows?"

Lynch twisted in his chair, turning around to look at him. "Maybe, maybe not," he said. "If the matter field has any similarities to actual armor, it will be subject to physical properties. However, if it's more like their cloaking device, a tool that requires huge amounts of power to activate and is therefore used sparingly, flickering on and off when needed—" Another barrage of enemy fire slashed across their armored front, rocking the bridge. "It's possible we could overload it," Lynch conceded. "Maybe."

Maybe would have to be enough. He touched his earpiece again, reopening the connection to Shao. "Captain, I'm sure you've seen those shields."

"Sure have," she said. "I'm hoping you have a solution for me, because they're really ruining my day."

"You know I always like to make you happy," he said, Ramirez's words flashing back into his head. *You're flirting...* That was a distraction. He put it aside. No time now. "But, uh, yes. Plan is to coordinate fire on one particular spot and overload their systems."

"Sounds good to me—"

A voice cut over her. "Admiral," said Commander Pitt, his tone urgent. "We're detecting a power buildup on the hostile ship."

His chest tightened. "Like the mass driver?"

"Yes, sir," said Lynch. "It's smaller. Lighter. Maybe an emergency system, but sir, it's charging *fast.*"

Shit. They were right in the enemy's face. There was no way to dodge. And their Z-drive systems wouldn't charge anywhere near fast enough. "Can we avoid it?" he asked, dreading the answer.

"It's not us we need to be worried about," said Commander Pitt, his face ashen. "They're targeting the *Fuqing.*"

"Shao," he roared, touching his earpiece. "Shao, listen to me, you need to engage your Z-drive system. Get out of there right now!"

"We're working on it," said Shao, desperation clear in her voice. Fear. "Standby."

It was too late. On his screen, the whole underside of the enemy ship opened up, revealing a mass no more than a hundred meters long, strapped to two long rails. It swung to one side, and with a flash, it fired.

The *Fuqing* absorbed the blow straight on the nose, the front of the ship crumpling in, hull plates buckling and breaking away. The ship lurched backward and downward, like a sick whale, the edges of the entry point glowing red hot.

Her guns went silent.

"Captain Shao," said Mattis, his heart in his throat. "Report status." Nothing but static on the line. The *Fuqing* burned on his monitors, red flares igniting in front of their windows. "Calling any soul on the *Fuqing*. Report status."

Nothing. He slowly took off the earpiece. "Mister Lynch," he said coldly. "Consolidate firing solutions on the hostile ship. Concentrate fire on the smallest area you can, firing as rapidly as you can. Melt our barrels if you have to. I want everything except the torpedoes shooting, even the point-defense guns, strike craft, you name it. Give them *everything*, and when they break, put a pair of torpedoes into them. Pound that son of a bitch back to the Stone Age."

Lynch did exactly that, cranking up the rate of fire on the *Midway*'s guns, explosive salvos flying. The rounds came together at a point right at the center of the ship's front, each impact sending up a blue flash as the shield blocked them.

"Keep firing," said Mattis. "Send them to Hell."

A round slipped through the shield. And then another and

another. Then, just as quickly as it had appeared, the shield flashed a bright blue and winked out.

"Torpedoes away," said Commander Pitt. "Strike craft recalled out of the blast radius."

Twin missiles leapt away from the *Midway*, each the size of a strike craft, their engines glowing brightly against the dark of space. At close range, they barely had four or five seconds in space before they plunged home, burrowing deep into the hull of the alien cruiser and detonating within. The ship bucked wildly, as though it were a living thing in pain, rolled over onto its side, and exploded.

The shockwave of debris washed over the *Midway*, shaking everything in a way that, to Mattis, reminded him of the way *Friendship Station* had gone up. Wreckage pelted the *Midway*, hitting its hull like rain, scraping and bouncing off the armor.

And then everything was quiet.

"Target destroyed," said Commander Pitt.

The bridge erupted into cheering. Mattis kept a cool, commanding posture during it all, but inside, he was yelling along with them.

And, of course, there was the matter of the *Fuqing*. "Report status on our allies," said Mattis. "Any word from Captain Shao?"

The request tempered the joyous exultations on the bridge. The glow of the fires on the *Fuqing* painted her hull orange, but that was a good sign, ultimately. Her hull was intact. The fires were probably on the surface. No radiation leakage from her reactors.

"Not yet," said Commander Pitt. "But early scans show the ship is floundering and adrift, but likely salvageable. They'll need a couple months in spacedock, a partial refit, and of course the front part of the hull will probably need to be repaired—but the *Fuqing* will live to fight again."

That was welcome news. They'd need as many ships as they could get.

"Although," said Commander Pitt, his brow furrowing as he further examined the scans, "I *am* detecting some strange readouts from their ship. A buildup of power. They might be attempting to…use their Z-drive, maybe?"

He scowled. "I hope not," said Mattis. "If they try to jump away with that amount of damage, they'll tear themselves apart."

"I don't think it's the Z-drive," said Lynch, studying his readouts with increased fervor. "It looks like it's coming from their reactor core, I think, or some kind of secondary system."

Damn. "What could it be?" asked Mattis. "Some kind of weapon? An emergency protocol?"

"I have no idea," said Lynch, as he and everyone else stared at the monitors which showed a energy build up deep within the ship. "What in the blazes?"

"Launch our SAR bird," said Mattis, taking command of the situation. "Continue to broadcast on all frequencies, all channels. See if we can raise someone—even if it's on handheld radio. There's no chance their whole crew is dead. Lots of Chinese are alive over there, and we're going to save them."

"Aye aye, sir," said Lynch. "SAR bird away. We're dispatching some of our dropships to serve as rescue shuttles. We should be able to dock with the Chinese airlocks, or if we can't, cut our way in. Our ships should be able to make a solid seal. If there's anyone alive in there, they should know to come to the sound of cutting."

Sounded like a good plan. "Make sure you send over medical teams as well," he said. "There will be casualties."

"Sir," asked Commander Pitt, "we could have our alert fighters do a sweep of the ship. See if they can see any escape pods launching, or otherwise provide assistance."

"Whatever we can do." Mattis took a breath. "Okay. Let's —"

"Sir," said Lynch, "the energy buildup. It's reached—"

The Chinese ship exploded.

Chapter Thirty-Four

Forward Infirmary
USS Midway

Although they both hurt, Guano cradled her left hand in her right all the way to the infirmary. Frost came with her. There was help that was closer and better, but this one had Flatline.

As she approached, the nurses came out to meet and remove her, but she held up her blackened hand. "Hey, legitimate, legitimate!" she said, waving one of her damaged hands around as protest.

"It's true," said Frost, although she looked nervous, hopping from foot to foot.

Dammit, woman, the goal here is to get my hands fixed, then check in on Flatline. Don't mess this up for me…

For a moment, she thought she'd get turned away, but perhaps seeing the bruises changed their minds. Reluctantly, one of them stepped forward to examine the injury.

"Looks painful," he said, blinking in confusion as he turned the hand over, causing her to grimace.

"Hey, careful, that's my throttle hand!" She held out her right instead. "See, this one too."

The nurse stared at the injuries in amazement. "What the hell did you do to yourself, Lieutenant?"

She saw no reason to lie. Not directly. "I hurt myself at the gym. Put too much weight at the bench, and I couldn't lift it."

The guy sighed. "You pilots are all the same. Here. This should reduce the swelling." He pulled out a needle and, without so much as a hello, injected it into her palm.

"Ow!"

He glared at her. "Baby."

"How's Flatline?" asked Frost. Guano was glad she was the one asking that question.

The nurse, however, was less than receptive. "Are we going to have to throw you out too?"

"No," said Frost, holding up her hands. "No, no, no."

Sighing, the nurse jabbed a thumb over her shoulder. "Head inside," he said. "They're fixing him for surgery now. Joker's waiting there."

She didn't need to be told twice. Guano bolted through the infirmary, with Frost right behind her. They skidded around the corner to the surgical ward, where Joker—one of their fellow pilots—was standing, her brown hair pulled back, face pressed to the window that look into the surgery room. Guano muscled her way in beside her.

"Hey," said Joker, shoving back, "I was here first!"

"He's *my* gunner," said Guano. Together, they managed to fill the window, Frost jockeying behind them for even a glimpse.

Flatline had his leg slathered in surgical gel and was hooked up to several IVs. The ship's doctors stood around him, hanging bags filled with all kinds of liquids. Blood in one bag, fluid in another, and a cloudy mixture in a third, likely some sort of medication.

"He'll be fine," said Joker, and, in a feeble attempt to clarify, "he's a big guy."

Guano spoke with confidence she didn't feel. "Yeah. Little boo-boo like that, he'll shrug it off. I'm just making sure he gets a real fucking sick scar. I'm going to make the doctor sew a little smiley face into him, so, you know, he can always look back on these good times and think of me."

"Yeah," said Frost. "When we rotate Earthside again, I was thinking of getting a tattoo. You know, something like, *Crew of the Midway*."

Guano twisted around to look at her. "How do you deal with being a"—she hated saying it but forced the words out—"replaceable gunner?"

"Simple," said Frost, beaming back. "Don't be replaceable. Anyone can shoot a gun, Corrick, but being part of a team? Even a team of two? That takes something else."

As they watched, Flatline was wheeled into the next room and, with an angry scowl, the doctor closed the blinds.

"Hey!" Guano banged on the window. "Hey, open up! We want to see!"

"He's not even in the room anymore," said Joker.

The nurse from the main infirmary came storming in, his hands on his hips. "You three. Out. You were warned."

"But I didn't do anything wrong!" protested Joker.

Guano sighed and, with a last look at the blinds, turned and trudged out of the infirmary with the other two.

"Wanna play cards?" asked Frost brightly. "It'll keep our minds off things. We can go until he's out of surgery."

"Great," said Joker. "I got more money to win off you soon-to-be-much-poorer idiots."

The very last thing Guano felt like doing was playing cards, but there was nothing she could do for Flatline. "Fine," she said, absentmindedly cracking her knuckles, before immediately regretting it. "I'll show you bitches how this game is played."

As she said that, another doctor stepped through the doors and into the surgical suite, almost running.

"He'll be fine," said Joker again, although Guano couldn't help but notice the slight tremble in her voice as she said it.

Chapter Thirty-Five

Bridge
USS Midway

Stunned silence filled the room, broken by a tremor as a shockwave from the detonation passed over the ship, creating a faint ripple that shook computers and rattled the various systems.

Nobody spoke. Only machines quietly beeped, almost mournfully, reporting the status of a ship that was no longer there.

"What the hell?" asked Mattis, bewildered. "Their reactor was intact, their core life support systems functioning… Was it a side effect of the alien weapon?"

"No, sir," said Lynch. "The projectile was just a standard ferrous lump of inert mass. It didn't cause the explosion, at least not directly."

Another long, languished period of silence.

"Get Modi up here," said Commander Pitt. "If anyone can

sort this mess out, he can."

"Do it," said Mattis.

For a moment, Commander Pitt yelled into a communicator, arguing with Modi. Mattis appreciated the time to think. To digest. Shao and he had almost—*almost*—become friends, despite their history. And her loss… Well, there would be time enough to think on that later.

He was using that excuse a lot. Deferring his problems onto Future-Mattis. Eventually, he knew, he would become that guy, but not today. Not right now.

Quiet pervaded until Modi arrived. It was Mattis's first chance to get a good look at him. He was tall, wry and impeccably groomed. He had a neatly trimmed mustache that, to Mattis, appeared slightly ridiculous. Still, he carried himself with a serious, almost distinguished air, his stride stiff and formal as he walked over to Mattis's chair.

"Commander Modi reporting as ordered, sir."

"Thank you for coming up here, Commander. We figured getting hands-on with the systems directly would be beneficial for you."

"I concur."

An odd phrase, but Mattis let it slide, giving a deferential nod. "Good. Our ally's ship exploded. Find out why."

"Of course, sir," said Modi. "Mister Lynch, please play back the recording of the explosion. I'm sure I can give you some kind of information as to what went wrong."

Commander Pitt typed on his console and, after a second or two, an image of the burning *Fuqing* reappeared on their monitors. Modi took Lynch's console and, examining it carefully, scrolled forward, playing back the ship's destruction in slow motion. A brief flash from within, and then a much bigger one, completely blowing the ship and all her crew to atoms.

"The only thing I can offer by way of explanation," said Modi, his tone apprehensive, "was that flash right before the explosion."

"Do you know what it was?" asked Mattis.

"No, but it does not seem consistent with a typical reactor overload." Modi switched the screens back to real-time mode. "Its presence is certainly…odd. It appears to be a secondary explosion of some kind, a trigger to the primary."

A secondary explosion? But the enemy ship's ordnance was inert. "If you have the answer, lemme hear it."

"I do not."

Mattis grimaced. "Got a reasonable guess?"

"Yes," said Modi, without elaborating.

Lynch rolled his eyes. "You damn cyborg! He's not asking for mathematical proof. A guess is fine."

"The admiral asked if I *knew* what it was," said Modi. "If he wanted my guesswork, he would have asked for that."

Mattis flicked his tongue from one side of his lips to the other. "Commander Modi, I'd appreciate any input you may have on this matter, regardless of certainty, so feel free to contribute whatever you have."

"As you wish," said Modi. "Admiral, that flash appears to be indicative of a Type IV shaped charge explosion. That kind of hardware is used in various roles, from breaching charges to demolition purposes, but its primary role in a ship of that size and configuration would be as a scuttling charge."

"You could have just said that," muttered Lynch.

Mattis's surprise was impossible to conceal. "*Scuttling* charge? You mean the Chinese blew up their own ship?"

"Why in blue blazes would they do that?" asked Lynch. "They were hit pretty bad, but not *that* bad. Certainly not so bad as to blow themselves to Kingdom Come when there were no enemy forces in the AO and a ship obviously attempting to organize a rescue effort for them."

"This is why," said Modi, his tone even, "I would prefer to avoid speculation in the future."

"Maybe," said Commander Pitt, "it was the very fact that rescue was so certain and so immediate. Maybe they didn't want us on board, sir. Maybe they had something to hide."

It felt strange to cast aspersions on the Chinese so soon after they were friends, with the debris swirling around his ship. But the truth was, for all her banter and friendliness, Shao had kept secrets from him the whole time he'd known her.

"I think you may be right, XO," he said, watching the last of the *Fuqing*'s debris field expand and disappear into nothingness. "We've got two mysteries on our hands now. Where the hell did these enemy ships come from? And what the hell are the Chinese hiding?"

Chapter Thirty-Six

Bridge
USS Midway

Despite the loss of the *Fuqing*, the atmosphere on the bridge was electric. They had defeated their first alien ship—assuming they *were* aliens and not another rogue nation state—and discovered a critical weakness in their shield designs. Mattis knew why they were happy, but despite it all, couldn't bring himself to feel much except a vague, hollow feeling in his gut.

It had been too easy.

Damage assessments and repairs were made, including an assessment of the front armor of the ship. It had taken quite a beating, but with a little field repair, it would be right as rain.

He did his job, transmitting a report to the fleet, which included a full breakdown of what had transpired. Everything he could think of was included, starting with the appearance of the enemy ships at *Friendship Station* and ending with the loss of the *Fuqing*. Mattis made specific note of Shao's skill and courage, especially in the face of adversity, but he couldn't bring himself to say anything positive about Admiral Yim.

Live by the sword, die by the sword.

Having sorted out as much as he could, he slept, which was the best thing in the world. Waking up and returning to the bridge, however…less so.

It had been cleaned. The whole thing had been scrubbed from top to bottom. Every scorch mark and blood stain had been scrubbed away and the whole room lightly scented with pine. The damaged consoles, even ones that were still working, had been replaced, and every scrap of debris had been meticulously cleaned up. It looked like a brand new ship.

Were the crew always this damn clean?

"Report," he said, his head clouded. Nobody had brought him coffee yet. It was difficult to think without his brain juice.

"Admiral," said Lynch. "The fleet has responded to your report. They've dispatched reinforcements, the USS *Alexander Hamilton* and the USS *Paul Revere*. They are expected to complete Z-space translation in approximately one hour."

He knew those ships. "The *Hamilton* and the *Revere*? They're sending us scout frigates?" Mattis frowned. "We're going to need something a little bigger."

"That's what they're sending for now," said Lynch. "The rest of the fleet is slower. We're expecting a much larger group of ships within a week."

Another week might as well be another lifetime, but there was an old saying: You went to war with the army you had, not the one you wanted. Same applied to the Navy. "Anything else?"

Lynch flicked through his reports. "Oh, wait, there's one more thing. A supply ship, the HMS *Somerset*, carrying fuel, repair crews, and a lot of interesting things…including a wing of strike craft. They were set to resupply *Friendship Station*, but we could really use those ships to replace our losses."

Some good news. The irony of a British ship coming with the *Paul Revere* was not lost on him. "The British are coming," he said, unable to keep a smile off his face. "Send word to the incoming ships, inform them of the tactical discoveries we've made and ensure they're briefed on the various weaknesses we've exploited. And regarding those strike craft, make sure we transfer them all, even if we don't have room to operate them yet. If we take more losses, I want to keep our combat effectiveness."

"Will do, Admiral."

"Very good. Dismissed."

Lynch bit his lower lip. "Um. Sir, there *was* one more thing that I was supposed to tell you."

Not good. "Proceed, Commander."

"Well, sir, it's just…" He held out a tablet with a response from the fleet on it. "GBC News wants an interview. Apparently details of the battle have leaked out, and people are panicking. To calm everyone down, they want an interview with you, just, you know, to reassure the public that this is being taken care of. They're paying fleet HQ top dollar, and since we already have one of GBC's representatives on board, HQ figured it would be…easier."

Ramirez. He had to give an interview with Martha. Mattis stiffened his back. Not again. "I'm not going to talk to her."

Lynch squinted. "You rabbiting from a reporter, sir? After

all that's happened?"

It was different. "Reporters and I, Lynch, we have... history."

Lynch leaned back in his chair, looking past him. "So I heard, you know, through the grapevine. But, unfortunately, HQ demanded, sir. So I think you're going to have to get through it somehow."

Great. Just great. "When's the interview?"

"Uh, now, sir." Lynch pointed over his shoulder.

Mattis twisted in his chair. Behind him, a film crew with cameras stood in the corner, their arms full of equipment. He hadn't noticed them come in. "On the *bridge*?"

"It's, uh, dramatic. It evokes a feeling of power and authority. And that the situation is well under control."

Well, that would explain why the whole bridge had been cleaned. "Don't suppose," he said, turning back toward Lynch, "there's any way I can order you to get me out of this?"

"Sorry, sir," said Lynch, shrugging helplessly.

"Right. Well, at least make sure someone brings me coffee. Black and bitter, like my soul."

"Aye aye, sir. I'll make it happen."

It took the crew several minutes to set up. Assembling a light here, placing a microphone there, and endlessly testing the camera. At any other time, in any other place, it would have been less infuriating. This was his work office. His command seat. His ship was essentially helpless while he spoke to reporters, and he was itching to chase down the rest of the alien fleet.

His eagerness was tempered by the realities of his situation. The smart play here was to wait for reinforcements and repairs. They had pushed their luck. Too much, and they would break. Having a pair of frigates at their side, even if they were small, would be extremely useful. More targets to shoot at, more guns to shoot back. Those little frigates were fast, too. Maneuverability counted.

Didn't mean he liked it at all.

Finally, Ramirez's team were ready, and she pulled up a chair opposite him, a too-bright light shining in his face.

"Okay," said Ramirez, smiling her reporter smile. "Just try to answer the questions as naturally as you can, Admiral Mattis."

Yes, this is totally natural. "Of course."

"Okay." Ramirez held up her fingers. "Uplink is good? Good. Okay. We're live in five, four, three, two…" She cleared her throat and almost became another person.

"Good evening. I'm here on the bridge of the USS *Midway*, a United States warship, and I'm joined tonight by the Commanding Officer of that ship, Admiral Jack Mattis."

A red light blinked on the camera that was pointed at him. He squinted in the glare, trying—less than successfully—to smile.

"Admiral Mattis, what can you tell us about the situation out here?"

What *could* he tell her? He didn't want to spread rumors that he couldn't verify, but he'd given a few press interviews in his time. He had two strategies to avoid giving out information. *No Comment* his way through it, which was a dick move, or just give indirect non-answers.

"Miss Ramirez, as you well know, this is a very difficult and unusual situation out here in border space."

"Certainly," said Ramirez, her face locked into reporter mode. "Although we're looking for something a little more specific." She knew what he was doing. "What can you tell us about *Friendship Station*?"

"Well," said Mattis, "as I'm sure you're aware, that station is no more."

"A tragic loss of life," said Ramirez. "It went down with all hands, is that correct?"

"That hasn't yet been confirmed," said Mattis.

Ramirez would know a dodge when she saw one, but for reasons unknown to him, let it slide. "And what can you tell me about the force that attacked it?"

"They're certainly unlike anything we've seen before."

"In what way?"

The heat from the light made him sweat. Was it normally that bright?

Ramirez was trying to make him say they were aliens, but he wasn't falling for it. "Well, we haven't encountered those ships before, in any service on Earth."

"Do you think they're from Earth?"

Ah, now they were getting closer.

"Their origin is unclear at this time."

Ramirez blinked, affixing him with a deathly glare that melted away the instant the camera flicked back to her. "How would you describe the battle at *Friendship Station*?"

"We took what the defense gave us, and responded to their play accordingly."

"So this is a game to you?"

Mattis folded his hands in front of him, giving her a thin smile. "Chess grew out of war. Almost every game we play is essentially ritualized combat. War *is* a game, Miss Ramirez. We play to win."

"But—"

Mattis cleared his throat. "Miss Ramirez, I've learned my lesson. I don't give vital information to reporters, lest the whole GBC network start printing it everywhere they can. This is an active combat zone and—"

"Thank you very much for your time," said Ramirez, cutting him off with a smile, her teeth ever so slightly clenched. "That was Admiral Mattis, Commanding Officer of the USS *Midway*. I'm Martha Ramirez from GBC News, good night."

The light, mercifully, flicked off.

"What the hell was that?" hissed Ramirez. "You're being a jerk. Do you really think the people of Earth are going to see that interview and go, *oh, that Jack Mattis guy, he's so great!*"

"What?" asked Mattis. "You can't honestly expect me to go on national TV and tell the world that there are aliens attacking border stations, do you? After what happened last time?"

"Yes! Yes, I do, Jack! The public has a right to know this!" She affixed a withering stare to his face. "I know I was out of line during the war, but I was young and I needed a story. That little titbit got my foot in the door—"

"And put my crew at risk," said Mattis. "Dammit Martha, you should have known better. If you're going to describe a ship as *heavily damaged*, the damn reds are going to hunt it down to finish it—"

"That didn't happen!"

"*That* time." Mattis folded his arms. "But damned if they

didn't try. I won't make the same mistake. Not again. Too much is at stake."

"Well," said Ramirez, shaking her head, "you should have said something. Everyone's blaming the Chinese."

"It wasn't the Chinese," said Mattis.

Ramirez stood and put her hands on her hips. "I know that, you know that, and you needed to tell the galaxy that. You could have just said it wasn't the Chinese, Jack. That's all you had to do." Without another word, she stormed off the bridge.

That could have gone better. Mattis sat back in his chair as the film crew awkwardly packed up the lights and cameras around him.

"Admiral," said Lynch, when he had a moment. "The *Hamilton* and the *Revere* are dropping out of Z-space. The *Somerset* is expected in the next few minutes."

"Good," said Mattis.

Now they had a fleet again.

Chapter Thirty-Seven

Bridge
USS Midway

Now there were three of them. The *Revere* and the *Hamilton* were sleek, fast frigates—tiny ships bristling with guns. The *Somerset*, however, was a squat, fat pig of a ship that was designed for only one purpose: getting equipment to where it was needed. As tempting as it was to keep that ship with them, she was barely armed and couldn't keep up with the faster warships. Once her supplies were transferred off, she would depart.

"Admiral," said Lynch. "Captain Katarina Abramova of the *Hamilton*, Captain Michael Fisher of the *Revere*, and Captain Caitlin Salt of the *Somerset* are all on the line."

The *Midway* was popular today. "Patch me through," he said, adjusting his earpiece.

"Well, well, well," said a woman with a thick Russian accent. Must be Abramova. "Guess who's the most popular man in space right now?"

Mattis blinked. "Surely you can't mean me."

"She ain't talking about me," said a man whom he presumed was Fisher. "Everyone's talking about *you*, Admiral. Admiral Mattis and the *Midway*, the lone ship out on the edge fighting the alien menace. Or the red Chinese menace—some disagreement on that point."

"Well," said Mattis, "you should know we were, at one stage, a massive ultra-modern space station and the Chinese flagship. Admiral Yim stepped out of that ship onto *Friendship Station*, and it was the last thing he ever did. Captain Shao took command of the *Fuqing,* and she's a bunch of free-floating atoms right now."

"Nice pep talk," said another woman with a clipped English accent. Captain Salt. "I feel so inspired."

"Just being realistic about the situation," said Mattis. "There's a lot of death out here and not much glory."

Salt spoke up. "It seems unlikely that the loss of the *Fuqing* is in any way your fault."

"You can delegate authority, but not responsibility." Mattis sighed. "I have my share of the blame, I suppose."

"Well, fortunately for you, I'm not here to judge you. I'm simply here to drop off some new toys, and then I'm off."

Abramova spoke up again. "So Admiral," she said, "they really *are* aliens?"

He nibbled on his lower lip. "We don't know what they are. All we know is what we've sent you. We've been unable to board their ships and investigate them, and our lone victory evaporated, so we don't have anything left of it."

"Very well," said Abramova. She sounded vaguely

disappointed. What stories had they been telling her? Been telling the population of Earth?

He felt vaguely bad. He probably should have treated Ramirez's interview with a little more gravity. She had called for openness. Maybe that was wise. Maybe…

Maybe he just felt bad for upsetting her. He'd been a dick. It was the news scoop of the millennium, and he'd shat on it for her.

"Admiral?" asked Abramova.

"Sorry," he said, "I was, uh, taking a report. Say again?"

"I was asking if the Z-space tracking you've been using is accurate."

This was an annoying question. "It has proved effective so far. It allowed us to follow and destroy a light cruiser."

"A man after my own heart," said Salt. "Amateurs discuss tactics, professionals discuss logistics."

Spoken just like the CO of a supply ship. Mattis was about to contribute more, but his comm flashed. "Excuse me, Captains, my chief of engineering wants to speak to me. Hold please." He switched channels. "Very important call, Modi."

"Very important information, Admiral."

Mattis was coming to see that Modi's way of speaking was something that required getting used to. "Concerning?"

"The position of the enemy fleet," he said. "According to Lynch's predictions, the fleet should be well ahead of where they are. But instead, they are behind."

"They're…slow?" He didn't want to repeat this conversation. "Hang on." With a switch, he merged the two calls. "Ladies, gentlemen, Commander Modi, the chief of engineering on the *Midway*."

"Greetings," said Modi. Was *he* the alien that everyone was talking about? Who said *greetings*?

"Mister Modi, please relay to the good captains what you just told me."

"The position of the enemy fleet," he said, in exactly the same tone he used earlier. "According to Lynch's predictions, the fleet should be well ahead of where they are. But instead, they are behind."

"What Mister Modi is trying to say," said Mattis, "is that our predictions about the enemy fleet were wrong. We've just discovered that their top speed is slower than anticipated."

A brief moment of silence as the group digested that.

"Good news, I take it," said Fisher.

"Seems like," said Mattis. "Means we can wait for more reinforcements before they get too far away for us to track."

"Speaking theoretically," said Modi, his voice flat, "it's possible that this is a side effect of the energy drain that Earth had a problem with while trying to develop cloaking tech. It might be effecting their engines."

"Cloaking technology?" said Abramova, Fisher, and Salt at the same time.

Mattis scowled. "It was in the briefing I sent through," he said.

"No, it wasn't," said Fisher.

Mattis saw Lynch trying to catch his eye, frantically. "Excuse me again, Captains. Modi, please bring the captains up to speed with what we've learned." He muted the connection. "Yes, Lynch?"

"Admiral. The enemy fleet has changed course."

"To?" asked Mattis.

Lynch didn't say anything for a moment. He might have been afraid to, as though speaking the words would make them real.

"Earth."

Chapter Thirty-Eight

Bridge
USS *Midway*

The four ships leapt into Z-space, stressing their engines
to the maximum, trying to make up for lost time.

Earth.

The cradle of humanity. The home of everything his
species had built. Every king, every tyrant, every doctor, every
scientist was there. Every father, mother, every child. For good
or bad, Earth was everything.

"Damn," Mattis said, for the thousandth time since Lynch
had told him. *"Damn."*

The *Somerset* fell behind, unable to catch up. Salt had
pledged her ship to the fight, even though it was essentially a
freighter with a single light cannon on it for plinking at
bothersome asteroids. Still, the quiet, reserved Englishwoman's
courage was not lacking. She had pushed her engines to the
limit, but pluck and courage could only account for so much.

Four ships became three. The remainder sped on, steel arrows in space, racing toward Earth.

"Sir," said Commander Pitt. "Due mainly to some creative overwork of their engines, the frigates USS *Spearway* and USS *Able* report that they will probably be able to rendezvous with us before we arrive at Earth. Unless their engines give out."

Always a risk when pushing their hardware. "If they make it, they make it. We could really use them. If not, we'll manage."

Lynch shifted uncomfortably in his seat. "And how exactly are we going to manage this, sir? Best case scenario, we are five ships. There are eleven of *them*, and they've likely rearmed their mass driver by now."

That was a problem. "We'll fight until we can't fight anymore. Worst case scenario, we'll just have to hope we soften them up enough that Goalkeeper can finish the job."

Lynch didn't seem convinced. "Goalkeeper hasn't been tested. There's a reason why there are still ships protecting Earth."

The reasons behind that were more complicated than a simple untested weapons system—said reasons were geopolitical in nature—but he didn't need to go into it. "I know. But I'm not trusting the lives of our whole species to an automated defense network, you hear me? Fancy guns and torpedoes and missiles, all run automatically. To alleviate… diplomatic pressures. That's a great way of saying, have our entire world defended by a thing we don't even know works."

"No argument from me, sir," said Lynch. "I don't trust that thing as far as I can throw it, and given how much it weighs that's not very far at all. When it comes to a brawl, I'd trust my fists before anything else."

That was basically how he felt. He returned his attention to the readouts in front of him. Analyzing the capabilities of the *Revere* and the *Hamilton*, running the plays over and over in his head. They would drop out of Z-space as close to the enemy fleet as they could. Launch as many of their strike craft as they could. Try to target the alien fleet with focused fire, as they had before, and have their strike craft attack their engines.

And then, eventually, be overwhelmed.

There *were* ships guarding Earth. And there was Goalkeeper. But none of those elements could be counted upon. The political situation on Earth was tense. The Sino-American War was twenty years past, but relics of history remained, and there was no way to be sure that the ships in orbit would stand beside one another and put their own lives on the line, that they would view the ships of competing nations as allies, and that nobody would try to exploit the situation for their own gain. Because no nation would *ever* do that. *No way.*

"Admiral," said Commander Pitt. "We're receiving a communication from Earth."

Direct? Well, that would be refreshing. "Who is it?"

Commander Pitt's face was a mixture of excitement, worry, and anticipation. "The President of the United States would like to speak to you."

Chapter Thirty-Nine

Senator Pitt's Quarters
USS Midway

What a joke. This whole thing was a joke. This mission, this ship, this commander. An unfunny joke.

Senator Pitt steamed, picking up the communicator again. He dialed another number. It rang out.

Finally, he called Chuck Mattis. It rang twice before the phone was answered.

"Your father," spat Senator Pitt, "is a stubborn-headed, ox-brained asshole."

There was a brief, cautious pause on the other end.

"I'm guessing you want to speak to Chuck?" said the guy, who was definitely too…foreign to be Chuck. Accent was hard to pick out. South American? Maybe?

"Yeah. Chuck."

There was some scuffling and moving.

"Hello?" said Chuck.

"Your father," spat Senator Pitt, although it lost a little something with the repetition, "is a stubborn headed, ox-brained…" He clicked his fingers. "I forgot what I said before. Oh, wait. Asshole."

"No disagreement here," said Chuck, with a tinge of sincerity to it. "What can I do for you, boss?"

What exactly *could* Chuck do? Why was he even calling? Pitt chewed on the inside of his cheek. "Eh. Honestly, I ran out of people to call. I just wanted to talk to someone who wasn't going to tell me I'm being paranoid. Someone who knows what he's *really* like."

"You're not being paranoid," said Chuck, "but you should know my dad's a good man. Deep down. I won't help betray him."

"I'm honestly not sure I believe in deep down." Senator Pitt shook his head. "I think we are the results of our actions, and Admiral Mattis is about to face those consequences. As are many others."

Silence on the other end. Then, "Sir, are you asking me to resign?"

"I'm not asking anything," said Pitt carefully, "but I'm just saying, this unpleasantness with the admiral is going to get worse before it gets better. Maybe you shouldn't be in the middle of it, forced to choose between your loyalty to me and your father."

"Okay," said Chuck. "Then I resign. Thank you, Senator." And then Chuck hung up.

Well, that was expected. No glowing letter of recommendation for him. Pitt massaged his temples.

He needed another play.

Another idea.

Something.

Maybe it was time to talk to the President again.

Chapter Forty

Bridge
USS Midway

Mattis pressed a switch on his command chair that isolated him from the whole bridge, deploying noise-canceling buffers that would effectively silence him from the outside world, and vice versa. With security established, he touched his earpiece with a reverence he didn't quite expect from himself. "Madam President?"

"Good evening, Admiral Mattis." It *was* her. President Edita Schuyler. That smooth, political tone that was, in some way, almost reminiscent of Ramirez, but *that* was a distraction he could absolutely not afford at this time.

"Good evening, Madam President."

"I'm calling you directly, Admiral, to speak on matters which you are far more intimately well versed than I." She paused, considering her next words. "Rumors are afloat, Admiral, and I wanted to consult with a primary source, as it were, so that I can make the right decision for our nation."

"Thank you for your confidence," said Mattis. "I hope, Madam President, that I can assist you."

A brief pause, and then President Schuyler spoke again. "I think we can dispense with some formality. Jack, I want you to tell me exactly what's going on out there, and don't bullshit me."

He took a deep breath and, as though worried that the bridge crew hearing him say it would turn him into a pillar of salt, told the truth as best he could. "There's an alien fleet out there with tech far beyond whatever we have, and it looks like they're coming for Earth."

"When you say alien," asked President Schuyler, "do you mean to say that they are French? Mexican? Indonesian?" She paused before lowering her voice. "Or are you suggesting they are *extraterrestrial?*"

"Sure looks like the *latter* to me."

That seemed to be enough for her. "I understand. The Earth Defense Fleet *was* en route toward you, converging on an intercept point, but according to your latest report, the alien fleet has, instead, decided to come to us for the party. Is that correct?"

"To the best of my knowledge," said Mattis, "it is."

The president hesitated. "Jack, you know better than I do that changing course in Z-space is difficult. The EDF won't be able to make it to Earth before the alien fleet arrives."

He ground his teeth together. "Probably what they were anticipating the whole time. They were baiting us, picking on the border stations, trying to provoke a response. First Capella, then Cor Caroli… They probably selected *Friendship Station* when they saw how much media attention it was getting. They knew we were watching. So they attacked, then they jumped away, leaving us as witnesses. They *wanted* us to come investigate, so they could jump in behind our fleet while our pants were down. We didn't win the battle at *Friendship Station*. We played right into their hands."

"My thoughts exactly," said President Schuyler. "They seem to know us quite well."

That thought nagged at Mattis, but he put it aside. The nature of their attackers was irrelevant. For now. "Madam President, I want you to understand the gravity of this development. There are three ships in my fleet, the *Midway* and two frigates. There are two more frigates who are likely to meet us at the rendezvous point, beating the aliens there and coming in with us. There are eleven alien vessels, including one substantially capable ship which possesses a mass-driver weapon, a particularly nasty piece of hardware that took out *Friendship Station* in a single shot. This is not a battle we can win."

"I understand," said President Schuyler. "Whatever happens in that regard, I know you have done honorable work."

"Don't say it like you're saying goodbye," said Mattis. "Say it like you're saying, 'So, I spoke to the other countries, and we're going to put aside our political bickering and work together, just like you and the *Fuqing* did, so that we, as a species, can survive. We're going to have to meet them before they finish their Z-space translation and exit near Earth. Which will leave Earth defenseless, should another country try to take advantage of this crisis. But we have to trust that they won't.'

That's what I want to hear from you, Madam President."

Her silence gave her answer before her words did. "It's not that simple, Jack."

"Make it that simple." Mattis leaned forward in his chair, knowing full well she couldn't see the gesture. "Tell the Chinese President, tell the EU, tell the Indian navy, the Russians, the Brazilians, tell every damn person on the planet: this is it. This is the moment we come together and push our problems into the *deal with it later* basket, or this is the moment we don't *have* any more problems, because we're all dead."

He clenched his fist so hard it hurt. "Madam President, Z-space translations are imprecise. The aliens aren't going to want to risk some of their limited fleet; they're going to drop out of Z-space some distance away from Earth. Outside the moon's orbit, in all likelihood. We need whatever the Chinese can muster there, waiting for them, and we need it urgently. We need every damn ship we can get—everything from tugboats to garbage scows. If it has guns on it, we need it. Even only to ram them."

"I'm working on it," said President Schuyler. "But this is a difficult negotiation. I can't convince everyone to move their ships out of defensive range of Earth on a whim."

"With respect," said Mattis, "work harder."

She took a deep breath. "I'll do what I can. But you realize what will happen if this turns out to be a hoax, or some kind of diversion. If we move those ships, the planet will be left to Goalkeeper and that's it."

"We need those ships," said Mattis, with all the strength and steel he could muster. "This isn't a joke."

President Schuyler hesitated and then, with palpable

reluctance, seemed to give in. "I'll plead your case one more time. Don't let me down, Jack. I'm staking my political career on you."

"Believe me," said Mattis, "you're staking a lot more than that."

Chapter Forty-One

Bridge
USS Midway

Mattis's eyes hurt.

Fatigue was a natural consequence of war. Of pushing the human body to its limits. He'd been tired before, the kind of tired where everything gets distant and fuzzy, where you function on autopilot, using the basest, most animalistic part of the human brain. He gave orders, barely listened to reports, and did his best to keep his eyes open. The ol' synapses weren't firing like they should have been.

The twin battles, followed by a long Z-space translation, were the most action he'd had in years. Back in the day, twenty years ago, he would go days without sleep. He would fill his gut with coffee and his lungs with a high oxygen mix, he would distract himself with work and danger, and push his body to the limit. It felt like the old days. For better or worse.

He was two decades further along now. Lynch,

Commander Pitt, and the rest of the bridge crew looked so young, even though many of them were almost old enough to have their own commands, especially Commander Pitt.

He rubbed his eyes for the third time, trying to massage the burn out of them. He'd almost forgotten how awful this part of war was. *The waiting.* He just wanted to get it over with.

"Admiral?" asked Commander Pitt. "We're stowing the supplies brought on board from the *Somerset*. We're running low on space to put some of these unassembled strike craft. The *Revere* and the *Hamilton* are both embarrassingly overstocked, as they were just beginning a long-range patrol to the colonies, so they don't have any room."

What was Commander Pitt expecting him to do? Conjure up more deck space with magic? "What's your point, Mister Pitt?" he asked, more snappish than he intended.

"Well, sir," said Commander Pitt, obviously trying to keep his own frustrations in check, "I was simply checking. Are we rendezvousing with any further reinforcements before we re-engage the alien fleet, or should I have the extra strike craft jettisoned into space?"

An annoying question, but one that was legitimate. Still, Mattis struggled to come up with a good answer. "Can we stow them in the hangar bay?"

"Well, that's where they are now," said Commander Pitt, "but if we have another crash, as we did in the battle of *Friendship Station*, then we're going to have a *massive* fire risk, and a lot more debris. We've got more junk than we can shake a stick at right now."

He *almost* had them jettisoned, but his rational, sane, calm commander's mind took over at the last second. "Keep them in the hangar bay," he said.

Suddenly, Lynch's eyes lit up. "Sir, I have an idea. What if we jettison them when we get to wherever we're going? We'll use them as decoys. If nothing else, hostile strike craft will shoot them instead of our actual ships."

The idea of wasting perfectly good strike craft for a minor tactical advantage didn't sit well with him, but in this significantly outmatched fight, he was happy for whatever he could get. It was clever. "Do it."

"Aye aye, sir," said Lynch. He stifled a yawn and then shook his head to clear it. "But I mean, this would be a lot easier if we could potentially transfer those perfectly functional strike craft to another warship before the combat, sir, or at least get some pilots for them so we can use them as something more than target practice. I mean, they're ready and rarin' to go."

Tell him something he *didn't* know. Mattis, despite his best efforts, lost his temper. "I'm sure that would be a lot better, Mister Lynch, but we *don't* have that luxury, so I'd appreciate it if you kept such speculation to yourself. I asked for help, and I didn't get shit, so we have to make do with what we have." He snarled and looked away. "Worthless politicians."

Commander Pitt stiffened at that comment and, for a split second, Mattis thought he might say something, but the man—to his absolute credit—maintained his composure.

You're being shown up by your XO, who's doing a much better job of maintaining the discipline required of an officer than you are, old man.

His own thought made him even more angry.

"But sir," said Lynch, "it's just—"

"Mister Lynch," shouted Mattis, turning back to him,

"stop worrying about things we can't change! I know the odds are long, okay? We're all *keenly* aware of the troubles this ship is facing, and we don't require a constant reminder of them. Acknowledge."

Lynch sat up straight in his chair. "Acknowledged, sir."

For some reason, all Mattis could think of was Ramirez admonishing him. *Yelling at your own people is not productive,* said his imaginary Ramirez. *Find some other way to motivate them rather than just shouting. You're better than this. You can do better.*

He could, too, and knowing that made it worse. Mattis took a slow, steadying breath. "My apologies, Mister Lynch."

"None required, sir." Well, now, that was mighty polite of him. "I should have thought before I spoke."

Mattis curled his toes inside his boots. "Well, honestly, if you want to make it up to me, find some way to get us the edge in this upcoming battle. The aliens won't be trying to bait us into running this time. They'll be playing for keeps. And we've gotta find some way of winning that game."

"Aye aye, sir," said Lynch. "The biggest threat is their mass driver. If we can find some way to disable that weapon, we can fight them without having to worry that we're going to have comets lobbed at us. I'll talk it over with Mister Modi in engineering. If anyone can solve this problem, he can. Pretty sure he's more alert than I am at the moment. Robots don't sleep, after all."

Mattis tiredly smiled. "Very good, Mister Lynch."

He let Lynch work, tuning out the conversation in the background, covering his mouth with his hand to prevent a yawn. Losing his temper at his bridge crew was a first for him. He had never done that back in the day. Probably. He couldn't remember.

For the first time since arriving, Mattis felt old. He felt stretched too thin, as though this was something best left to younger men. Had he just been fooling himself more than anyone else? The last, desperate grasp of an old man trying to cling to the glories of the past?

But what glories *were* there? The younger generation didn't fear the Chinese. His own son knew Mandarin and would probably teach it to his grandson. His grandson… Now he had a *grandson*… His kid had a kid… He closed his eyes for a brief moment, thinking about that. About meeting Javier, playing with him on a beach, taking him out to the holopictures…

"Admiral," said Modi beside him.

Mattis jerked awake. He'd nodded off and, obliviously, in the intervening time, Modi had come to the bridge. The man stood with his hands folded behind his back, looking perfectly rested. Maybe he really *was* a robot. "Uh, report."

"Admiral," said Modi, "we've figured out a way to stop the mass-driver projectiles."

Lynch grimaced. "But you aren't going to like it."

Chapter Forty-Two

Bridge
USS Midway

"The answer," said Lynch, "is that we ram the lead alien ship with our cap ship before it can fire on the frigates, and use the four frigates to take out the remaining ten smaller ships, also by ramming them. That leaves five alien ships, smaller ones, which should be an even fight for the Earth Defense Fleet and Goalkeeper."

Mattis had spoken to the Joint Chiefs about using ships as battering rams before, but when the prospect was in front of his face, suddenly it was a lot less appealing. "No way in Hell," he snapped. "The *Midway* is one of the few battle-tested, combat-capable ships to have faced these bastards and lived to tell the tale. We're not sacrificing it."

"Admiral," said Modi, "I concur with your assessment. However, you should realize that the probability of us surviving a direct engagement with the enemy in a pitched battle, based on a frank assessment of their previously displayed capabilities, is low. An unorthodox tactic like this may tip the scales into a favorable range."

"I understand," said Mattis, mentally reminding himself that he was tired, grumpy, and perhaps, just maybe, a little defensive about this ship and its fate. "Now hear this. I understand the *Midway* may be lost in the upcoming battle. I've played my share of poker. I understand the odds are long. If we fail, we'll fail safe and secure in the knowledge that we tried our damnedest, and that every single member of this crew performed heroically. But deliberately sacrificing this vessel while she can still fight is off the table. Am I clear?"

"Aye, sir," said Lynch.

"Yes, sir," said Commander Pitt.

Mattis rested his hands on each of his chair's armrests. "Very good. Keep working on a solution."

Lynch's face was as resolute as it was skeptical. "Aye aye, sir," he said, turning around and going back to work.

It was a difficult task. There was no question about that. They were outnumbered, outgunned, and in a poor tactical situation to boot. Everything about this engagement screamed failure.

Maybe it *was* the right call. Deep down, Mattis knew that luck could only carry them so far.

Was he letting his personal feelings get in the way of doing what he knew was the right thing?

"Admiral," said Commander Pitt, his voice charged, energy cutting through the lethargy. "Sensors show that the alien fleet is exiting Z-space."

They were stopping? Z-space was nonlinear. That they had

spent only a few days of travel didn't necessarily mean their reinforcements were coming faster, or that the alien fleet was going to be where they were expected to be. Everything was a guess. "Best estimate on their exit location?" he asked.

"It's in the Sol system," said Lynch, confusion coming into his voice as he read out what the ship's sensors were telling him. "But it's *not* Earth."

Now that surprised him. He'd always assumed—everyone had always assumed—that any attack on the Sol system would be directed at the crown jewel, Earth. Sure, there were colonies and outposts scattered throughout humanity's home system, but the vast bulk of its population lived on their home world.

"Where?" asked Mattis. "Are they going to use the moon as a staging ground? Or take out the lunar gun batteries from Goalkeeper?"

Lynch read further and then looked up. "Jupiter."

Chapter Forty-Three

Bridge
USS Midway

Jupiter. What the hell were they doing *there?*

"Confirm that," said Mattis, drumming his fingers on the armrest of his chair. He didn't like that one bit. If the aliens really were stopping at the gas giant, they must have a good reason for doing so.

Anything that was good for the aliens was bad for them.

"Confirmed," said Lynch. "The alien fleet is completing their Z-space translation in high orbit of Ganymede, on the far side of Jupiter relative to Earth."

"What's there to be concerned about?" asked Mattis, almost as much to himself as anyone else. "Ganymede's a ball of ice and rock. It's millions of miles away from anywhere. There's no strategic value there, no resources anyone cares about, no ships, no stations…nothing. Worst of all, it's within sensor range of Earth, accounting, of course, for the light-speed delay." It was seemingly a huge tactical error, and one highly bizarre for an enemy who had displayed nothing but cunning and ingenuity at every step of their assault so far.

"I'm not sure," said Commander Pitt, looking over Lynch's shoulder. "All I can see here is a small mining colony, nothing major. It's mostly automated. Thirty-six souls stationed there, all civilians, and...apparently a Siamese cat named Rudolf. It's a corporate venture, sir, just like thousands of others all around the colonies. Nothing of any military value whatsoever."

A mining colony but no military bases. Why would they stop there? What was their play? Mattis churned the facts over in his head. What would *he* do, if he was attacking Earth in this way?

Maybe the aliens figured the human defenders would catch them before they reached Earth and decided to try to set up an ambush. Maybe this fleet was luring them into a trap.

Mattis brought up the Goalkeeper scans of the area. But there was nothing there, had been nothing for years. If there were alien ships there, waiting, they would have been discovered long before now.

He pulled up the chart of Ganymede on his command console, examining it carefully. There was the mining colony, as clear as day, its lights shining in the darkness of the moon like a beacon. He switched to EM view. There were probes and markers and relays, including Z-space anchors, but nothing of any significance that would affect a battle.

The mining colony was *there*, with its no-doubt cute cat. The solution was right in front of him, he knew it, but... where? There had to be something else. Something there they had all missed.

The alien fleet was coming up on Ganymede. They didn't have long to figure this mystery out before they, too, had to exit Z-space and engage.

His warrior's instinct, his gut, told him there was more to this—though that was an assertion he could not back up with anything firm. And, somehow, the whole thing stank of politics.

"Mister Lynch," he said, pointedly choosing him instead of Commander Pitt. "Get Senator Pitt up to the bridge."

Chapter Forty-Four

Bridge
USS Midway

Senator Pitt looked sour as a lemon as he was marched onto the bridge, which suited Mattis just fine.

"Senator," said Mattis, pointing at the image of Ganymede on his monitor. "Do you know what we're looking at?"

His stony glare told him he did. "It's one of Jupiter's moons," he said. "Some ball of ice and dirt out in the middle of nowhere."

Exhaustion and a short patience for the man made it difficult to keep his voice even. "Is it?"

Senator Pitt shrugged. "You think I know everything about every little backward outpost in the galaxy, Mattis? What's the big idea, huh? You think you can just drag me up to the bridge of your ship, act like a big man, and bully me into giving you what you want?"

"Yup."

Senator Pitt snorted. "Go to Hell."

"Already been there," said Mattis. "Twice, in the last few days, and we're about to go there again. You should know: the alien fleet has decided to pull up at that moon, Senator, and we are going to engage them at that location. As to why they're there—I need to *know* why. It could give us the advantage. Because as it stands, this is likely to be a fight we lose." He rose from his chair, bringing himself to his full height, glaring down at the little man. "And let me remind you, Senator, if this ship blows, you go along with it."

Senator Pitt shook his head. "I'm sorry, I don't know what you're talking about. Like I said, there's nothing there."

Mattis bit the inside of his cheek, staring the man down, but...nothing.

"Dad," Commander Pitt cut in, "you're a shitty liar."

Mattis raised an eyebrow, looking to his XO. "You got something to say?"

Commander Pitt affixed a scowl on his father. "Ever since I was a kid, I could always tell when the old man was lying to me. It's that crease above his brow. It gets a *little* more noticeable every time he's spinning a tale."

Senator Pitt didn't say anything, but for a split second, a look of surprise flashed across his face.

"You know what's there." Mattis took a step toward the Senator, conjuring his best glare. "You sniveling little worm. You *know* what the aliens are looking for, don't you?"

"Dad," said Commander Pitt, "we need to know. This hand is all-in. If we fold, we lose everything. *Everything.* Whatever's here on Ganymede, you can bet that the aliens aren't going to accomplish their mission here and then just leave us alone forever. Earth is *right there*. They'll swing on past, drop a few thousand nukes, and all of humanity will be a footnote on some grey-skinned asshole's history books."

Slowly, the bricks that comprised Senator Pitt's stone wall started to fall away. "Yes," he said, his tone bitter and frustrated, "there's something there, but it's beyond top secret."

"Great," said Mattis, folding his arms. "Spill. Don't worry, I'll vouch for you at the trial."

The mention of judicial punishment almost seemed to make Senator Pitt reconsider, but then, slowly, he nodded.

"Okay. I'll tell you."

Chapter Forty-Five

Bridge
USS Midway

"Clear the bridge," said Mattis, gesturing for the junior officers and enlisted crewmen to vacate. "Senior staff only."

It took some time for the bridge crew to totally rotate out, and he didn't like having the ship so unready to handle any kind of challenge. Still, top secret was top secret. When it was clear, Mattis waited for Senator Pitt to spill the beans. The whole of the bridge was quiet, save for the whirring of machines and the beeping of computers. Every eye and ear was upon him.

He waited. And kept waiting.

"C'mon," said Mattis, tapping his foot pointedly. "More words, less stalling. Time is a precious commodity here."

Senator Pitt looked to his son, perhaps hoping to see support, but Commander Pitt's face was only full of accusations and anger.

With a resigned sigh, Senator Pitt ran his hands through his hair. "Are you aware," he began, "of the Svalbard seed bank?"

Svalbard was part of the educational curriculum. A giant vault in the frozen wastes of northern Earth where a variety of seeds were stored as an emergency backup for the planet's flora. Should the worst happen—a nuclear war, massive climate change, or a runaway biological agent—there existed a repository where, if all other options were exhausted, viable seeds could be recovered and used.

"Learned about it in school," said Mattis. "What's that got to do with Ganymede?"

"Well," said Senator Pitt carefully, "you remember the Sino-American War, yes?"

"No," said Mattis flatly. "I totally forgot about it. Remind me again?"

His sarcasm was not well received. The edge of Senator Pitt's mouth turned down. "You don't remember it the way I remember it, Admiral. As you so aptly put it, war is hell, especially for the women and men who fight it, but one thing people always forget is the price paid by those who are left behind."

"Yeah," drawled Mattis, "those poor bastards safe and secure in their homes while the rest of us are getting shot at. My heart fucking bleeds."

"*It should*," snarled Pitt, the words flying out with absolute sincerity. "You have no idea what life was like for the common folk during the Sino-American War. The rations. The bread lines. The withholding of basic medications because they were needed by the military. You might have seen combat, Admiral, but you haven't held a sick, crying baby in your arms, knowing that a single pill could cure them, and looked up at the night sky, at all those hundreds of warships orbiting Earth, held in reserve for coming battles, aware that each one of them carries a thousand of those pills because, you know, *they might need them*."

It was tempting to argue the point, but Mattis knew that Ganymede was coming up fast. "What," he asked, "does that have to do with Svalbard, or Ganymede?"

Senator Pitt looked away for a moment, seemingly unable to match Mattis's stern gaze. "Well, the United States came a lot closer to being annihilated during that war than you and many other people realize. Not from losing an armed conflict, but from these…circumstances. Outbreaks of disease for which the cures were allocated to the military. A sharp reduction in fertility rates due to malnourishment. Birth defects from herbicide contamination. The media played it down— which is always a bad sign—but we knew how bad it *truly* was. So we made plans."

"What kind of plans?"

"The kind of plans," said Senator Pitt, his tone carrying a distinct darkness to it, "that you hope you never have to use. The kind that *should* be buried away in some safe somewhere, old and rotten, the key lost to time. Unfortunately, we were not so lucky." He took a breath, steadying himself. "We made, for lack of a better term, an ark. Our very own Svalbard right there on Ganymede, where nobody would even dream of looking—just not for plants. For people. DNA from healthy humans, frozen, stored up for the day when we may need it."

An interesting tale, to be sure, but one that made little

sense. "Okay, so, I understand that there's human DNA there, but so what? What use is that to aliens? They could have taken our DNA at any of the places they attacked. Hell, if they'd asked nicely, we just might have given it to them! They attacked us instead. What else is there?"

"Nothing," said Senator Pitt, and for the first time, Mattis actually believed him. "That is what's on Ganymede, Admiral. The future of humanity."

"The future of humanity?"

Senator Pitt nodded, but there was a hint of hesitation there. "Yes."

Mattis studied him carefully, trying to draw the truth out of the Senator with a stare. "You don't seem sure."

Senator Pitt backpedalled. "Look," he said. "I don't know *everything* that happens in the galaxy, okay? They didn't…" He looked almost embarrassed. "My source was evasive about a lot of the details."

"That's where the devil hides," said Mattis.

Senator Pitt replied, "Does it look like the devil lives there?"

"That is something only time can tell."

Chapter Forty-Six

Bridge
USS Midway

It may not have made much sense to him, but very little in war did.

"Very well," said Mattis. "So, okay. There's this human seed bank on Ganymede. I understand that. More importantly, I feel, *you* understand the significance of this installation better than most. Yes?"

Senator Pitt nodded. "I think so, yes. I was one of its most outspoken advocates." His tone turned sour. "And accordingly, one of its most trusted secret keepers."

"Part of being a good secret keeper is knowing what secrets *should* be kept." It was difficult to say, but Mattis forced the words out. "You did the right thing, Senator."

"Thank you," said Senator Pitt.

"But," said Mattis, "I, unfortunately, have to ask one more thing of you." He gritted his teeth, taking a wild stab at what might convince the good Senator. "And I'm afraid I'll have to *owe* you one for this."

"Indeed," said Senator Pitt, his eyes lighting up in a way Mattis had not seen before. "Well, ask away. I'm all ears."

"I spoke to the President earlier today. Despite my best efforts, she won't move what few ships we have in orbit around Earth for any reason. Even to get a tactical advantage. Because of the political implications."

Senator Pitt mulled over that. "It's likely that she doesn't even know about the seed bank. She's on her first term; there's a lot of information that gets passed to a new president, and frankly, this is something that is a very low priority. Nobody needs to know about it, nobody needs to do anything for it. The mining colony on Ganymede, they're our people. *They* are the ones who keep watch over the seed bank, but even *they* don't know what they're guarding. The whole thing is essentially a giant sealed box."

"Everyone's awfully paranoid about this thing," grumbled Mattis.

"At the time it was made, there was a good reason to be paranoid. Besides, paranoia is the delusional fear that someone's out to get you. If the fear is rational, and there really *are* people trying to make mischief in your plans, then it's not paranoia. It's justified caution."

"Everyone's awfully *justified caution-y* about this thing then," said Mattis. "But it doesn't matter. Do you think, if the President knew about this facility—and you could convince her that it's real and worth defending—she would move the fleet from Earth?"

"She can't know." Senator Pitt shook his head. "This thing

is *need-to-know* only. She can't be told of this. She's not authorized."

"Time we made an exception. Besides, she's the President. She kind of has the right to know."

"You can't," said Senator Pitt. "I won't allow it."

Mattis tilted his head. "And what, pray tell, are you going to do about it? I'll call her up right now and tell her everything you just told me."

"And you'll be thrown into a hole so deep no one will ever find you, Admiral."

Threatening a Commanding Officer on the bridge of his own ship. That took some stones. Even Mattis acknowledged that. "I think I'm comfortable with whatever punishment gets thrown my way, Senator." He leaned forward slightly. "Are you?"

Senator Pitt, obviously shaken, closed his eyes for a moment. "I can talk to her," he said, "but she's only going to step in if she's sure Earth is safe." He grimaced. "That makes sense, right? If the aliens aren't after Earth, then we can move whatever ships are defending it."

"It's a risk. She won't like it." Mattis took off his earpiece and handed it to him. "But you need to make her do it."

Rather than taking the device, Senator Pitt pulled out one of his own and clipped it on. "I'll try," he said, turning and walking to a corner of the bridge.

With that unpleasantness out of the way, Mattis moved over to Commander Pitt. It couldn't have been easy watching his Commanding Officer and his father argue in front of him.

"You going to be okay?" he asked.

"Yeah." Commander Pitt touched the tip of his hat. "With

you, sir."

Mattis nodded in acknowledgement, and with a friendly clap on the shoulder, moved away.

"Sir," said Lynch, "the *Spearway* and the *Able* report they are in position to commence Z-space translation. Recommend we exit first, followed by the *Hamilton* and the *Revere*. Of course, the sooner we all come out, the better."

Hopefully Senator Pitt could come through for them. "Righteo," said Mattis. "ETA?"

"We're two minutes out, Admiral. The aliens are beginning their attack on Ganymede."

Chapter Forty-Seven

Bridge
USS Midway

Two minutes until they were back in action. Two minutes until the three warships, and their two allies, dropped out of Z-space and commenced their attack on the aliens who had destroyed *Friendship Station*.

Four frigates and a cruiser versus ten light cruisers and a heavy. Not good odds.

Mattis touched his earpiece. "*Midway* actual to *Spearway*, *Able*, *Alexander Hamilton* and *Paul Revere*." He made sure to patch in the *Somerset* too, as a courtesy to Captain Salt, even though her ship was long behind the rest of them. She deserved to at least hear what was happening, even if she couldn't help.

All the captains acknowledged.

"In one minute, we will be dropping out of Z-space. We've discovered the primary objective of the hostile forces that have attacked us. It isn't Earth. It's a facility on the surface of Ganymede. The exact objective they are after is unknown, but we understand it to be a genetic seed bank. A vault of human DNA taken during the Sino-American War."

There was a brief silence on the other end of the line.

"Sir," asked Abramova, "if I may ask, what's the strategic value of this…seed bank?"

Mattis knew this would be a hard sell. "That's unclear at this time." He paused, gathering his thoughts. "But I know this: these aliens murdered a *lot* of people to get to it, and they had a very intricate, complex plan designed to fake us out at every step. Striking the border regions, then heading to Earth, then to Ganymede. They *want* whatever's in that box in the ice, and they want it badly. To be perfectly frank with you all, I don't have a perfectly clear picture as to *why* at this time. But I know if they want it, we don't want them to have it. Denying the enemy is a legitimate goal in this case."

"That's it?" asked Fisher, skepticism in his tone.

Mattis cast a glance over his shoulder. Senator Pitt was still huddled in a corner, talking in hushed whispers to someone he presumed to be the President of the United States—or someone else. He had a worried look on his face and the call was taking way longer than it should. Either the President could not be convinced, or…

"I understand, Captain Fisher," said Mattis. "I know this is a hard sell to all of you, asking you to risk your ships, your lives, for an unclear objective in the face of overwhelming odds. All I can promise you is"—he kept his eyes on Senator Pitt—"there's more to this than we initially suspected."

"That's good enough for me," said Abramova.

"Aye aye," said Fisher. "We're with you, sir."

"Acknowledged," said the captain of the *Spearway*.

There was dead air as everyone waited for the captain of the *Able* to report.

"I'm with you," he said finally.

Then it was settled. "Very well. We're beginning our Z-space translations. All ships to follow, and be prepared to engage the moment we enter real-space. Come into it kicking and screaming. We want to capitalize on the element of surprise as much as we can."

Everyone on the line signaled their acknowledgement, and then Lynch spoke up.

"Sir, we are beginning our Z-space translation."

"Acknowledged," said Mattis, as the multihued spectrum of Z-space began to give way to its real equivalent. The bright lights vanished, and the moon Ganymede suddenly appeared before them, a small body of blue and grey. Behind it loomed the massive striped sphere of Jupiter. Mattis had never really appreciated just how *massive* the gas giant was until he was, metaphorically, standing right in front of it. Even at this distance, it dwarfed Ganymede in their sight.

The radar screen lit up. Eleven ships, red dots on the screen, firing streams of projectiles down to Ganymede's surface.

"Scramble all fighters," said Mattis. "And engage targets of opportunity."

Chapter Forty-Eight

Pilot's Ready Room
USS Midway

"Raise." Guano threw a handful of coins into the center of the table. "C'mon, Frost. Show me you have some balls."

Frost whimpered, her fingers hovering over a card, then another, then back to the first. "Hang on, hang on…"

"Raise, call, or fold," said Guano, affixing her most withering poker face on her last remaining opponent. "You know how the game's played."

Tick, tock. Tick, tock. Finally, Frost laid down her cards. "Fold," she said, reluctantly showing her cards. Nine of hearts straight through the five of hearts.

Was Frost joking? The whole table erupted into laughter. Guano cackled along energetically, fanning out her cards and laying them on the table. Two black aces, two black eights, and a joker. "You folded a straight flush, you moron! Hah, I'm going to enjoy spending all this."

Suddenly, the laughter died out. Everyone was staring at her.

"What?"

"Aces and Eights," said Joker, sitting back in her chair, blinking in shock. She looked at the cards like they were a grenade with the pin out. "The Dead Man's Hand."

"The…what?" Guano asked.

Frost's eyes were as wide as saucers. "The Dead Man's Hand," she said. "Eight and ace of spades, eight and ace of clubs, plus a hole card. It's the hand that Wild Bill Hickok was holding when he was murdered." Frost glanced to all the players in turn, then finally Guano. "It means you're going to die. Within the day."

Guano snorted dismissively, poking a finger at the joker card. "Surely that means that Joker's going to buy the farm," she said. "I mean, it's right there, *joker*. Plain as day."

"No way," said Joker, shaking her head emphatically. "Believe me, as the official Joker on this boat, I can tell you officially: the joker card represents the fool, which frankly, is Frost. Look at how easily she folded. She's an idiot who can barely shoot straight."

"What?" shrieked Frost, suddenly turning her attention back to Guano. "The joker card symbolizes a literal *wild card*. Given how you've been flying lately, and what happened to Flatline, you're the wildest card of *all*." Frost repeated herself for emphasis. "It means *you*."

Fucking superstitious idiots. Guano started scooping up her coins. "You're both just deflecting."

"I'm not going to die," said Frost, although there was just a tiny tremor in her voice when she spoke. Everyone knew how superstitious the pilot was. "It… It's going to be fine. It's one of you two. Not me."

Roadie stuck his head around the corner. "Okay, losers," he said, "it's time. Last briefing before we head out."

Joker groaned audibly. "But sir, we already know what we're doing." She shook her head. "Nah. We should skip it. It's bad luck, after Guano dealt herself the Dead Man's Hand."

"I wasn't the dealer!" she protested. "That was Frost!"

Roadie scowled right at her. "Guano, you dipshit, did you get yourself dealt the Dead Man's Hand?"

"It wasn't me!" she said again.

"Every one of you idiots, inside." Roadie ducked back into the briefing room.

Everyone got up and made their way inside. Guano finished stuffing her pockets with coins and then, wealthier but downhearted, she stared at her cards.

"Just a stupid game," she muttered, and flipped them all over before she headed to the briefing room.

All the pilots and crew had gone over this exact briefing again and again and again. Guano was sick of hearing it, but *finally*, after nearly three days of being in space, this was it. The last briefing.

Yet, despite it all, Roadie went over *all* the details one more time.

"As many of you know," Roadie said, "the AO has changed from high Earth orbit to Ganymede." This change made it easier for her to pay attention. "But the engagement is still the same. Ten light cruisers, one heavy. Four frigates on our side, and the *Midway*."

She tapped her foot impatiently and tried not to think

about if Flatline was going to be there or not. Roadie hadn't assigned her a new gunner yet, which was a good sign, but it might also mean she wasn't going to participate at all.

Roadie droned on. "Combat launches will be the order of the day. We will launch in three waves, designated Alpha, Bravo, and Charlie. Don't get mixed up. Stay off the radio unless you need it. And for God's sake, call your targets. We expect a *lot* of fighting here. Four friendly frigates will be launching their own strike craft, plus we'll be deploying the additional Warbirds we picked up as decoys. They have no pilots in them, just autopilot, and you don't need me to tell you that robots can't fly for shit. Not to mention, of course, our enemy—the aliens are very likely to give everything they have. This is going to be a massive furball, ladies and gentlemen, with a lot of distractions, contacts, and friendlies, so bring your A game."

She'd already planned to. Didn't she always plan to?

"One more thing," said Roadie offhandedly. "Some of you might know that Lieutenant Deshawn Wiley got himself shot, and despite what you might be thinking, it *wasn't* by me. Well, I have some news about him that might be of interest to you. Or not. I dunno."

Guano sat upright, her back like a rod. Flatline? He was okay?

Roadie raised his voice. "Get your black ass in here, Flatline, so we can loudly berate you."

Wild cheering filled the room as Flatline, his foot heavily bandaged, limped inside, arms held high like a triumphant boxer. Everyone crowded him, dispensing insults, compliments, and boyish claps on the shoulders and back.

"The king is back, baby," he said, grinning from ear to ear. "Two heart attacks and going *strong*."

Frost leaned close to Guano. "Which one of us is the fool again?"

Would they just shut up? Guano silenced her with a death glare, and then patted the seat next to her. "It's a good thing you don't need your feet to shoot your guns," she said, talking over the laughter. "We were going to replace you with a robot. One beep for shoot left, two beeps for shoot right, and a bonus: a lot less talkative."

Flatline slid into his seat, groaning softly, regarding her with a cheeky grin. "You missed me, Guano. Admit it."

"No." Guano casually picked at her fingernails. "Gunners are a dime a dozen, you know. Washed-up pilots who couldn't hack it at a stick."

He laughed, thumping her in the shoulder. "Yeah, you missed me. I heard you ran *all* the way to the infirmary, crying and shit, tried to fight a bunch of the nurses like some kind of jackass."

"Bite me."

"Say please," said Flatline, grinning and putting his arms behind the backs of the chairs beside him. "I'm just glad my dick's okay. Shrapnel hit the artery and nearly killed me, but missed my joystick by an inch. Thank God."

Guano grinned. "Nice."

Roadie clapped his hands together. "A'right," he said, "a'right. Calm down." He pulled out a tablet, tapping it to light it up. "Okay, so, back to business. Those of you who have damaged ships, hope you weren't too attached to them, because we're swapping you out with brand new ones."

Groans and complaints all around. Fighter pilots loved their ships and got very weird about them. Guano's gut ached when she thought of hers, in pieces somewhere.

"Those of you who lost your ships, well, this is your lucky day. One get out of jail free card, courtesy of the US taxpayers, those morons." Everyone laughed, even Guano, although being reminded that she'd been shot down hurt. "So. Final kill count for our last engagement: Joker and Shrapnel bagged one, two kills for yours truly—thank you Frost, you're the best—and…" Roadie held up his hands dramatically. "Three confirmed space-to-space kills for Guano and Flatline."

More cheering, wild exultations.

"No, no, no, you dickheads, quiet up, quiet up!" He held up a hand to silence them. "As you all know, Guano and Flatline crashed their ship like idiots, and Flatline was too fucking stupid to dodge a bullet, so that's a minus one to them! So we're even! Two each!"

Boos rang out.

"That ain't how it works," shouted Guano.

"Lame," bellowed Flatline. "Lame, lame!"

"Shenanigans! Shenanigans!" cried Frost.

Roadie flicked his wrist and turned away. "Fine, fine, fine. Okay. Okay! Final tally stands for three for Guano and Flatline." Cheering drowned out whatever he said next. "Holy hell, can you believe it?" Roadie bellowed over the din. "We fought aliens! We fought real-life aliens, motherfuckers, and we killed them!"

Raucous shouting overwhelmed everything, with Roadie leading it on. "A'right, you know what to do! Get to your ships. We are doing this thing for real! Let's go get some!"

Her blood pumping, so full of energy she could burst, it was almost physically painful for Guano to have to wait until everyone else had left. She offered Flatline her hand.

"You ready to do this?" she asked, grinning like a jackal.

"You bet." Flatline pulled himself to his feet, limping as he made his way toward the door. "Let's go get five. Ace Aircrew Flatline and Guano, coming through."

"That's *Guano* and *Flatline*," she said, helping him walk. "That's why idiot gunners ride in the back, like luggage, shit you haul around all day, worthless junk you know you should throw out but you're just too lazy to."

Flatline smirked at her. "I knew you missed me," he said.

Despite it all, she couldn't help but smile too. It was good to have him back.

Chapter Forty-Nine

Bridge
USS Midway

Senator Pitt did not like this.

He was not a warrior. He was not a soldier. He'd been on more than enough trips through Z-space to know when exiting it was normal, and when it wasn't. Seeing the ship come out of the strange, nonlinear, warped unreality that was Z-space was unsettling enough—some found it beautiful, if one could imagine that—but coming out of it in the middle of an alien fleet was profoundly disturbing.

"Are you still there?" asked President Schuyler. "The line crackled for a moment."

"For now," whispered Senator Pitt, and he tried to summon as much of his strength as he could. "We just exited Z-space. Listen! Listen, the battle's starting; things are about to get hot. Just remember what I told you and *send help*. You'll be well compensated when it comes to election time."

"You must think I'm a whore," said President Schuyler, an amused edge to her tone. "To be bought and used at your pleasure."

He prepared the usual platitudes in his head. *No, Madam President, of course you're not. Of course you're an upstanding woman and a proud President.* Strangely, as the first volleys of fire started to ring out all around him, all those platitudes melted away. "Everyone's a whore," he spat, still whispering. "Everyone in this world trades something for something else. Sometimes it's money for dick, sometimes it's far more subtle, intricate things. And I mean *everyone*. You, me, each and every one of these muscle-headed saps you send into battle. You think they're here because they like being shot at? Like watching their friends and coworkers die? They're here because they're useless muscle-heads who lacked the acumen to achieve at a college rate. They're whores of the state, getting fucked in the ass to save us all.

"So maybe you didn't suck a dick to get the presidency. Maybe you sucked fifty. God, it wouldn't be the first time. It doesn't matter. Whatever you *think* of your position, I can tell you this: you don't understand the truth of what's going on right now. In time, things will be made clear to you—in time— but not right now. You're just going to have to trust me." He paused. "And if you don't trust me, you're going to have to trust that I have the capability to have you re-elected, or not. Do I make myself clear?"

"I think you're bluffing." President Schuyler's voice hardened. "You're a desperate, cornered old man trying to save his skin. You have nothing on me, nothing, and I'm not going to jeopardize the whole planet just to save your wrinkled old ass."

"Call Spectre," he said, laying a massive card on the table. "Call Spectre and ask her if what I'm saying is true."

Silence on the other end of the line. Then, "How do you know that name?"

Now, finally, the shoe was on the other foot. "I know a lot more than you can imagine," he said. "You should know, if I die out here, Spectre will dump everything she has on you. You won't be able to get elected to your local school council. Impeachment will be the last of your worries; you'll be *lucky* to live out the rest of your life in a prison cell." He let the threat dangle. "Do you know the United States still practices capital punishment for treason?"

A long silence, punctuated only by the shouting of the bridge crew—which he tried to shield the microphone from—and the rumbles of incoming weapons fire.

"Take your time," said Senator Pitt, dipping his voice in sugar. "Not like we're being shot at over here or anything."

More nothing. Maybe he was actually on hold.

He tried to catch his son's eye, but each time he did, the result wounded him. The man's face was painted with disgust, bitterness, anger…distrust.

You don't understand, son… You're a man, but in some ways, you'll always be my boy. I've kept all the secrets for all these years. But I can't imagine what you'd think about me if you knew what was really at Ganymede…or what was really at stake in all of this. There's a reason you're here, son, and you have a lot to do yet before I fully pass the torch. But you'll be ready soon. Soon.

A faint click signaled the end of the hold.

"This call never happened," said President Schuyler, and

the line went dead.

Pitt slowly took off the earpiece and stared at it. A blinking red light on the side confirmed it: the call had been disconnected.

That was a good thing, right? She hung up because she was sending help, right?

Right?

Chapter Fifty

Lt. Patricia "Guano" Corrick's Warbird
Hangar Bay
USS Midway

Guano's brand new ship shot out of the hangar bay like a dart, Roadie on one wing and Joker on the other.

"Alpha wing is away," said Roadie. "Bravo flight, get ready to launch. Alpha wing, check in. Alpha-1 is go."

It felt good to be promoted to Alpha wing, although strange, given that she'd lost a ship. But a 3:1 kill:loss ratio was good, right?

"Alpha-2 is go," said Joker.

"Alpha-3, go," said Guano, switching on her radar.

Her screens lit up like a Christmas tree. Red and green and blue everywhere. Red for hostiles, green for friendlies, and blue for decoys. A steady stream of strike craft poured out of the two frigates, and as she watched, two quick flashes of light signaled the arrival of their other two frigates. Gunfire flew across space in wild, jagged streams, the friendly cannon tracers white streaks, the hostile particle weapons a sizzling red.

"Jesus, what a shit show," said Joker.

Roadie turned and Guano turned with him. "The nearest hostile ship is twenty-two kilometers away," said Roadie. "Lock it in, designation Skunk-1."

"Looks like we're going to be late to the party," said Joker.

"A fighter pilot is never late," said Guano. "Nor is she early. She arrives precisely when she means to."

The three of them laughed.

"That's my joke," said Flatline, sounding vaguely offended. "It's meant to be about gunners."

Guano adjusted the gain on her targeting radar, locking up Skunk-1. The front of it opened up, and like some kind of beast, it began belching fighters out into space. "Tally," she called, "bandits, one o'clock low. We got fighters."

"Guns check," said Roadie. "Everyone clear your throats. Might as well aim it at that skunk."

She dipped her nose, aligning her ship to the alien cap ship, and gently squeezed the trigger on her guns, sending a short burst out into space. "All good here," she said.

Roadie fired too. Then Joker. They were ready.

"Ready to get our ace?" said Flatline.

"Always," said Guano, her voice pitching up in excitement. "Let's frag these bastards!"

"Light up those contacts with your long-range missiles," said Roadie. "Mark your targets and knock 'em down."

She did so, tapping buttons on her console with one hand and flying with the other. She selected one, two, three, four of the closest alien fighters and, with as many presses of her button, fired off all of her long-range missiles. "Fox three," she called, like a mantra. "Fox three, fox three, fox three…"

Four little streams flew out, splitting off as their targets tried to evade. The missiles disappeared inside the swarm, detonating against things she couldn't possibly see.

The ship's computer would tell her if they were kills, but she knew—she just *knew*—that she'd gotten two more, and become an Ace.

Flatline exalted behind her. "Nailed 'em," he shouted. "Great shooting!"

It was, too. Her missiles were perfectly timed, as close together as possible so as to confuse any defenses they might have, but far enough apart that they wouldn't strike each other. She drank in the feeling, the rush, the energy flowing through her. No fears. No worries. Only a desire to get in close to those fighters and blast them to atoms. It was like electricity.

And then, just as quickly as it arrived, the feeling vanished, being replaced with something else. A strange *calm*. Like a trance, a tranquil embrace that washed over her, dissolving all her fears, uncertainties, and doubts.

She stared at the massive innumerable rush of incoming fighters that threatened to wash over the three of them like a tidal wave, and she felt nothing but calm.

"Ready to close to heat-seeker range," she said, her voice strangely airy. "Let's get in there."

"All craft, break and engage," said Roadie, pitching his nose up.

She pitched her ship down, then up again, splitting to attack from below. With no more long-range missiles, she switched to heat-seekers, and then to guns. Way, way out of effective range, she gently squeezed the trigger.

"Guns, guns, guns."

"Whoa!" shouted Flatline. "Hey, Guano, relax—we're way too far away for those rounds to…" The rounds splashed into the alien swarm, little tiny flashes, pinpricks of light at that distance, as they raked a streak of fire across all of them. "… hit."

Flatline twisted in his seat, looking around at her. "Holy hell, that was a nice shot! I think you nailed, like, four of them!"

Not enough to kill all the ones she hit, but several of them broke away from the fight, belching smoke and debris, so that was something. She tilted her ship up, rolled over, and spun as the alien horde descended. Guano pushed her left foot on the rudder, tilting her ship, narrowly avoiding a red stream of fire that streaked past their cockpit by meters.

It was like listening to Celtic music while being stoned. So smooth, so easy, everything a gentle motion, everything a deliberate action, her decisions planned out six moves in advance. A total lack of adrenaline. She'd felt more excited idly watching baseball games at home.

"You okay?" shouted Flatline, swinging his turret around and firing a stream of rounds at a pair of fighters, the rounds flying wide.

"Totally fine," she said, keeping the ship steady so Flatline could shoot.

Another burst from him shattered one of the fighters into a billion tiny pieces, and the other one—damaged by one of Guano's earlier bursts—broke in half. Flatline gave each half a half-second burst, then Guano swung the nose of her ship around, squeezing off a missile without even a proper lock. "Fox two."

The missile flew about thirty meters, then an alien fighter she hadn't even seen flew up in front of her nose, perfectly smashing into the missile, destroying it in a huge flash of energy.

Then she saw the main capital ship, the leading ship with its mass driver, moving to the front of the alien fleet, its weapon ready and aimed at the *Midway*, the ship surrounded by an endless swarm of fighters.

"Shit's about to get real," said Flatline.

Guano took a shallow breath and let it out slowly. "Couldn't have put it better myself."

Chapter Fifty-One

Bridge
USS Midway

"*Hamilton*," said Mattis, pressing on his earpiece with his finger so hard it hurt. "Ready forward gun batteries. *Revere*, likewise. On my mark. Three, two, one, mark."

All three ships fired at once, a barrage of shells that flew out like an angry swarm, impacting against the shield of the nearest light cruiser. Several shells slipped through the shields, splashing against the hull and carving out great chunks of the enemy ship, but it wasn't enough.

"Repeat," he said, and the guns spoke again.

"Sir," said Lynch, "the *Spearway* and the *Able* are completing their Z-space translations in three, two, one…" Twin flashes lit up the various monitors on the bridge, bathing the whole room in light that quickly faded. Two new frigates, their guns firing the moment they entered real space. "They're in the fight."

Good. It evened the odds a little. Another barrage of enemy fire struck their front; two of the alien light cruisers were moving around them, like the pincers of a giant crab. A much more aggressive stance than they'd previously seen. This time, the aliens were playing for keeps.

"Target the port skunk with our broadside guns," he said. "Maintain all other weapons fire on skunk alpha. We're starting to crack that ship's shield, let's keep it up. I want that ship burning before we switch targets, but I also don't want to get flanked."

"Aye aye, Admiral," said Commander Pitt. "Let's frighten away the port ship with some torpedoes. Maybe they'll know what happened with their friend."

Good plan. "Make it happen," said Mattis, settling into his chair, doing his absolute best to project an atmosphere of command. Morale was important. Impressions, a critical part of that.

Helm moved the *Midway*, shifting it to port, trying to avoid the flank. The ship twisted, aligning its nose to the enemy ship, and fired a pair of torpedoes.

"Torpedoes away," said Lynch. "Ten seconds till impact."

More than enough time for the enemy to reposition their shield, but hopefully it would distract them for a little while…

…and it did not.

The alien light cruiser didn't change its heading at all, continuing to move implacably up beside them, its nose still pointed at the *Midway*. The torpedoes struck home, blue flashes of light absorbing the blinding detonation of the twin warheads.

"No effect, Admiral." Commander Pitt folded his hands

behind him. "I'm afraid we're being caught in a pincer."

Probably the oldest tactic in the book that wasn't a frontal assault. Attacking from two sides would increase their surface area, making them easier to hit, and the armor was softer there. And all the while they couldn't effectively bring their torpedoes to bear unless they presented their rear to one, which would make things even worse.

It wasn't only the alien ships that had minimal armor toward the rear.

He couldn't focus entirely on the pincer, though. The battle raged around them. Their strike craft met hostile strike craft, and kill reports started to flow in. The two signals merged, becoming a dogfight in the middle of space.

And then Mattis saw the enemy flagship moving forward, into the gap, toward the front of the fleet, its mass driver loaded and charging.

"Admiral, they're about to fire," said Lynch. "They must have pre-charged!"

Of course they would have. They knew they were being pursued, just as the humans knew their course.

"Options," said Mattis, practically shouting the word. "Can we avoid it?"

"Not at this range," said Lynch. "But we're executing an emergency maneuver. We might be able to turn it into a glancing blow, especially if we angle our armor, increase the chance of a deflection."

That would be enough, hopefully. *Midway* heaved as she moved, trying, almost pathetically, to avoid the blast—

A white flash. Mattis shielded his eyes instinctively.

But a second later, the flash faded. A ship had dropped out

of Z-space, interposing itself between the hostile cap ship and the *Midway*. Steam poured from its engines, and it looked liked it had been flogged for days, almost to the point of overheating, but its massive bulk obscured their enemy completely.

"This is the HMS *Somerset*," came the voice of Captain Salt, its small single cannon spitting shells defiantly at the enemy. "Late, but in earnest! We are engaging the enemy. For King and Country."

Mattis could hardly imagine the faces of the enemy on the other ship as this massive, squat, ugly transport appeared right in front of them, firing away with their little pop-gun. The event must have shocked them so much they didn't fire, giving the *Midway* precious seconds to move out of the way, hidden from view by the bulk of the cargo hauler.

"Captain Salt?" asked Mattis, scarcely believing it. "What the hell? How did you get here?"

"It's a long story," said Salt, the sound of wailing alarms in the background of her ship. "In short, the crew and I decided that it would be bad form to miss this engagement, so we took our reactor off containment and pushed the old girl a little harder."

Without their reactor being contained, she and all of her crew would have already received a lethal dose of radiation poisoning. A dozen full servlets or more, and increasing by the hour. She must have been in agony, throwing up and with uncontrollable shaking, tortured by the knowledge they were walking corpses, but her voice was cool and in control.

Mattis resolved never to doubt English courage. "Very good," was all he could say. "Maintain effective weapons fire. I think you being so close to their ship is spooking them."

"Confirmed," said Salt, hiding a faint cough. "Weapons, maintain fire, target their mass driver!"

A searing yellow light stole his attention. The *Spearway* took a hit to its port side, and flames burst from the hull. He could do nothing to help them. The ship continued to return fire, but several of its guns were now silent. *Able* moved in closer to her sister ship, guns spitting fire, but that ship, too, bled atmosphere through several holes in her hull.

The frigates were hurting. The *Alexander Hamilton* and the *Paul Revere* had been largely spared so far, presumably because of their proximity to the *Midway*, but that protection would only last so long.

Waves of red fire came in from both sides as the two light cruisers continued their bombardments, their flanking maneuver complete. Mattis had to ignore them for now. "Frigates, fire another barrage against the primary skunk. All guns. Let's crack this egg so we can break the pincer."

Another heavy volley of fire came out, focused on the very front of the light cruiser directly in front of them. The fire overwhelmed the shields, and a stream of rounds found their way inside, igniting fires within the ship and blasting its insides, leaving a scorched hole, unshielded and vulnerable.

"Torpedoes away," said Lynch, and this time the missiles flew true, spearing into the ship one after the other, burrowing in deep before bursting, blinding flashes combining into one, and when it cleared, the ship was no more.

"Target destroyed," said Commander Pitt. But they had no time to celebrate. Red streaks tapped a staccato beat on both sides of their hull.

"Sir," said Lynch, pointing at his monitor. "We have a problem."

"Go," said Mattis. As though they didn't already have enough.

"The alien cap ship," said Lynch, "it's charging up again!"

"To fire on the *Somerset*?" asked Mattis, guessing the likely target.

"No, sir," said Lynch, his voice trailing off, eyes fixed on the display. "They're turning toward Ganymede."

Chapter Fifty-Two

Lt. Patricia "Guano" Corrick's Warbird
16 kilometers from the USS Midway

She was one with the universe. Or something. Or maybe she was having a stroke. But whatever was happening to her, Guano almost felt time slow down around her, the whirling storm of fighters seeming to be a fairly predictable cloud, drifting along. She aligned one with her guns and, with barely a breath on the fire button, blew it to shreds.

"Nice shooting," said Flatline, his rear gun chattering away as he swung his quad barrels from side to side, "real nice!"

"Seems like I'm getting the hang of this," she said, spinning the craft inverted and pulling the stick gently back into her stomach. The Warbird looped, coming back around, and she neatly dodged the debris of her previous kill. Almost. A piece struck the outer edge of her port wing, bouncing off with an audible *ting*.

Well, not even her weird battle trance was perfect.

The alien cap ship was there, its mass driver radiating energy. It was aiming at some ship she didn't recognize, except by its type. Standard Royal Navy cargo ship, Mark VIII. *York* class. What the hell was that doing there?

It was right in front of the enemy cap ship. Physically blocking its mass-driver launch port, as though it might sacrifice itself to protect the *Midway*. Brave, but that was only one shot.

Then the cap ship began to turn, and she knew, suddenly and without error, what its target was.

Guano opened the throttle, racing toward the massive sphere that was Jupiter, the acceleration crushing her into her seat. "Flatline," she said, her voice weirdly calm, "the enemy capital ship is preparing to fire on Ganymede. We have to get closer to it. We gotta ignore these fighters and plug that bastard in the engines, just like we did with the other ship."

"Are you crazy?" asked Flatline, but there was an edge of rhetoricalness to it. "No, it's okay. I know you are. Just…" He whined loudly. "Don't get me shot again, okay? I hate getting shot!"

She raced toward the cap ship, her craft's exhaust trailing a silver line across space, an arrow heading straight toward their biggest, and most heavily defended, enemy. As the massive ship turned its rear toward them, she fingered the trigger on her guns, but knew that—at that extreme range—it would take minutes for the shells to arrive. Pointless, even with her newfound zen. Without radar-guided missiles, there wasn't anything she could do at that range.

Heat seekers? Not enough range. The rocket motors would burn out before they got close and, if her ship continued to accelerate as it did, she would actually overtake them—possibly risking being struck by her own missiles. Semi-active radar-guided? Too weak. Could never hurt a cap ship.

Calmly, methodically, she worked through all the plans in her head and came up with nothing.

All she could do was watch despairingly, her hand gripping the throttle, as the cap ship fired toward the surface of Ganymede.

Chapter Fifty-Three

Bridge
USS Midway

The aliens were turning to attack Ganymede. He couldn't let them do that.

"Lynch," said Mattis, a sudden decision made. "On my authority, position the ship between the hostile cap ship and Ganymede."

His helpless face told him it was a pointless decision. "We can't, sir. Our sublight engines will never get us there fast enough, and our Z-drive isn't powered. It'll take too long to charge."

Dammit. Dammit. Damn, damn, damn, damn, damn…

"Admiral," said Salt over the line, "we have an idea. The *Somerset* is in ideal ramming position. We're slow, sir, but we're heavy. We can throw ourselves at them."

He could scarcely imagine the courage that would require. Conditions aboard that ship would have to be wretched. Hot, irradiated, reeking of puke and coolant. Half her crew would have been fried by now, or more, even with the most powerful anti-radiation meds.

Maybe, in this case, it was a mercy.

"Do what you need to," said Mattis through gritted teeth. "And get your ass to an escape pod. You've done enough."

"Ships this old don't have an autopilot," she said, stifling another wracking, pained, wet cough.

"The inertia will be enough," he said. "Just set a course and go. That's an order."

"Sorry, Admiral," said Salt, over the perfectly clear connection. "You're breaking up. Missed that last part…"

"Sir," said Lynch. "An alternative. The *Somerset* could possibly maneuver itself and block the shot to Ganymede. But it would require precision piloting, up to the last second, and… nobody would be getting off that ship."

"Then no," said Mattis, snapping at him. The injustice of it appalled him. Salt may already be dead, but her bravery, her loyalty, was admirable. She shouldn't die like that. "Not unless there's an evacuation plan for the crew."

Lynch's answer was, then, silence.

He'd made his choice. There was nothing more he could do for Ganymede. Nothing anyone could do.

Mattis fixed his eyes on his monitor as the alien ship fired.

Chapter Fifty-Four

Outside the seed bank
Ganymede Colony

Lucas tried again, pressing in the ignition on his transport. No dice. It wouldn't start.

Typical. The moon's harsh conditions could even interfere with things inside the protective shield of the colony, and would often play havoc with a transport that regularly went outside.

Still, despite that, he'd always been able to coax the thing into starting up before whenever this happened. It was important for his job, a weird part of his duties for the mining colony, the administration of the CEO's little pet project. He didn't know what lay beyond the thick steel doors tucked at the end of the box canyon. All he knew was that it was his job to read the numbers on the display, write them down on paper— *actual* paper—and send them via the post to Earth.

The actual postal service. It seemed totally absurd to him;

the CEO of a mining company was obviously rich enough to afford a Z-space relay, and there were only a few reasons to send actual letters by the painfully slow postal system. Tradition, or accountability, or its *opposite*—someone had something to hide.

His lawyer had assured Lucas that, no matter what was happening beyond those doors, he had no knowledge of it, so he was legally in the clear. Besides, he was paid an extra five hundred euros a month for twenty minutes work, so… definitely worth it.

He set the paper off to one side and, closing his eyes, did the one thing that almost always worked.

In de naam van de Vader, de Zoon en de Heilige Geest. Amen.

If God was out there, watching down from the stars, he might help. Or the engine might be flooded and need time to clear itself. Either way, things would work out.

Lucas tried the ignition again. The engine choked, spluttered, and sprang to life.

Phew. That one was close. He'd have to remember to log the form to request a replacement. No sense in trying to repair the busted old thing. Like with most things these days, it was just cheaper to throw it away. Park it somewhere and leave it. Then there would be no more need to bother the Almighty with his annoyances. God preferred to help those who helped themselves.

Slowly, the transport began to trundle back toward the mining outpost, its six wheels spinning occasionally on loose gravel and rocks. Lucas adjusted his space suit and sang quietly to himself.

What if all the world were dried whitefish,

And each tree a sausage,
And every puddle made of pure shoe polish
That quenches the thirst?
That is the question, ladies and gentlemen,
Over which for seven years,
Seven professors
Have scratched behind their ears.

A traditional nursery rhyme. It might have seemed weird to an outsider, singing a children's song as he drove a rover across the barren landscape with the massive striped gumball—that's what they called Jupiter, the gumball—taking up half the sky, but his kids liked that song, and it helped pass the time.

Ahh, his kids. Dutch stock, through and through, a rarity in these modern times. Mixed race people were far more common, just due to the demographics of everything. Not that that was a bad thing—he wasn't bigoted—but it was nice to know where he came from.

The Dutch were the first settlers on Ganymede. No strangers to hard work, they enjoyed the challenge. It was a big task bringing his kids to this place—many would ask why, and question what kind of life they could have here—but the two boys had a small school, plenty of space, and it was safe. Nothing could ever hurt them here.

A bright flash stole his attention. Another meteor impact, so close? That could be an issue. Lucas pulled over and popped open the door. More flashes from above, more light. He'd seen this kind of thing before, twenty years back, as a child. When the US and China decided that diplomacy and peace were less preferable to posturing and war.

A space battle, in high orbit. A firefight so close made

staying here dangerous. Vacuum had no resistance; a round fired in orbit would travel forever until it hit something, and if a quarter of the sky was Ganymede...*well*. The average battle could put out a lot of rounds. The odds weren't good.

And then something happened. Something he had not seen before. A glinting thing, getting larger and larger. Big. Reflections of ice and rock, heading directly toward him. Toward Ganymede Colony.

Men and their tools of death. Lucas closed his eyes. Time to ask God for a big one. Not for him, but for his kids.

"*Wees gegroet Maria, vol van genade, de Heer is met U. Gezegend zijt gij boven—*"

Then there was only white.

Chapter Fifty-Five

Bridge
USS Midway

Mattis watched in helpless, stunned silence as the alien ship hurled a mass of rock and ice down from space, through Ganymede's vanishingly thin atmosphere and to the surface. It struck silently, almost anti-climatictally, and from their position in high orbit, they could see the barest flash from the surface.

At that distance, the blast must have been thousands of megatons if it was visible from so far away. A bright light on the dark surface of the moon, quickly fading away to nothing.

Maybe it had missed. A planet was a big place. Mattis pulled up the display on his command console, zooming in on the position of the colony. A dark grey mushroom cloud, the pulverized upper kilometer of the facility and surrounding colony, rose up through the atmosphere like a living, growing thing; a time-lapse of actual growth, blooming on a lifeless world.

But this flower symbolized death, not life.

"Damn," said Commander Pitt, summarizing exactly how they all felt.

Mattis slumped in his command chair. The *Spearway* burned, its guns silent as it slowly spun, over and over, in space, drifting inexorably down toward Ganymede. Escape pods flew out of it in all directions. Some relief, then, at least…not that it counted for much.

"Sir," said Lynch, breaking the tense silence. "We have an incoming transmission from the *Somerset*."

"This is Salt." Her voice sounded weak, strained, as though all the life was being drained out of it. "Admiral, we can't let them fire again. Here, or anywhere else. That ship must be stopped. Do you understand what I'm saying?"

Mattis couldn't say it. He couldn't say yes—he couldn't doom the dying woman to a fiery death—but he couldn't say no, either. Salt was right. "Just… do what you feel is best," was all he could manage.

"Aye aye, Admiral. *Ah,* this was a bad day to give up the scotch." The *Somerset* accelerated, big and bulky and leaking atmosphere from several holes in her decks. The massive transport lurched toward the capital ship, sublight engines flared, maneuvering thrusters at full. It continued spitting at them, its little cannon splashing ineffectively off the larger ship's shield, until the two met.

Her hull crumpled, her superstructure buckled, her small gun fired one more time, and then the whole ship evaporated in a searing flash of white light.

The alien cap ship remained, blackened and scarred, but the *Somerset* had done its work: the rails of the mass driver were bent and warped. Salvageable, maybe, but its accuracy would be well down.

A seemingly petty sacrifice for a whole ship and its crew.

The remaining alien ships, all nine of them, began to turn and, in seconds, jumped away.

Now all that remained was the burning wreck of the *Spearway*, three heavily damaged frigates, the *Midway*, and a cloud of strike craft mopping up.

And the terrible, crushing guilt.

"Oh, nice work," said Senator Pitt, his voice equal parts venom and sarcasm and…something else Mattis couldn't identify. Fear? "Very well done, you damned *idiot*. Great work, ordering that woman not to ram the ship when it would have counted, then waiting until *after* they'd fired!" He started to shout. "What were you *thinking*, Mattis?"

Good question. Mattis knew he'd made a terrible error, but it was—it was the right decision at the time. He had no idea they would fire at Ganymede mid-battle. Why would they want to destroy the seed bank? He'd always assumed they wanted what was there—to take it, to use it for nefarious purposes. To simply bomb the repository of human DNA was pointless. What did that prove? Their actions made no sense to him.

"Get him off the bridge," said Lynch.

"To hell with you," spat Commander Pitt, glaring at his father with a dark look in his eyes. "You have no idea what you're talking about."

"No, son, *you* don't know." Senator Pitt hissed in anger, his eyes meeting Commander Pitt's, holding his gaze. For a brief moment, Mattis thought there might be a fistfight, but then Senator Pitt turned back to him. "If my son was in command,

Ganymede Colony would still be there. Captain Salt was dead the moment she turned her reactor off containment, and you were too damn stubborn to realize it. You sacrificed everything on that planet for the life of... of someone you'd just barely met. And look what happened. She died anyway, and the damn aliens blasted the moon."

It was true, but what could he do? He couldn't undo the past. Couldn't bring back Salt, or the Ganymede colony, or the seed bank, or anything.

Senator Pitt stalked closer to him, his face twisted and bent out of shape. "This is all your fault, you broken-down fool."

At a signal from Lynch, the bridge marines grabbed the Senator and dragged him off and through the door, but his words lingered.

"Orders, Capt—I mean, Admiral?" asked Lynch.

Captain. The position he'd inherited from Malmsteen. And taken from the man who'd really deserved it, Commander Pitt. Mattis's voice stuck in his throat. Commander Pitt, the whole bridge crew, they sat there, waiting, as their CO said nothing. Despite it all, the only thing he could think of was Chuck and Javier.

"I have to...I have to make a call," he murmured and pushed himself out of his chair, heading for his ready room.

Chapter Fifty-Six

Captain's Ready Room
USS Midway

What an idiot he'd been.

How had it come to this? How had he come to this place, this ship, taken command…and for everything to go so horribly wrong?

I did my best was the refrain of those who had failed, and that was what he'd done. Failed. The seed bank had been blasted to ruins. The *Spearway* was abandoned and burning, drifting down toward a fiery grave on Ganymede's unforgiving surface.

He sat on the bed, head in his hands, playing the mass-driver strike on the seed bank over and over in his head. That huge mushroom cloud, the debris. The sight of the *Spearway* tumbling end over end, her bow aflame, like a falling candle in the dark.

What had he done?

Mattis snatched a coffee mug from the end table and flung it across the room, roaring angrily. The mug smashed into a million pieces against the far wall, showering the room with tiny sharp shards of porcelain.

Well. That didn't solve anything. And it didn't feel any better. He grabbed the little table and upended it, the wood splintering as it hit the unyielding steel, smashing into flat panels, spilling its contents all over the floor. Dozens of sheets of paper. A calculator. Pens of all colors.

A chromed revolver, the faintest gleam of brass cartridges visible in the chambers.

Mattis stared at the gun for a split second. It was Malmsteen's sidearm. His service pistol. The symbol of his office. The symbol of the ship's authority, really. Gleaming metal, polished to a mirror shine, perfectly well kept. Loaded and ready to fire.

Wouldn't be the first time for a seasoned commander on the verge of defeat. Nobody would blame him, and—

No. *No.* Mattis shook his head, trying to clear out the bitter thoughts, but they clung like spider webs over his thoughts. Sticky. Tenacious.

In the quiet of the ready room, he finally noticed his communicator vibrating in his pocket, the noise a nuisance. A distraction. *Vrrt. Vrrt. Vrrt* Mattis snatched it up and got ready to hurl that thing away too, but saw a text message on the front. A series of them. They had been there for a while.

He brought them up.

M. Ramirez: *Hey, what the hell kind of interview was that?*
M. Ramirez: *Talk to me, Jack.*

M. Ramirez: *Jack!*

Damn. He should really check his messages more often. These had been sitting there for ages. He kept scrolling.

M. Ramirez: *Jack, hey… I'm sorry, okay? I know that must have been difficult for you. But my job is to be a reporter. My job is to find the truth.*

M. Ramirez: *I don't know. Maybe I went too far with this one. It… I didn't mean to. I wasn't thinking of the last time. I just wasn't. I didn't realize you were either.*

That softened him a little. It took a lot for someone to admit they were wrong. He had trouble with it. Such a stubborn old fool.

M. Ramirez: *You're right to be mad. You have every right to be, I guess, I just…*

M. Ramirez: *I just want you to know, this has been difficult for me too. Being around you. Being in your space. It…reminds me of what could have been.*

There was a long gap between texts. Almost an hour.

M. Ramirez: *I wish things had turned out differently between us.*

Mattis's hands shook slightly, and he had to swallow his feelings. This wasn't the time to second guess himself. It wasn't a good place to be, especially with the thing he'd found. The gun. His eyes drifted back to it unconsciously. That might still be the best option…

No.

A brief knock on the door stole his attention. "Yeah?"

"Hey," said Ramirez on the other side. "Sorry, I just… You weren't answering your texts, I just need to talk to you."

He wasn't sure about this. "Briefly," he said, a little more angrily than he meant to. Then, quieter, "Sorry. Come in."

She pushed open the door and stepped into the ready room. Her make-up was all smudged.

"You okay?" asked Mattis.

Ramirez looked at the smashed stuff scattered around. "Are *you* okay?"

He smiled. She smiled.

"Sure," said Mattis.

"Did you read—"

"Yeah."

"So, I was thinking—"

"Yeah."

They stood there awkwardly, exchanging a long, held smile.

"Good talk," said Ramirez, and then, with a playful smile, she left.

It was weird, awkward and cringeworthy, but Mattis couldn't help but chuckle. It reminded him of when he was younger. When they were both younger. Of things that could have been. Of the things that could *be*…

He wasn't sure how long he stood there, torn between walking out after Ramirez and picking up the weapon, but the ringing of his communicator broke him out of the trance.

Temptation to throw the thing came back, but he resisted. "What?" he asked, snapping into the line the moment it opened. "This better be fucking important."

"It's Chuck," said his son, the mere sound of his voice bringing Mattis back down to reality for a moment. "Is this a bad time?"

People who asked that question were usually ill prepared for the answer to be *no*, but as Mattis took a breath, he realized that speaking to Chuck was exactly what he needed. "It's a perfect time, son. What can I do for you?"

"Two things, Dad." The joy in Chuck's voice was almost infectious. Almost. "The surrogate gave birth. And I know we should have talked to you before we dropped this on you, but there just wasn't time. We…uh, we named him Jack."

Despite it all, that brought a confused smile on his face. "I…I thought his name was Javier," said Mattis, a little quiver in his voice that was entirely unbecoming of an officer of his standing.

"That's my boyfriend's father's name," said Chuck, the awkwardness of his sentence obviously designed to deflect attention away from the guy. "But we talked it out, and we think—we *both* think—that it'd be better if Javier was his middle name. Jack Javier Mattis. That's what we put on the birth certificate. It's official, Dad, you're a grandfather."

Well, now, wasn't that something.

Mattis couldn't help but smile and, ever so subtly, kick the pistol under the bed where it was out of sight.

Jack. Jack Javier Mattis.

In the midst of all this chaos, it was nice to hear some good news. But Chuck had said there were *two* things, and people usually lead with the good news first, especially if the bad news was particularly bad. "You said there was something else?" he asked, almost dreading the answer. What if Javier—or Jack, rather, he had to remind himself—had been affected by a birth defect? Herbicide overuse had made this an unfortunately common outcome. One in a thousand, or something. What if Jack was the one?

"Well," said Chuck, his tone apprehensive. "I just…" Please, no. Please, no. Please, no. "It's something I shouldn't even be talking to you about."

"Just spit it out, son."

"It might cost me much more than my job to even mention it, but there's…something that Pitt's office just received. It came in a little envelope. We opened it, of course, and the first page was a series of numbers and letters. Like a code."

Mattis tried to make sense of it. "Any chance of decoding the message?"

"I don't think it's like that," said Chuck. "I don't think it's a coded message, it's too short, just twenty characters long. I think it's more like an access code. It says: D5G-KXZO-WPW."

An access code? "Did it say anything else?"

"Yes," said Chuck. "It says: *I couldn't send ships, but I could send this.* Does that mean anything to you?"

The President. She'd come through for them.

"Anything else?"

"Yeah," said Chuck, "on the second page. Hang on, I'll scan it and text it to you. One sec."

Mattis waited, and then the text appeared on his screen. The more he read, the more confidence came back to him. This was perfect. Exactly what they needed.

"It was signed," said Chuck, "by someone called Spectre."

Spectre. That was a strange name. A codename, obviously, and written in the British spelling rather than the American. But the information they'd given was very useful. "Thanks, son," he said, and closed the connection.

Mattis walked back onto the bridge of the *Midway*, his shoulders held high and his confidence restored.

Jack Javier Mattis. Has a ring to it, I guess.

Every eye fell upon him as he entered, and he knew he hadn't exactly inspired them with walking out, but hopefully what he had when he came back would help bring their morale right back up again.

"Retrieve our strike craft," he said, trying to bring with it the air of command and a confidence that was only just starting to return. "Patch up our frigates as best we can, and lay in a pursuit course for the alien fleet."

"Aye, sir," said Lynch. Although the man's tone was flat. Hollow. He thought they'd lost.

He thought wrong. "Get us to Earth. Don't spend time trying to track them—we all *know* that's where they're going next."

"Sir?" asked Commander Pitt, obviously confused. "What's happened?"

Mattis took a deep breath, jaw strong and back straight. "I know how to stop that weapon."

Chapter Fifty-Seven

Lt. Patricia "Guano" Corrick's Warbird
16 kilometers from the USS Midway

Guano slumped back in her chair, watching the explosion on Ganymede, followed by the flashes as the ships jumped away.

"What happened?" asked Flatline, squirming in his seat, trying to look past her headrest.

"We weren't quick enough," she said simply, and took a steadying breath. "Okay. We gotta get back to the *Midway*." She thumbed her radio. "Hey Roadie, we have to RTB. The fleet's gone. No reason to stick with them."

"Damn straight," said Joker in her ear. "Guano, I'll form up on your wing. My port gun was giving me some trouble when I warmed it up. I'd appreciate a hand."

"No worries," said Guano. "I'll walk you in." The two of them formed up, and turned toward their mothership.

"Why are you so calm all of a sudden?" asked Flatline, his

voice tinged with a little apprehension. "You don't have to do it for me, you know. I'm okay. I'm cleared for duty."

"I know," said Guano, trying to get a handle on herself. Even her gunner noticed something was odd. "It's just, well…" She almost said something but shook away the feelings. "No, it's fine."

"You sure?" asked Flatline. "Because if you're acting weird, and we get into the shit, I don't want to have to shovel it, you know? I gotta rely on you."

"You can rely on me," said Guano, glancing over her shoulder. "I promise."

"Okay," said Flatline, rolling his eyes. "If we die, though, this is your fault. Remember the Dead Man's Hand?"

That was okay with her. "We won't die," she said. "It'll definitely be Frost."

"Hey," said Frost over the line, "screw you guys!"

"Sorry, Roadie," said Guano, grinning to herself. "You can have my gunner if she bites it."

Everyone started shouting at once, which made her smile even more.

But nothing could hide the faint glow in her rearview mirror. Ganymede, where so many lives had just been snuffed out. While they were joking around and being dicks.

Suddenly it didn't feel very funny at all.

Chapter Fifty-Eight

Bridge
USS Midway

He could have heard a pin drop. Nobody said anything—they all looked at each other, exchanging skeptical glances. Mattis knew it must have been difficult for them, after seeing Ganymede burn, to accept what he was telling them, but he needed his crew to believe him if he was going to pull this off.

"Bring Senator Pitt back up here," said Mattis. "We're going to need him." He added, almost as an afterthought, "And Modi, too. I don't care what else he's doing."

"But sir," said Lynch, eyes flicking to the door, "we just had the marines drag the senator kicking and screaming out of here."

"Great," said Mattis, "so have the marines drag him kicking and screaming right back here. I've received new information that might tip the balance in our favor. And that information requires the senator if it's going to be put to good use."

Lynch made the call, talking in hushed tones into his earpiece, and a few moments later, a shouting, swearing Senator Pitt was brought back to the bridge.

"What do you want?" roared the senator, throwing off the marines attached to his arms. "Want to show me your latest failure, Admiral?"

Far from it. Mattis glared at Senator Pitt, slowly reached into his breast pocket, withdrawing the half-finished cigar he'd been storing there, took the lighter out of his pocket, and lit the cigar, puffing smoke across the bridge.

"You were right," said Mattis coolly. *That* surprised Senator Pitt. Mattis saw his rage momentarily abate. "If your son had been in command, or if I'd made a different decision, things might have turned out for the better. But we're not in that universe, Senator Pitt. We're in *this* one, and in this one, we have to make do with what we have."

"And what is it we have?" asked Pitt. "A bunch of bloodied ships, a crew that's three-quarters in the grave with exhaustion and running on adrenaline, and—"

"And," said Mattis, letting the words hang in the air, "access to a little toy the Chinese have cooked up." His lips curled up in a wide smile. If only Shao was here to see this. "It turns out that the Chinese aren't the only ones who engage in nation-state sponsored espionage."

That drew a lot of attention. "What kind of weapon, sir?" asked Commander Pitt, pointedly refusing to look at his father.

"It's called a gravity pulse weapon," said Mattis. "It's similar to the artificial gravity on our ships in terms of operation, and actually quite similar to the mass driver, but rather than magnetically accelerating masses to high velocities, it emits gravity waves and uses them to push things around. It's much less powerful and still in the prototype phases—the Chinese built it to attack strike craft, to basically disorientate them and make them an easy kill for flak guns and other things —but, given the nature of the threat we're facing, I reckon it can be used to deflect the masses we're seeing."

Commander Pitt's skepticism was clear. "How exactly is it supposed to do that?"

"That's what I need Modi for."

"And what," asked Senator Pitt, "do you need *me* for?"

Now that was the question. Mattis turned to face him squarely, cigar in his teeth. "I need you to talk to the Chinese. We have the access code. We just need the reds to be on our side with this, and okay with us using their weapon."

"Can't they fire it?"

"It's more complicated than that," said Mattis, inhaling bitter smoke. "Are you in, or not?"

Senator Pitt's eyes narrowed. "I don't suppose I have much choice."

Less choice than he realized.

Modi appeared on the bridge. For the first time since Mattis had met him, he'd started to look tired, little bags around his eyes. "Sir," he asked, "reporting as ordered."

Mattis tossed Modi his communicator, open to the plans of the gravity pulse weapon. "Let me know if this will deflect the masses we're getting shot at us."

He seemed to like that style, simple, direct commands with no wishy-washyness about them. "Yes, sir. I'll get right on it."

With that, Mattis turned back to the bridge crew. "So. This

plan requires a lot of cooperation with the Chinese—and a lot of trust. We're going to be working with people who are our enemies. When we had the *Fuqing*, it was one thing, because we were fighting alongside them, our guns aimed at the same things." The memory of the *Fuqing* firing her batteries to clear the *Midway* from the scaffolding jumped back into his head. "More or less. But this time, they're going to be behind us. They're going to have all the cards, and if they don't like the deal we're about to offer them, we are screwed. For all they know, *we're* the ones who iced *Friendship Station*, just like lots of our folks back home suspect *they* did." He took a deep breath. "It's also against Navy regs. Big time. If we make it through this, we're probably going to end up in courts martial facing disciplinary action. Anyone uncomfortable with this, speak up now, and I'll make sure your objections are noted in my log."

Nobody said anything for a moment. That was okay. Mattis let them have time to digest what he was saying. Throwing away one's career was an action not taken lightly.

"With respect," said Commander Pitt, "Admiral, humanity is a brotherhood. Like family. I can talk all the shit I want about my brother, but if someone else does? That's not ok. The Chinese know this."

Mattis nodded firmly. Nothing like a common enemy to bring everyone together. "You okay with this?"

"Yes, sir."

He turned his gaze to Commander Lynch. "How about you, Commander?"

"Those aliens are threatening Earth," said Commander Lynch, his accent slipping out once again. "Them's fighting words. Earth is where Texas is. Ain't nobody mess with Texas."

"Very good, Commander." He looked to Modi, hunched over in the corner, writing on a notepad, Mattis's communicator balanced precariously on his arm. "Mister Modi?"

"Mmm." He didn't even look up.

"That's…a yes?" asked Mattis.

"I concur with everything you, and Mister Lynch, have said." He scribbled frantically. "However, my thoughts on Texas are neutral."

"Hey now," protested Commander Pitt, but Mattis just shook his head.

Mattis turned his attention toward Pitt Senior, who still looked annoyed. "This is a battle only you can fight, Senator. You know these people. You work with them."

Senator Pitt started to protest, but Mattis silenced him with a raised hand. "I don't care about the details, at the moment. But we're going to need their help to properly deploy this deterrent."

Slowly, reluctantly, Senator Pitt dipped his head. "This is outside my area of speciality," he said, "but I'll do my best."

That was all he could ask for. "There's the communications system," he said, gesturing to Lynch's console. "Go for it."

Senator Pitt stepped up to the console. "Contact Chinese High Command. Tell them: Lower. Inconvenience. Nominal. One. Update. Accounting. Pale. Over."

"What's that?" asked Mattis. "Some kind of code?" Lower being a ship, inconvenience being…a fight?

"Randomly generated words. Don't worry about it. It's a signal to them that we need to talk to them urgently."

Trust was the name of the game at that moment, so Mattis let it slide.

There was a tense silence that smothered everything. Seconds ticked away as they waited.

Lynch glanced at Mattis. "The Chinese are responding."

Chapter Fifty-Nine

Bridge
USS Midway

Everyone worked in silence. The fleet gathered around the *Midway* and, with their engines spun up, quickly jumped. Z-space was nonlinear and unpredictable, but trends could be observed. The trip to Earth from Jupiter's moon would be short. Bright energy enveloped the ship as the fleet jumped.

Mattis, with little else to do as the ship travelled, walked over to Modi. "How's it going?" he asked.

Modi held up his finger to silence him. Normally a rude breach of protocol, Mattis let it go. This was important.

"No, eight," said Modi, clearly talking to someone on the other end of his earpiece. "We require no less than eight ships." Pause. "I am aware of that." Another pause. "And I am also aware of that. I have the readouts from the alien ship in front of me; we will require no fewer than eight gravity-equipped ships to effect the kind of deflection we require."

Pause. "I concur. However, I'm telling you, you will need to pipe the weapons directly into the main reactors of your ship. They can handle the strain, I assure you. The calculations support it." Pause. "That is not necessary. The calculations support it."

Mattis waited patiently until Modi terminated the call. "How did it go?"

"Well," said Modi, "the theoretical problems are sorted. That leaves only the political ones."

Which meant his next port of call was the good senator. With a thankful nod to Modi, Mattis marched to the other side of the bridge.

"Right," said Senator Pitt, and then he looked up as Mattis walked over. "They want to know who'll be in command of the operation."

Mattis's pride wanted him to offer himself, but he knew he would need to play this card eventually. A show of face for the Chinese, to get them to agree to let him use their weapons. "Whoever the highest ranking flag officer is," he said. "Treat the Chinese fleet as though they were Americans, and put the *Midway* under the command of whoever they want. Their highest ranking officer, presumably."

"Actually," said Senator Pitt, his tone confused, "they're specifically asking for you. Apparently the Chinese High Command received some kind of transmission from Captain Shao right before her ship exploded, vouching for you. Apparently her recommendation comes with a lot of weight."

Well. Mattis was genuinely surprised. "I see." Problems one and two sorted.

"Sir," said Lynch. "We're about to complete our Z-space

translation. Our frigate escorts report they are ready to translate on your command."

It made sense that almost as soon as they entered Z-space, they were translating out of it. "Execute," said Mattis.

Lynch touched his console. The gossamer splashes faded away to reveal Earth, the blue and green ball of life. They had appeared over Africa, the continent lit up at night, a patchwork of light and shadow on a planet floating helplessly in space.

Surrounded by ships, debris, and weapons fire.

Chapter Sixty

Bridge
USS Midway
High orbit of Earth

"Patch our ships into Goalkeeper," said Mattis. "And give me a status update."

Lynch went straight to work. "It will take some time to integrate our fire control computers into the system," he said. "But based on the amount of debris in the upper orbit path, it doesn't look like Goalkeeper is faring well."

A quick glance at the tactical radar made it hard to disagree with that assessment. A sizable portion of Goalkeeper's network of floating turret platforms had been blown to bits. The aliens were making mincemeat of their automated systems, as Mattis had suspected they would. As usual, the hard lifting would have to be done by the humans.

"How's the Earth Defense Fleet?"

"They're a long way out," said Lynch. "They definitely

won't make it. But, some good news… it looks like they didn't commit everything. There are some ships left in Earth orbit."

They'd split their fleet. Kept some in reserve. Paranoid bastards… but, fortunately, it had worked to their advantage. "What do we have?"

"Not a lot," said Lynch, looking over the readouts. "Four battleships, two cruisers, ten frigates…a mix of Chinese, Indian, Russian, and American vessels. Some of them are undergoing repairs or overhauls, or have suffered mechanical failures. That's why they're here. And there's us."

The *Able*, *Alexander Hamilton* and *Paul Revere* dropped out of Z-space in perfect formation. All ships began pumping out wings of strike craft, including the *Midway*. Their pilots must be getting fatigued, tired, stressed, but they launched regardless.

Everyone was tired. Yet everyone was working. Even the thought of it made him tired. The human body could only produce so much adrenaline. Could only last for so long without rest. There were limits, and he was rapidly approaching them. Or had exceeded them completely.

"Strike craft away," said Lynch. "Engaging targets of opportunity."

"Good," said Mattis. "Spin up our gun batteries. Target the enemy cap ship. Order all ships to engage that vessel. Target their mass driver. Try to overwhelm the shields in that area so we can punch through." He gripped the armrests on his captain's chair. "This time we're making *sure* they aren't getting their shot in."

Streams of gunfire leapt away from the *Midway*, all their shells converging at the bent and damaged rails. Blue discs of energy blocked the shells and none slipped through. Damn. This one's shields were stronger, as one might expect for a much larger ship. Mattis zoomed in on his command console. He could see thousands of automated drones working away at the rails. Bending them back into shape. Welding and cutting and fixing.

"Keep firing," said Mattis. "Bring the frigates and the Earth Defense Fleet into this. Hell, get whatever's left of Goalkeeper firing, too—those damn robots are too stupid to consider focus firing on a fixed point. We'll have to guide them. Slave their targeting systems to ours."

"Aye aye," said Lynch. "Firing."

Another barrage flew out, this time joined by similar shots from a dozen ships. Nearly a hundred shells slammed into the cap ship's ventral racks. The light of the shield flashes was like a miniature blue sun, forcing Mattis to squint, washing the monitor out.

When he opened his eyes fully and the view returned to normal, the rails were gone. All that was left was their mountings and a few meters of twisted, broken metal.

"Again," said Mattis, a surge of adrenaline blasting away his resurgent lethargy. "Repeat that last barrage. Keep shooting."

The *Midway* rumbled, loudly complaining as they became a target for the enemy ships, those red lines of hostile fire slamming into their hull, carving out bits of it.

This time, Lynch's voice carried a certain urgency. "Admiral, we have a major hull breach on the forward section. We are losing atmosphere."

It was the third battle the *Midway* had been involved in, in short succession. Most of the damage they had suffered had been patched haphazardly, or not at all. There was only so much their damage control teams could do. "Seal those sections," he ordered. "And dispatch evacuation crews. Make sure the crew get out." That was protocol, but as Mattis looked over the readouts, he knew the truth.

Nobody had survived.

A third barrage of fire roared toward the alien cap ship, more than half the shells skipping past the shield and striking the vulnerable underside. Yet the ship held. Tougher than its brethren.

A half-dozen white flashes burst all around them, and the bridge was illuminated by the glare.

"Report!" said Mattis, shielding his eyes.

The white light faded.

"Sir," said Lynch. "There are six vessels joining the battle."

"Reinforcements for the aliens?" he asked, dreading the answer.

"No, sir," said Lynch, his voice charged. "They're squawking Chinese signals."

Chapter Sixty-One

Lt. Patricia "Guano" Corrick's Warbird
Hangar Bay
USS Midway

Guano hadn't saved Ganymede. She'd failed.

Her combat landing was perfect, as though whatever trance she was in had allowed her to touch down without error. She'd been the first to get her ship in. With the destruction of Ganymede Colony replaying over and over in her mind, she sat in her fighter for agonizing minutes, until they were finally ordered to launch again.

In reverse order. So she was now last. Right next to Joker.

"What a bummer," said Flatline, as another wave of their strike craft flew out into space, joining the fight. "Just having to sit here. We really won the lottery."

"Actually," said Guano, "winning the lottery is far *less* likely. Like, okay, trying to win the lottery to get rich, right? It's like trying to kill yourself, flying commercial exosphere shuttlecraft."

"Yeah." Flatline tapped on the back of her seat with his foot. "I'm just trying to pass the time."

She appreciated it, but there was no point. The view through the open hangar doors was enough. Even that tiny window offered a beautiful, and terrifying, view of the battle outside. White streaks of cannon fire like falling stars, red streaks crisscrossing the black of space, and sparkling fields of debris flying in every direction.

Minutes passed. Wings of craft went out. Finally, it was her turn.

"Let's do this," said Joker. "C'mon, let's get out there!"

Guano couldn't agree more. "Hotel-1 requests permission to launch," she said. *Hotel.* So far down the list it was almost an insult.

"Not so fast," said Roadie, his voice carrying a strange, mysterious air to it. "Guano, I got a special mission for you."

Chapter Sixty-Two

Bridge
USS Midway

No matter what they threw at the alien cap ship, it kept coming. Their shield had burned out completely—the barrages of fire the fleet sent its way all speared in, finding the hole in the hull and puncturing through into the inner workings of the vessel. And yet, as mighty as their attacks seemed to be, the ship absorbed as much of that punishment as they were willing to deal out.

So it was time for the coup de grace. "Ready torpedoes," said Mattis. "Aim for their underbelly. Get ready to sink that bastard once and for all."

"Torpedoes loading," said Commander Pitt. "Stand by."

"Fire when ready," said Mattis, chewing on the end of his cigar, teeth digging in, the taste of tobacco on his lips.

Mattis's command console flashed an angry red. The *Paul Revere* had been hit, and hit bad, by the looks of it. Its superstructure was burning, a white cloud of leaking atmosphere drifting into space.

"Report," he asked Lynch, anticipating the man's question, his heart in his throat. "The *Paul Revere*?"

Lynch spent a moment reading, and then looked up, ashen faced. "One of the light cruisers nailed them with a mass-driver shot. It went straight through their superstructure, sir. Right to their core."

Their bridge. "Get Fisher on the line," said Mattis. "I want to talk to them. Make sure they're okay."

Sadly, Lynch shook his head. "The connection won't even authenticate. Scanning." He grimaced. "I'm sorry, sir. The shot went straight into the bridge, and beyond. They're gone."

Mattis closed his eyes for a moment. When he opened them, the *Revere* was, amazingly, still firing. "Hail anyone on that ship. Who's ordering those guns to fire?"

Lynch tapped at his console for a second, and then a panicked, youthful voice filled his earpiece. "Hello? Hello?"

"Calm down, son," he said, putting on his best CO's voice. "This is Admiral Mattis. Who do I have?"

"Uh, Petty Officer Clevon Price, Admiral."

"Price. Who's in command over there?"

"I don't know, sir!" The man's voice became shrill. "Nobody's answering their comms, nobody's talking to us, we can't raise the bridge—"

"Calm down." Mattis had seen this kind of thing before in the heat of battle. Everyone lost their damn minds. That was, after all, why ships had officers. To keep order, to give the orders, and to project a calming presence that allowed everyone else to function.

The *Paul Revere* needed a new captain. Mattis's eyes flicked, almost subconsciously, to Commander Pitt. Some unspoken communication occurred between them, a signal of their mutual understanding.

"Sir," said Commander Pitt slowly, "request permission to go aboard the *Paul Revere* and assume command."

Mattis smiled. Commander Pitt had performed admirably this whole mission, despite extremely adverse conditions…and Mattis had practically stolen the ship from him. It was time he had his own command. "Nobody more deserving," he said. "Get a shuttle and go. I'll have one of the remaining fighters escort you across."

"Wait," said Senator Pitt. Mattis had almost forgotten he was there. The man gestured to the screens scattered around the bridge. "Look at that! In case you have forgotten, Admiral, there's a battle raging out there!"

Mattis ground his teeth and ignored Pitt Senior. "Get to the shuttle," he said. "Maintain discipline. Establish order. Assume command. Take a small cadre of junior officers with you to help. That is all."

"Over my dead body!" shouted Senator Pitt. "He'll be killed out there!"

Commander Pitt's lips drew themselves into a thin line, his face tightening as he tried to conceal his excitement, excitement that was married to fear, but also pride. He straightened his shoulders and gave a crisp salute. "Yes, sir. Thank you, sir. I won't let you down."

"I know you won't."

With that, and with barely a glance at his father, Commander Pitt practically sprinted out of the bridge.

Mattis touched his earpiece. "Petty Officer Price, stand by. A new CO has been dispatched from the *Midway*, my own XO as a matter of fact."

Relief flooded his ear. "Yes, sir!"

Senator Pitt gave him a withering glare, but Mattis was happy for his XO. Yet whatever brief time he had to celebrate ended with a call from Lynch.

"Sir, the alien flagship is moving into a firing position on Earth."

A worrying call, but one he wasn't too concerned about. "Good luck without their mass driver."

Lynch shook his head. "Sir, it's charging up anyway. It's still gaining energy, just like as if it was going to fire…"

As they watched, the whole top of the alien ship blew off, detaching itself and floating off into the void, tumbling as it drifted away.

Revealing a whole mass-driver gun, loaded and charging.

The fucking ship had two mass drivers.

Lord help them all.

Chapter Sixty-Three

Lt. Patricia "Guano" Corrick's Warbird
Hangar Bay
USS Midway

"Special mission?" Guano fiddled with her throttle, yearning to open it and join the battle raging just out the window. "What's that?"

"Stand by for instructions," said Roadie. In the background, she could hear gunfire and the warble of the missile lock alarm. Damn guy was getting all the kills.

"Roger that," said Guano. "Cooling my heels in the hangar bay."

Time ticked away, seconds turning into almost a full minute. Roadie accumulated another victory, a guns kill. His fifth. Now he was an ace too. A thought crossed her mind. That wasn't it, was it? He wasn't trying to keep her in the *Midway* so he could get the most victories, and claim the title of the *Midway*'s chief ace?

Pilots could be awfully petty about these kinds of things, but Roadie was a great CO. He was stern but fair, and always tried to encourage his pilots to do their very best. He wouldn't jack all the glory for himself. It wasn't his style.

Was it?

Finally, Roadie spoke to her again. "Apologies for the delay, Guano. A shuttle is leaving the *Midway*, designation Zulu-1. Aboard it is Commander Pitt. The USS *Paul Revere* has suffered significant damage and requires a new Commanding Officer. Your mission is as follows: launch with Joker and that shuttle and protect it as it makes its way toward the *Paul Revere*, and then again on its return journey. When its mission is complete, join the engagement."

Joker practically vomited into the microphone. "Are you serious? Are you *serious*? Escort duty? No way."

Roadie's tone turned sour. "Don't fuck with me right now, Joker. I'm serious. Escort that shuttle."

"This is bullshit," said Flatline right behind her. "C'mon. We're all reloaded, refueled, rearmed. Let's get back out there. We have a full compliment of guns and missiles. Let's do this!"

Guano clenched her teeth, ready to shout and scream and protest, agreeing with Flatline and Joker—but then, just as it had before, the battle-calm came over her, and her anger evaporated. "This is Hotel-1, we are ready for launch and escort duty."

"What?" shouted Flatline.

"No way!" said Joker, her tone incredulous. "Unreal."

But she was ready. The shuttle lifted off. Guano fell into formation with it, sliding onto its wing. The three ships drifted out of the hangar bay. Shuttles were so much slower than fighters. The three of them turned toward the *Paul Revere*, the burning ship growing gradually closer in her cockpit.

Their charge flew at almost a snail's pace, drifting among the debris, past the occasional red streak and stray cannon shell. She took the opportunity to get a good look around. It was beautiful, in a strange way. Like watching a fireplace on a warm winter's eve.

"Zulu-1," said Guano, "be careful of that debris field."

"No worries," said their pilot, an excited-sounding man with a thick Asian accent. She didn't know him. Utility drivers and fighter pilots didn't mix. "We're going around it. Thanks for the cover."

They weren't doing anything at all but flying straight and level. It felt wrong to accept the guy's thanks, but she should reply to his transmission. "Acknowledged. Don't worry, buddy, we got you."

The shuttle docked. Guano and Joker fell into a protective formation, turning slow circles around the USS *Paul Revere*, but none of the alien craft came close to them—they had probably discounted the *Revere* as a burning wreck.

Zulu-1 undocked, and then the three of them began the slow trundle back to the *Midway*.

"Holy shit," said Flatline, his voice stressed. "I can't believe they pulled us out to escort this guy."

"He's a VIP," said Guano, still basking in the unnatural calm. "They want their best guarding him. Same reason you want your best pilots to be your instructors, not combat personnel. Because you want your strength to grow, not decline. Roadie picking us is a compliment."

"Man," said Joker, "fuck compliments. I'd rather get into

this fight, not babysit a shuttle."

"I can hear you, you know," said Zulu-1.

Guano studied her radar instead of engaging with the chatter. The Chinese had sent reinforcements, a bunch of ships now flagged as allied on her screen. They seemed to be tipping the odds.

The rest of the trip back to the *Midway*, a trip taken through the writhing maelstrom of battle, was almost soothing to her. She stifled a yawn.

Zulu-1 disappeared back into the *Midway*'s hull, and she was free to engage.

Chapter Sixty-Four

Hangar Bay
USS Paul Revere

Looking at the dismal state of the tiny hangar bay, bereft of strike craft, Commander Jeremy Pitt had never felt such *presence* in himself. He adjusted his heavy space suit and beckoned the four officers behind him to follow. Two Ensigns, and two Junior Lieutenants. Just kids, really, but better than nothing.

He strode over to the airlock, cycled through it, and stepped into the ship proper. His air safety indicator told him he could remove his helmet, and he did so.

The moment the air hit his nostrils, he regretted that. The ship stank of burning wire, melted plastic, and roast pork, and Pitt was confident they were not organizing a cookout.

"Let's go," he said, clipping the helmet back on.

"Sir?" asked Junior Lieutenant Cloe Burnett. "Shouldn't we change into our uniforms?"

He didn't have an easy way of telling them about the stink of the ship, and it was best that he didn't upset the junior crewmen. "Best we stay suited. We don't know many of these rooms have pressure, and if they're going to stay that way."

"Aye aye, sir," said Burnett, eyes darting around in the smoke-filled corridors. She looked for all the world like a scared little mouse.

"This way," said Pitt boldly. He wasn't *entirely* sure of the direction—the layout of most ships was similar, with the bridge at their heart and the auxiliary CIC toward the rear— but officer school had taught him well: confidence was contagious.

The five of them strode into the rear of the ship, Pitt leading the way. They passed several areas that had obvious battle damage, and several shaken crewmen, but curiously absent was weapons fire. The aliens, possibly believing them to be destroyed, were ignoring them.

Time to change that perception.

Soon, they reached the CIC. It had been abandoned. The crew within sealed themselves into the escape pods but, bizarrely, they hadn't launched yet. A response to panic. Nobody wanted to be the first one to abandon ship, but they'd probably forgotten that, once sealed, the pods couldn't be opened again from the inside.

No worries.

"There," said Pitt. "Ensign Ward, take the helm. Ensign Sexton and Lieutenant Haney, you're on weapons. Haney, if you need to navigate, move between them. And Burnett"—he gave a cheeky smile—"hope you're ready to help me work this ship, XO."

Everyone was being thrust way, way above their experience level—most of these kids had only been at their "duty posts" when the *Midway* was in dock, and Burnett hadn't been in command of anything more complicated than a coffee machine—but they all took to their assigned roles with courage and gusto, sitting in seats that still had the original owners looking on. Pitt shrugged over his shoulder. They didn't have the keys necessary to open the pods and couldn't spare the time to cut them all open.

The *Paul Revere* was so similar to the *Midway* in every way that sliding into the command role was as natural as breathing.

"Weapons online," said Haney, at weapons. "I think."

Sexton coughed. "They're definitely online. I'm bringing up a targeting view now." He typed on the keyboard. "Sorry, sir, this kind of thing is usually done on the bridge…"

"I know. Don't apologize. Just get results."

"Yes, sir." Sexton tapped at keys frantically.

There was one thing to do. One important thing. Pitt touched the side of his spacesuit helmet, bringing up a menu, and tapped into the ship's intercom system. "Attention all hands," he said, projecting his best captain's voice. "This is Commander Pitt. I am your new CO. Be advised: we will be rejoining the battle imminently. Be prepared. Remain at your stations, do your duty, and I look forward to meeting you all soon."

The silence felt good.

"Sir," said Ward, "communications are up."

"Good, Ensign Ward. Signal the *Midway*. Tell them we've arrived and link fire control computers. Then put me on the line to them. I want to talk to Mattis myself."

"Aye, sir."

Sexton tapped a final key and all the screens around them lit up.

The battle was still raging. The *Paul Revere* floated in the void, ignored by all, surrounded by debris. Goalkeeper flashed wildly, automated turrets firing at capital ships and strike craft alike, its guns slaved to the *Midway*'s systems.

"Lieutenant Burnett," he said. "Prepare to re-engage the enemy."

Chapter Sixty-Five

Bridge
USS Midway

"Shit," said Mattis, staring in confusion and anger at the top of the alien cap ship. "They have a second gun."

"The lower part of the ship probably had a similar cover," said Modi, whom Mattis had utterly forgotten was still there. "It would have been jettisoned during the attack on Capella, most likely. Look at the way it's shaped, and try to imagine that it was clipped on the underside too—"

"Fascinating," said Mattis, trying to shut him up, "but we should do something about it."

"I concur."

For once, Mattis completely agreed. "All ships, all ships, target the cap ship. Give them everything. Mister Pitt"—he wasn't here anymore—"Mister Lynch, rather, patch me into the Chinese fleet."

Almost immediately, a chattering voice speaking Mandarin

filled his ear. "Lynch, autotranslate, please."

The computer turned Chinese into English and vice versa, but it always did it with a cold, dispassionate air that, at least to him, was a little disconcerting. "This is Admiral Mattis," he said, keeping his speech slow so as to be easily translated. "Engage the gravity pulse drives. Ensure they are targeting the mass driver's projectile."

"That's the comet, right?" said the computer, translating for one of the Chinese captains a fraction of a second after he spoke.

"That's right," said Mattis. "Big ball of ice is the target. We need all eight ships to be firing the gun at maximum power. All eight of them, you understand?"

"Lucky eight," said the Chinese captain in the computer's voice. "Ready."

Mattis watched his screen intently. "Steady," he said, hoping that such a command would be translated well. "Steady. Watch for the flash."

Then it came, a white light as bright as a searchlight from the ship's dorsal rails, and the comet was flung down toward Earth, a visible tail erupting as soon as it emerged into sunlight.

"Now!" Mattis affixed his eyes on the mass. It was traveling slower than expected, even right from the moment it launched, leaving a long icy tail behind it. "Modi, velocity of that mass."

Right as he issued the command, he noticed the object slowing visibly. An optical illusion? Or maybe the top system was a weaker backup. Or—

He had no time to worry about such things.

"One hundred twenty kilometers a second," said Modi. "One hundred ten, one five…"

It was slowing. But it was also getting awfully close to Earth. Space was big and the distances involved were huge, but even 37,000 kilometers would get eaten up quickly by something traveling that fast.

"Ninety. Eighty. Another gravity pulse is joining the original eight, sir, to great effect. Fifty. Twenty. Sir, the mass is starting to break up."

He could see that. All the rapid acceleration and deceleration couldn't be good for it. But the pieces that were coming off were mostly fragments, small enough to either burn up in the atmosphere or cause minimal damage if they did land. As long as it was one largely contiguous piece, they would be fine.

"Son of a bitch," said Mattis, pride growing in his voice. "It's working."

"The mass is now stationary," said Modi. "More or less."

The imprecision was appreciated. "Keep pushing," said Mattis, seized with a sudden idea. "Throw the damn thing back against them. We had the energy to slow it right to a stop. We should be able to speed it right *up*, shouldn't we?"

"Math checks out," said Modi, nodding his approval. "Package marked return to sender. Object is reversing at twenty kilometers a second. Thirty. Forty…"

A flash out of the corner of his eye caught his attention. One of the Chinese ships burst from within, its gravity pulse signal winking out. The whole stern broke away, careening into another frigate, the second doomed ship cracking in a spiderweb, atmosphere leaking from the cracks.

"Sir," said Modi, an alarmed edge growing in his voice. "The object is decelerating again. The aliens are pushing it back to Earth."

Chapter Sixty-Six

Bridge
USS Midway

Seven Chinese ships. Seven wasn't enough. Mattis touched his earpiece. "We need more pushers," he said, eyes fixed on that huge mass, watching it tumble end over end, slowly coming to a halt once more.

"Translation error," said the computer in his ear.

Dammit. He tried again, slower. "We need more ships to engage. You hear me? More gravity pulse weapons. Go."

"Only one more ship with the weapon aboard," said one of the Chinese captains. "And then that's it."

"Okay," said Mattis, drumming his fingers on his armrest. "So do it."

A brief pause. "It's not that simple," said the Chinese captain. "We haven't finished linking it to the others yet."

Slowly, inexorably, the mass began to move back toward Earth, its long tail streaming out to one side, pointing away from the intense, piercing light of the sun. It really did look like a massive comet. "How can I help?"

"The work is being done by damage control teams," said the Chinese captain. "But if we can have a ship cover us, we can work faster."

He knew just the man for the job. "Commander—no, *Captain* Pitt," he asked, pointedly stressing the *Captain* part, "are you listening in?"

Senator Pitt's eyes widened slightly, but he said nothing.

"Just got comms working over here," said Captain Pitt, sounding almost like a proud Texan, as if Lynch had rubbed off on him. His blood must *really* be up. "What do y'all need?"

In command for less than ten minutes and already asking what he could do for someone else. "One of our Chinese friends is experiencing distress," said Mattis. "And if we can't get that ship back into the fight, we're going to have a hard time pushing the mass driver projectile back where it belongs. Can you move out there with the *Revere* and give them some coving fire?"

"Can do," said Pitt.

"Try to do it without killing yourself," said Mattis, taking a deep breath. "We need the Chinese to come through for us on this one."

"I'll do my best, Admiral."

The absolute sincerity in his voice gave Mattis confidence. "Godspeed, son. You're a credit to your uniform."

Now, all Mattis had to do was keep the rest of the fleet alive until he got there.

Chapter Sixty-Seven

CIC
USS Paul Revere

Captain Pitt adjusted his space suit and increased the oxygen. He was breathing heavily. Time to focus. Time to get it done. "We got a mission," he said to his bridge crew—and although they were recent transplants from the *Midway,* that was truly how he saw them—putting all other considerations out of his head. "Let's make it happen."

"Aye aye, Captain," said Burnett, folding her hands behind her back in a way that *perfectly* reminded him of himself. "Ensign Ward, bring us forward and up, positioning the *Revere* between the cap ship and the damaged Chinese ship. Ensign Sexton, Lieutenant Haney, we're going to need fire laid down on the closest alien light cruiser—make them look at us. We're pretty." She did so well, but right at the very end, her eyes flicked to him for approval.

"Couldn't have done it better myself," said Captain Pitt

genuinely. He felt the ship move beneath them—there must have been some kind of problem with the artificial gravity generators, normally used to dull inertia—and then rise, his weight intensifying, the suit suddenly like it were made of lead. He held out as long as he could, and the sensation faded quickly. "Well done."

Lieutenant Haney tapped at keys on her keyboard. "Dammit," she hissed. "Sorry, sir, I disabled inertial compensation by accident. Stand by. This console is different from what I'm used to."

It was understandable. "Here," said Sexton, pointing. "Right here. The red one." Then he pointed somewhere else. "Wait, I think it's this one, Lieutenant."

Haney pressed it, and fire retardant foam sprayed down from the ceiling, splattering over everything. Including the visor of his suit. Captain Pitt wiped the stuff away from his visor with as much dignity as he could muster.

"I think," said Sexton, "it was the first one."

Haney pressed the first button. "Sorry, sir. The disruptions should stop from now on."

"Very good," said Captain Pitt. "Status on the maneuver?"

"Going well," said Sexton. "We're almost in position."

His comm chirped. "This is Mattis," came his former CO's voice, a grave edge to it. "We got a problem."

"Send it," he said.

"The Chinese ship reports they won't be able to get their gravity pulse weapon fixed any time soon, so they're scuttling the boat." The bitterness in his voice was palpable. "I think that's game."

Captain Pitt considered. "How much force does the sucker

need to push it?" he asked.

"More than we can give with the gravity pulses," said Mattis. "It's eight, pushed to the max. Seven just won't cut it. They're overstretched as it is."

It was simpler to just go straight to the source. "Put Modi on the line, please. I got a plan."

A little bit of futzing around on the other end—probably difficult to get that damn robot to talk to someone on the other end of the line, or something—and then finally he heard him.

"This is—"

"I know who it is," snapped Captain Pitt. "Listen, you chowder head, I need to know: how much velocity are we missing?"

"Five kilometers a second per second," he said, as easily as though he were reciting the weather. "We're missing acceleration, not velocity. Acceleration depends on—"

"No physics lecture is necessary," said Captain Pitt. "These frigates are fast, right?" He paused. "I don't suppose you know the speed of one of these ships off the top of your head, do you?"

"Of course," said Modi, sounding vaguely offended. "Six kilometers a second per second, at full sublight and thrusters." Captain Pitt could almost hear the gears turning over in the guy's head. "You aren't seriously considering—"

"I am," said Captain Pitt, flicking foam off his fingers. "Is it possible?"

Modi hesitated. "Such an act will heavily damage the front of the ship."

Captain Pitt had become quite attached to the *Paul Revere*

in the short time he had come aboard, but knew, ultimately, the ship was disposable. "Eh, it's a rental."

"But yes…in theory."

He'd heard enough. Captain Pitt closed the connection and gestured to Sexton. "You heard all that, right?"

Sexton nodded. "Already maneuvering, sir. The mass is stationary, so it's an easy target."

"All hands," he said, "brace for impact." Another glance at Sexton. "A *gentle* impact, please."

Captain Pitt watched as the ship shifted, this time with no distortions, coming up behind the mass. It was broken, fractured, but still one contiguous lump, which would serve them fine. It grew on his screens, larger and larger, until it swallowed the black at the edges and all they could see was the rock.

"Captain Pitt," said Mattis in his ear, "I'm moving all my strike craft to your location, giving you extra cover."

He appreciated it. "Thank you, sir. Be advised, we're about to make contact. In three, two, one…" The ship and the rock collided with a roar that rang throughout the ship like a bell, the very deck below their feet rippling with the impact.

"Sir," said Ward, "we're attached."

"All engines full ahead," said Pitt. "Thrusters, sublight, give me everything you got."

"Yes, sir," she said, pushing several buttons all at once.

The *Revere* shuddered, shook, and the mass began to move back toward the alien cap ship.

As Captain Pitt watched, the alien ship lit up with a fiery explosion from its dorsal mass driver, and the force—the invisible hand—the aliens had on the rock disappeared. He felt the ship jerk forward, the comet moving away from them, toward the enemy ship, gaining speed as it moved farther from them.

"We did it," said Sexton, his eyes lighting up. "We did it!"

And then the *Revere*'s port engine exploded.

Chapter Sixty-Eight

Lt. Patricia "Guano" Corrick's Warbird
Hangar Bay
USS Midway

Guano turned her ship toward the dogfight and switched on her targeting radar, the familiar whine filling her ears. The battle was silhouetted against Earth, the whole quadrant of space filled up with the planet, lights and flashing cannon fire of battle framing the world for a brief moment.

Then Roadie called her again, ruining it. "Hey, Guano, you're just in time. Come on, we're forming up around the *Paul Revere*, they need our help."

She was ages away from the *Revere*, being only a hundred meters or so away from the *Midway's* hangar bay. "Maybe you should reconsider that. By the time we get there, the action will be over. There are enough fighters out here for her to be perfectly safe. What's two more?"

"Oh, thank *God*," said Flatline behind her. "Escort this,

escort that… What the hell is wrong with Roadie today?"

"And me, too," said Joker, chiming in. "I'm with Guano right now. Similar situation."

"If you think you can handle it," said Roadie, a little caution creeping in. "Be advised, you two will be acting alone and without support. All other strike craft have been repositioned."

She could take on the whole galaxy right now. "Confirmed. We are both full on missiles and guns, and if I don't give him something to shoot at, Flatline is going to murder me."

"Roger," said Roadie. "Good hunting."

She'd finally, finally, been cut loose. Yet she didn't feel the rush of joy, didn't shout or yell—she just opened her throttle and sped away from the *Midway*, Joker tightly on her wing.

"Let's do this," howled Joker. "I got radar contacts for *days*, my friend!"

Flatline laughed over the line, singing. "Clowns to the left of me, jokers to the right, here I am, stuck in the middle with…bat poo."

Guano normally would join in such levity, but she just… didn't feel it. Cool and even, she lined up four targets for her long-range missiles, firing them all one after the other. She didn't bother to track if they hit or not, but instead, powered up her engines, switching to guns. "Let's get in there," she said.

"Yeah," said Flatline, although he hesitated slightly as he spoke. "Hey, Guano, are you okay? You've been really weird since Ganymede."

"It's fine," she said, speeding toward the alien strike craft. Way too far out for guns, or heat-seeker missiles. She had to get closer. No other way.

"Okay," said Flatline unconvincingly. "Just make sure you get checked out when you get back, okay? Combat Stress Reaction is a real thing."

"This isn't…" She let the sentence trail off. "I'm fine. Let's just kill these guys, yeah?"

Flatline said nothing, which was actually more concerning than anything.

"I'm fine," said Guano again, and then she frowned at her instruments. "Hey, check out the cap ship."

"Mmm?" Flatline tapped on some keys behind her. "What am I looking for?"

She pointed at her screen, even though he couldn't possibly see that. "Their mass driver. It looks like it's emitting a *lot* of heat…straining to push the comet thingie at Earth."

"So?"

"So," she said, clicking her tongue. "We're carrying a full load of *heat*-seeking missiles, and that thing is one giant target, even at this range. And the ship's not moving, so we can hit it…"

"I don't follow," said Flatline.

Idiot. She casually dialed up the range on the missiles, locking in that massive heat signature. It glowed like a beacon in the dark, flashing and pulsing as it tried to cool itself. Must have been nearly a thousand degrees.

"Cover me, Joker," she said, and loosed four missiles, all she had. She fired them all at once, quad streaks leaping away from her ship toward the target.

"You got it," said Joker, pulling up above her, protecting her top.

The missiles traveled toward the cap ship, four little

streams getting smaller and smaller in her cockpit canopy. Guano focused on them, watching them fly straight and true, almost too small to see—and then all four missiles blew, blasting into the side the mass driver.

It wouldn't be enough to destroy it, probably, but it might disable the thing long enough—

"Contact!" shouted Joker, almost making her jump. "Two bogeys, coming in fast, two o'clock high! They're firing!"

Shit. She'd been so fixated on watching the missiles, she hadn't been paying attention. Guano kicked at the rudder, swinging her craft to the left. A dozen red streaks streamed past her cockpit, missing her ship by only a few meters.

"Wait, dammit!" Joker said, hissing as she spoke. "My port gun's jammed! Hang on, coming around!"

"Shit!" shouted Flatline. "I don't see them. I don't see them!"

She didn't see them either. Guano rolled inverted, flipping her ship, pulling the stick back. This was bad. She couldn't dodge what she couldn't see. Cracks began to appear in her calm exterior. This wasn't good, this wasn't...

The flaming wreckage of Joker's ship drifted past her, her ship riddled with holes and missing a wing, fire pouring from the shattered cockpit canopy. She was close enough to see the blood on the glass.

The Dead Man's Hand flashed back into her mind with terrifying clarity.

Guano twisted in her seat, neck on a swivel, trying to find the enemies. She floored it, trying to put some distance between her and the wreckage, and whatever just killed her wingman.

A faint glint above caught her eyes. The enemy fighters, they were right above her, practically in spitting distance. How had they gotten so *close*? Flatline's gun chattered, firing wildly.

"Hang on," she shouted to Flatline, pitching the nose down, and then up again, rolling her ship, dodging another alarmingly close wave of fire. "We're too far out, dammit! So stupid!"

"We have to get back to the *Midway*," said Flatline, gasping from the g-forces. "Their guns can protect us."

"No!" She knew it wouldn't work. They were too close. Shrapnel from their own guns would shred them. "That's stupid!"

"If stupidity got us into this mess, how come it can't get us out, huh?"

She went to answer, but the g-forces stole her words. Guano pulled the ship upward, and she saw a flash of red.

Her Warbird convulsed, throwing itself to one side as a deadly stream of fire caught the rear of the ship, blasting through her hull. Alarms screamed in her ears. She kicked her left foot out at the rudder. Nothing. Kicked the right. Nothing. She shook the stick wildly. Nothing.

Slowly, her ship began to turn over and over, leaving a long trail of smoke behind it, the rear glowing with flame, the starboard engine alight.

"Guano," said Flatline, his voice panicked. "They're coming around again. Fix the ship. Fix it!"

It couldn't be fixed. Not like this. Her ship was a smoking ruin. Her readouts flickered ominously, full of static. She could feel the heat of the fire behind her, radiating through the ship's hull…

Above her, she saw the enemy fighters twist around, bearing down on her disabled craft, their guns glinting in the light of the sun, lit up by flashes from the surrounding space battle, silent predators coming down to finish her. Nothing she could do to save the ship.

Nothing to do but reach down between her legs and yank the ejection handle.

Chapter Sixty-Nine

Bridge
USS Midway

Mattis watched in mute fascination as the comet reversed course, pushed away from Earth by a combination of Chinese ingenuity and American courage, Captain Pitt's ship's engines flaring as hard as they could, creating a second tail for the comet, this one pointed away from Earth.

It got closer and closer, and then smashed into the alien cap ship, traveling at hundreds of kilometers a second. The ship's blue shields tried their best to stop the impact, protesting it feebly, contesting its own demise—but such forces couldn't be resisted. The cap ship burst in a fiery flare, turning the night of space into daytime and casting long shadows over everything, a second sun right in the heart of the battle.

The alien command ship burned and, by God, it was satisfying.

"Got 'em," said Lynch.

"We certainly did." Mattis couldn't fight the massive grin that spread across his face. "That was some mighty fine work, Modi. You did good."

"More correctly," said Modi, his tone completely serious, "I did *well*. Although in this case, given the adversarial nature of the unknown ships, it's likely that we also did *good*."

Mattis let him have that one. He'd earned it. He settled back in his chair, exhaling a breath he didn't realize he'd been holding. He closed his eyes a moment, just a moment, a little bit—

"Wait," said Senator Pitt, pointing at one of the screens accusingly. "Is that my son's ship?"

Eyes open. Job's not done yet. Mattis forced himself to look, despite a sudden wave of fatigue.

The *Paul Revere*, smoke belching from one of its engines, drifted in space. She'd obviously worn herself out. The ship wouldn't get far on half power, but fortunately, Earth had a comprehensive shipyard. They'd be able to get it fixed.

But, as he watched, the readings in the other engine increased, growing in power.

"Captain Pitt, you okay over there?" asked Mattis.

No reply. Their comm system must be out. A swift glance at the radar showed help would be nearby. The Chinese battleship *Jianghu*. The same one who had suffered the malfunction with their gravity device. They were right there.

"USS *Midway* to *Jianghu*," said Mattis. "Our ship, the *Paul Revere*, is in severe distress. We'd appreciate it if you could dock with her and take aboard survivors."

"This is *Jianghu*," came the voice, speaking English, accented but clear. "Stand by."

Chapter Seventy

Bridge
Chinese Flagship Jianghu
High Earth Orbit

Captain Yeung rubbed the stubble on his face, watching the American ship, the USS *Paul Revere*, burn with a significant measure of concern. The Americans had come through for them today. The alien cap ship was floating debris and they largely had the *Midway* and the *Revere* to thank for it.

Time to repay the favor.

"Patch me through to high command," he said to his communications officer. "And get ready to move in and provide aid to our allies."

"Yes, sir," she said, and in a moment, he could hear a faint hissing in his ears.

"This is Captain Yeung of the *Jianghu*," he said. "Request permission to break formation, move in and render—"

"Denied." The woman's voice that came back was flat and

emotionless. "Remain on station."

It took Yeung a second to process that. The request hadn't even been finished, and it was being denied. Surely High Command could see what he could see; they could see the burning ship, listing to one side like a sick beast. The fire on its engines was dangerous. If it reached the reactor core, the ship would become a firework.

"Ma'am," he said, trying again. "I understand—"

"Captain Yeung," said High Command, her tone suddenly venomous. "Is Commander Xiu Yu present?"

He and his XO, Commander Yu, exchanged a brief, incredulous glance. "Yes. She's…uh, right here."

"Captain Yeung, allow me to be perfectly clear: You are hereby ordered by High Command of the People's Republic of China Army Navy to hold your position, to not shift your position for any reason, and specifically, to not assist the floundering American ship in any capacity. You are also ordered to, immediately upon acknowledgement of your orders, commence radio silence until directly relieved by a superior officer. If you violate any part of this request, Commander Yu is ordered to draw her sidearm and immediately relieve you of your command." There was a brief pause. "Acknowledge your orders."

What the hell? mouthed Yu, her eyes wide as moons.

Yeung clenched his fists tightly, his monitors full of the burning American ship. What the *hell* was this? This was an unnecessary cruelty. Letting their allies die just as he had promised to help… It was not just a slight on him, it was a loss of face on the whole People's Republic to let their allies suffer like this. And no other could help. No other ship was close enough. It was the *Jianghu* or nothing.

There should be honor among those who wear the uniform, regardless of country. A nation was just a flag. Letting men die for a piece of cloth struck him as the height of stupidity.

But he had his orders.

"Acknowledged," said Yeung, his voice half bitterness, half regret. "Establishing radio silence."

Chapter Seventy-One

Bridge
USS Midway

As the fire spread along both engines of the *Paul Revere*, Mattis found his patience running out.

"They should be moving by now," he said, for the tenth time. "What are they waiting for?"

"Not sure, sir," said Lynch, staring in confusion at his monitor. "They *did* say they would help."

Mattis avoided looking at Senator Pitt, who was doing his best to catch the eye of anyone foolish enough to glance his way. "Open the channel again," he said. "In fact, broadcast on all channels, all frequencies. I want everyone to hear this." He touched his earpiece. "I say again, mayday mayday mayday, relaying for the USS *Paul Revere*. All craft who can respond, do so immediately."

Yet the Chinese ships, all of them, remained in their formation, their lead vessel so close to the *Revere* that it seemed like she could reach out and touch her. It would be so easy to send over a shuttle or two. That was all that was needed. Just a little bit of help.

Escape pods blasted out of the *Revere*, a sight that filled him with considerable relief. He hadn't seen any launch until then, but the event was proof positive that at least some of the crew would be okay. There was a good chance that Captain Pitt and the *Midway*'s junior staff were aboard one. It was going to be okay.

"Lynch, Modi, scan those escape pods. I want to know if our people are on board any of them."

"I already have been," said Modi. "They have not escaped yet."

The ship continued to burn, the flames trickling down the ship's spine. The minutes ticked away. Another set of pods launched, thin little slivers of metal flying out from the bottom of the *Paul Revere*, a cluster of six.

"Is that them?" asked Mattis.

Right as he did, a bright light grew within the *Paul Revere*, and the whole ship blew itself into atoms, scattering itself over space like a thousand little stars.

Modi looked up from Captain Pitt's old console, right into Mattis's eyes. His answer was blunt.

"No."

Chapter Seventy-Two

Bridge
USS Midway

Mattis stared at the expanding debris cloud, a hardness crossing his heart. There was no evidence to suggest it—just scans which, Modi was quick to remind him, were inconclusive —but somehow he *knew*. It wasn't in Captain Pitt's character to leave before all of his crew were off, even if they had only been his crew for half an hour.

There was no way he got out.

The ships of the Earth fleet were battered, bruised, and fatigued, but the alien cap ship had been blasted to nothingness, scattered across its high Earth orbit like garbage. The smaller ships, leaderless, seemed to lose much of their initiative; they shot randomly at Earth ships, or at nothing, their effectiveness significantly reduced. One jumped away in a flash of light, an action that seemingly inspired the others. They began to turn listlessly, exposing their weak engines, getting ready to leap away to the stars and safety.

It was time for the smaller ships to join their big brother.

"Modi," said Mattis, his tone dark. "I want to check something. The gravity pulse weapon. It emits a continuous beam of energy, yes? A beam strong enough to push huge rocks around?"

"That's right," said Modi.

"Strong enough," asked Mattis, "to turn on the alien ship's shields, keeping them on, draining them, overheating them, so we can put a pair of torpedoes into each ship?"

"That," said Modi, considering for just a second, "seems plausible."

He touched his earpiece. "All ships, this is Admiral Mattis. Focus your gravity pulse generators on the alien craft. Half power, but continuous output. Push them, drive them together, all together, so we can finish them once and for all. Coordinates to follow."

The voices of the fleet, mostly speaking English, some Chinese, echoed in his ears. The notable exception: the *Jianghu*. It hung there in space like a wart, unmoving, worthless. It didn't react to his transmission. Every other ship did. Not them.

Mattis had half a mind to turn his guns on that ship and claim it was an accident, but he didn't.

Gravity pulses leapt out from the seven remaining Chinese ships, latching onto the light cruisers that remained. Blue disks of light sprung up to protect them, shielding their hulls from the invisible waves of force, but the constant barrages hit again and again. The force was enough to move the ships, slowly corralling them, buffeting them off course and out of formation.

The first two collided with a shower of sparks and metal. Their shields trembled like a leaf in the wind, shaking and wobbling, and then winked out. A third ship joined the pile, slamming its bow into them, the metal crumpling with the impact.

Four. Five. Six. Slowly, the surviving alien fleet, minus the one that had escaped, were rounded up like a child playing marbles. Clumped together. Held in place by ghostly, invisible hands, taking out the garbage. The gravity waves pummeled them as they sat there, scrunched up like used newspaper, their guns firing futilely. The distortions blew their red streaks off course, sending them toward the stars.

Space had no air resistance. No friction. Those hyper-accelerated particles would travel onward until they *eventually* struck *something*. Regardless of how many decades, centuries, or tens of millions of years it took. Mattis was watching the whole galaxy, in some minor way, potentially change, just because of a few stray rounds.

"Ready torpedoes," he said, glaring at the pile of twisted metal and broken ships that the Chinese had gathered for them.

A blue light on his command console indicated the weapons were loaded, aimed and ready. Normally, the call would be made across the bridge and his XO would fire them —that way, everyone was clear about what actions were being taken by who, so that the relevant parties could be notified— but his XO was dead, now, wasn't he?

Mattis pressed the button himself, watching with savage satisfaction as the twin missiles leapt off toward their target.

Similar streaks flew from the ships in the rest of the fleet, massive nuclear-tipped missiles that struck in waves, flashes of white light obliterating the ships, pounding them into dust, leaving absolutely nothing to show they were ever there.

He pumped his fist in the air as the monitors cleared, showing only empty space filled with occasional spinning debris.

"Sir," said Lynch, the man's fatigue suddenly clear, slurring his words. "We're detecting dozens of active escape pods, along with one of our ejected pilots with her gunner. Their vitals are strong, sir, but there's a lot of radiation and debris floating about. We should prioritize their retrieval."

He nodded, sinking back into his chair. "Dispatch the SAR bird," he said. "Pick up our pilots, then secure the other escape pods." Bitterness found its way to his tongue. "Don't let the Chinese pick them up. American forces only. You got that?"

"Yes, sir," said Lynch.

For the first time since the *Revere*'s fiery end, Mattis looked over to Senator Pitt. The man stood there like a tree, rooted in place, unmoving, unblinking, staring at the monitor.

Perhaps, as though sensing Mattis's eyes upon him, the man slowly turned and faced him, his body weird and rigid, almost unnatural.

"You'll pay for this," said Senator Pitt, his tone the flat, empty, hollow voice of a man making a...not even a threat, or a promise. Merely an observation. "You killed my son. Directly, or indirectly, you *killed* him. And you'll pay."

"Get him out of here," said Lynch.

Marines once again took Senator Pitt off the bridge, but this time, there was no struggle. No resistance. He went willingly, calmly, without fighting.

Silent and exhausted, victorious but left with a vague empty feeling in his chest, Mattis watched the debris field slowly expand on his monitors, a billion tiny sparkles spreading farther out, the force of the terrific explosions scattering the debris across the whole solar system.

Victory.

Chapter Seventy-Three

High Earth Orbit
Space

Guano woke up spinning gently in space, her head throbbing like it had a spike through it. She was surrounded by debris, the blown-up remnants of her ship, and below her, Earth.

The blue marble. A beautiful, fragile ball floating in space. The sun was high over Africa and Europe, with the dawn line just past Morocco. The golden white of the Sahara was so bright, so daunting.

It was peaceful. Quiet. No sound except the beeping of her emergency locater beacon and her own soft breathing.

Slowly, groggily, she remembered how she'd gotten here.

Oh shit. Flatline! She fumbled for the transmit key on her wrist.

"Hey, anyone out there?"

"Corrick!" shouted Flatline, his breathing heavy. "Holy

shit, I thought you were dead. You weren't answering your comms. Jesus, don't scare me like that."

She was groggy but okay. Being knocked unconscious was a typical risk of ejection. And a fairly substantial number of ejections resulted in death. But it was better than the alternative: becoming part of the debris field that floated all around her.

"Where are you?" she asked.

"In space," said Flatline. "What do you want me to say? There's no landmarks out here."

She tried to locate him, but all she could see was debris. Guano squinted through the fog of her aching head, trying to spot him.

And then she saw a faint glint, and a white-suited guy outlined against the black. He wouldn't have been able to see her, since she was silhouetted by the Earth, but she could see him.

That was enough to make her smile.

Then, behind her, a spotlight turned on. A shuttle that had been retasked for SAR.

"This is Zulu-1," said a transmission in her ear, a familiar accented voice making her chuckle. "Time to repay the favor, Guano."

"Make it fast," she said as the shuttle turned around, opening its rear doors, backing up to swallow her.

"Don't forget me," protested Flatline.

She slipped into the ship's interior, grabbing a hold bar to keep her in place. "Onboard," she said. "Don't worry, buddy. We're coming to get you."

"Great," said Flatline. "Um. I guess that means we won?"

"Yup," said Zulu-1. "We won."

Awesome.

Epilogue

Arlington National Cemetery
Virginia
United States of America
Five weeks later

"And so," said President Schuyler, reading from a small crumpled piece of paper Mattis could barely see at this distance, "we discovered we were not alone in this universe."

President Schuyler. A short, blond woman with a slight frame and skin seemingly too pale to be outside. Yet here she was, on an overcast Virginia day, a US Marine holding an umbrella for her as she spoke.

"As was typical, when one civilization met another, there was bloodshed. And some of our finest women and men, members of the United States Navy, stood ready to shield us from this cost. Two of our starships were lost, with substantial casualties, and fifteen strike craft. Every ship involved in the battle suffered some kind of damage, and every ship involved, regardless of size, has crewmen being buried here today.

"Yet not a single person who stood on this planet during

these calamitous events was harmed. Despite the debris falling to Earth, despite the attempts of the aliens to destroy us…not a single civilian on our world was injured. We were shielded by our service personnel in orbit—shielded, in some cases, very literally. They paid in blood, willingly, so that we did not have to."

The President paused. The only noises were the wind moving through the grass, and the distant *crack* of rifles as another ceremony was getting underway.

"Unfortunately," said President Schuyler, "the Sino-American War was not the last war we will have to fight, but at least, this time, we'll fight it together. I would like to acknowledge our allies, the People's Republic of China, for their brave contributions to our cause, as well as their losses. For Captain Shao. For Admiral Yim. For all they are burying today, and other days.

"And I would also like to honor Captain Caitlin Salt of the Royal Space Navy for her heroic actions, actions which, directly, cost her her life. So rarely is so much asked of so humble a command, but Captain Salt showed us all the strength of mankind. Our courage."

Another pause. Mattis closed his eyes, thinking of Salt. Thinking of Shao. It had been weeks, and yet the events of the battle seemed to be just yesterday. It was difficult to believe they were all gone.

"We will bury more souls in the future," said President Schuyler. "I know this. We have won a battle, but not a war. We do not know where these attackers came from, or if more remain, so we must prepare for the possibility that more war is coming. That strife and conflict will rear its head once more.

No one can tell me otherwise. But I am dedicated, as your Commander in Chief, to ensuring that we defeat this threat, should it ever return. And we shall meet them with our allies, with new weapons, and with an endless determination and upright zeal."

She lowered her piece of paper and seemed, almost, to be looking directly at him. "The enemy may come, but they will not find us wanting."

The crowd clapped. Mattis did as well, politely. He'd been at so many of these funerals. His hands hurt. But this one, this one he clapped louder for. This one was special.

This one was for Commander Jeremy Pitt.

More words were said. Wreaths were laid. Mattis did his duty, quietly and respectfully waiting for the job to be done. If Senator Pitt was here, burying his son, there was no sign of him.

With the coffin lowered into the ground and the rifles fired, Mattis took his coat and prepared to leave.

"Just a moment." A man wearing dark glasses, a fancy suit, and a conspicuous earpiece held up his hand. "The President wants to speak with you."

Does she, indeed? Mattis had seen her at so many of these dedications—they were called dedications, often, because there was no body to bury—but they had not yet spoken. From the crowd, she emerged, flanked by two towering bodyguards. Surprisingly, she stepped away from the guards and, with simply the two of them, she led him away from the crowd, holding the umbrella over both of them.

"Madam President," said Mattis. "We finally meet in person."

"We do," said President Schuyler, inclining her head respectfully. "I wanted to take a moment to thank you, personally, Admiral, for everything you did during these tragic and tumultuous events. An excellent campaign, well fought."

Had it been? Mattis couldn't say the same, but he knew he had to maintain a certain level of politeness. "If you say so, Madam President. A pity about the…secretiveness of our allies, and their reluctance to help the *Paul Revere*, right when they had saved us all."

"Things," said President Schuyler simply, "are more complicated than they seem. I share your pain, Admiral, and believe me, I am investigating with all the resources at my disposal."

"I hope that's enough," said Mattis. Maybe some of his disappointed sarcasm made it through. Maybe.

She considered, folding her clipboard under her arm. "I understand that it might have seemed," she said, at length, "that I was not as supportive of your efforts as I could have been. That, at certain times, such as when your ship was at Ganymede, I did not help you as much as you might think I could have."

Mattis kept his mouth shut, and she obviously seemed to take that as what it was.

"I couldn't send ships. Simply couldn't. And it turned out to be a good thing, too, because Earth needed them. But I got Spectre to deliver something else. The gravity pulse device which, ultimately, won the day." President Schuyler looked away for a moment, to the sea of white gravestones. "I hope that's worth something to you."

Again, Mattis said nothing.

"You should know," said President Schuyler, clicking her tongue, "that Senator Pitt hasn't forgiven you. He's assembled a veritable army of lawyers from six states to take you down. To get you thrown off the *Midway*, off the service, and even attempt to get you deported to Canada, if you can believe, under some strange, archaic law that's been on the books since 1831."

"I'm not afraid of Senator Pitt," said Mattis.

President Schuyler affixed him with a firm stare. "You should be."

He said nothing, and she waited.

"Is there anything else, ma'am?" asked Mattis, curious.

"There is," said President Schuyler, seemingly at odds with how to say it. "The lone alien ship that escaped."

"Yes," said Mattis. "I do recall."

"Two days ago, the USS *Guam* tracked it down and, with twenty other ships, destroyed it." She weighed her next words carefully. "Under my explicit orders, they were told to disable it using conventional weapons fire only—no nukes. No gravity pulse weapons. Accordingly, substantial wreckage was recovered."

Potentially a huge source of intelligence. Or technology. Or—a thought hit him like a thunderbolt. "You've *seen them*," said Mattis, suddenly understanding what she was going on about. "You recovered an alien body."

"That's just the thing," said President Schuyler, her blond hair swaying in the gentle breeze. "They did tests on the most intact corpse recovered, which showed that parts of the mitochondrial DNA of these beings… Well, it suggests that they're…" She reached up and pushed a stray lock of hair out of her eyes. "They're *human*. Human, but from approximately one thousand years in the future… near as we can tell from extrapolating from the changes in their DNA. They're as far removed from us, and as close to us, as we are to people who lived in the Middle Ages."

"They're from," asked Mattis skeptically, "the *future*, ma'am?"

She adjusted her tie. "I wouldn't be telling you this if the best available evidence we have didn't support it. To be honest, much of the science is beyond me, but I have been told other parts of the DNA are human as well, but highly corrupted. Some of it is totally unrecognizable. The significance of this is not yet known at this time." She withdrew a thin tablet, handing it to him.

Displayed on the screen, washed out, slightly out of focus, was the image of a humanoid form labeled *Sample A*. Black and blue and sickly green, as though crafted out of rotten mold. Its skin was mottled, misshapen, deformed; it resembled a monster from an old zombie flick, skin drooping and withered, teeth jutting out at strange angles. Horrifying to look at but distinctly, in some way, human.

President Schuyler pocketed the tablet again.

He let that information sink in. Humans…from the future? That looked like *that*? The mere fact the President had voiced this seemingly ludicrous conclusion to him, shown him the picture, proved that she, on some level, trusted him. Trusted him not to run to the press with this information. Or just laugh and laugh and laugh.

That trust should be returned. If only slightly. What she had said was true—the gravity device had allowed them to defeat the aliens, in the end. "Thank you for the weapon," said Mattis, inclining his head respectfully. "That gadget turned the tide."

A ghost of a smile. "You're welcome. Good job out there, Admiral," said President Schuyler.

Mattis turned to leave, but she reached out and touched his arm.

"One more thing." Her expression tightened. "I mentioned the possibility of war. I'm saying it to everyone I can, in vague terms, but that ship, Mattis? The one that got away? It sent a signal. Outbound. Deep into the void. It was a Z-space transmission, but it didn't have any words. It was something else."

"What was it?" asked Mattis, suddenly uncomfortable in his uniform, as though it were a little too tight.

"It was a Z-space *beacon*. The same kind we use to navigate. It was a rallying cry." Her eyes caught his, as though trying to communicate a serious matter. "More are coming. I'm sure of it."

Maybe it was the cool air, or maybe it wasn't, but Mattis felt a distinct chill run down his spine. "I…can't help but agree."

"Mmm. So you see, Admiral Mattis, I am confident we will have further need for your skills in the future." She gestured for her bodyguards to come, and then, wrapping her coat around her to shield herself from the rain, the President departed.

Mattis wandered back to Commander Pitt's grave. By the time he got there, everyone else had disappeared. Gone back to their lives.

He caught a brief glimpse of Senator Pitt, in the distance, about to get into a waiting cab. Their eyes met, and Mattis felt the man's gaze burn into him. The palpable hatred. The barely contained fury. Then he got into the car, slammed the door, and Mattis was alone.

The wind picked up slightly. He, too, pulled his coat tighter around him and, after a pause, made his way toward his car. Chuck was there, cradling a beautiful baby in his hands. Jack, his grandson, who he was just getting to know.

The sight should have made him smile, but the farther he got away from the cemetery, the more he could not shake a strange feeling that, every step of the way, he was being watched.

Thank you for reading *The Last War*.

Sign up to find out when *The Last Hero*, book 2 of *The Last War Series*, is released: smarturl.it/peterbostrom

Contact information:
www.authorpeterbostrom.com
facebook.com/authorpeterbostrom
peterdbostrom@gmail.com

Made in the USA
San Bernardino,
CA